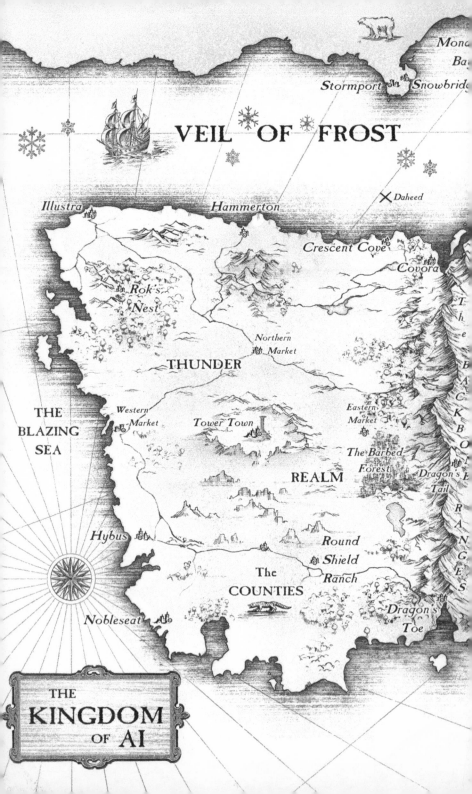

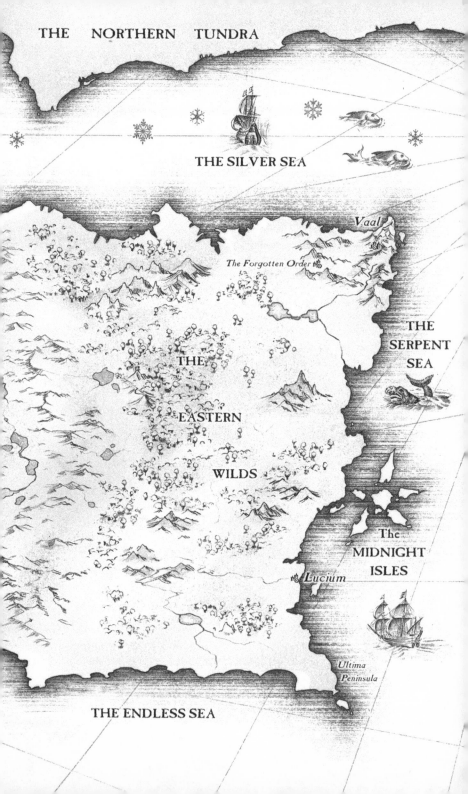

For Max
Welcome to the world, kiddo

———

Paladero:
The City of Night Neverending
first published in 2016
this edition published in 2020 by Hardie Grant Egmont
Ground Floor, Building 1, 658 Church Street
Richmond, Victoria 3121, Australia
www.hardiegrantegmont.com

 A catalogue record for this
book is available from the
National Library of Australia

Text copyright © 2017 Steven Lochran
Design copyright © 2017 Hardie Grant Egmont

Cover design by Kristy Lund-White
Cover illustrations by Jeremy Love
Internal illustrations by Milenko Tunjic
Typeset by Cannon Typesetting
Printed in Australia by Griffin Press, part of Ovato, an Accredited
ISO AS/NZS 14001 Environmental Management System printer.

3 5 7 9 10 8 6 4 2

 The paper this book is printed on is certified against the Forest
Stewardship Council® Standards. Griffin Press holds FSC chain
of custody certification SGS-COC-005088. FSC promotes
environmentally responsible, socially beneficial and economically
viable management of the world's forests.

PALADERO

THE CITY OF NIGHT NEVERENDING

STEVEN LOCHRAN

Hardie Grant

EGMONT

—

CHAPTER ONE

A LONE MAN

T HE attack came just before midnight. The pyrates swept so silently into the township of Crescent Cove that nobody saw them coming. Not until they burst through the crowd of revellers with weapons drawn, cutting a bloody path as they set the thatched cottages ablaze with their flamecannons. And, amid the screams of terror, a rough and terrible voice bellowed, 'Grab everything you can! *The Shadow God must have his tribute!*'

As fearsome as the words were, Joss had no time to consider them as he ran for the stables, whip in one hand and sword in the other. The Champion's Blade was a ceremonial object, not meant for battle. But it would still carve through anyone looking to stop him. The whip was to make sure it didn't come to that.

Villagers fled all around him. They became a rapid river in their panic, pushing and pulling him in every direction. But with great effort he forced his way towards a small side street. He could see the stables at the other end, drenched in shadows and untouched by the chaos.

It was only as he was nearing them that a figure sprang from the darkness. He was dressed the same as all his comrades: chainmail made of crustacean shells, worn beneath a bronze chestplate stained green by salt water. His helmet was the same rusty hue, the faceplate evoking a creature from the deep with its bulging glass eyeholes and jagged mouthpiece. He gripped the handle of a long metal barrel, a large tank fastened to its casing, a flame flickering at its muzzle.

'Drop your weapons!' the pyrate growled from behind his visor as he squeezed the trigger. The night was lit up by a sizzling jet of fire. *'Now!'*

Joss considered the flamecannon and the lone man wielding it. He looked back at the panicked villagers, at their burning homes. He turned again to the pyrate.

'I don't think so,' he said, and raised his sword.

CHAPTER TWO

———

A CROSSBOW BOLT TO THE CHEST

Earlier ...

THE straw of the thatched roof crunched beneath Joss's weight, pricking his palms as he shifted around, blinked the sleep from his eyes and shivered at the touch of the early morning wind that was blowing through Crescent Cove.

It had only been a fortnight since he had returned from the Way with his Bladebound brethren, Drake and Hero, nervous at the prospect of being denied the rest of their training by the Grandmaster Council. But that hadn't happened. Instead, their continued instruction had been approved, though not without some heavy deliberation. Grandmaster Eno had seemed particularly dour as he described what lay ahead for the aspiring prentices.

'We'll make arrangements with each of your individual orders to begin your training in earnest. Together you'll learn the finer points of riding, mustering and song sword technique. Consider yourselves fortunate that you hail from such disparate regions, as it will give you a broader range of knowledge. If you're wise you'll stay silent, listen well and learn.'

That last piece of advice had no doubt been aimed directly at Joss, given the way that Grandmaster Eno had stared at him as he delivered it. Still, Joss had been unable to resist asking further questions.

'Which order shall be the first, my lord?' he'd said, making sure to maintain an even and respectful tone. The last thing he wanted was to bait the old man, but his excitement to get started had simply been too much to contain.

'Starlight Fields,' Eno had replied, grinding his jaw on the answer, while Drake – standing at attention beside Joss – visibly straightened his posture. His pale face had been a mask of perfect composure, leaving Joss to speculate as to his friend's feelings about returning home. 'A season spent herding mammoths should serve as a solid introduction to all that's expected of you.'

The Grandmaster had gone on to explain the travel and accommodation arrangements that would be made for them, as well as to ask if they had anyone to appoint as their steward, a younger prentice who would assist them throughout their training. It was a largely thankless role, though it would stand the prentice in good stead when they eventually applied to go on the Way themselves, and Joss knew the perfect candidate. It seemed only right to put his name forward after all they'd been through, not just at Round Shield Ranch, but also in setting Joss on his path to becoming a paladero.

Thankfully, Eno hadn't outright rejected the suggestion, saying instead that it would be taken into consideration. Their audience at an end, the prentices had left the council to their business only to find Sur Verity waiting for them in the antechamber. Her face was twisted around her eyepatch in an expression that Joss had rarely seen in all the years he'd served as her prentice. Concern.

'So?' she'd prompted him.

'We start with a season's worth of training at Starlight Fields,' Joss had replied, expecting her to be as gruff in her response as she'd been when Lord Malkus, the leader of their order, had put Joss forward as Round Shield Ranch's nominee for the Way. Perhaps she'd be dismissive, lamenting how much more rigorous the training was back when the Bladebound would number a dozen or more and would be schooled by just as many paladeros. Most likely she would offer dire and cryptic warnings that would leave Joss feeling uncertain about himself and his chances at succeeding.

But she did neither of these things. Instead, her concern only intensified.

'Starlight Fields?' she said. 'That means you'll be stopping at Crescent Cove before you cross the Silver Sea …'

The name hit Joss like a crossbow bolt to the chest. 'It does?'

'Is that a problem?' asked Hero, who had been characteristically silent until that point, her polarised goggles and mess of black hair rendering her as impossible to read as Drake had been. Joss could only stare at her, dumbstruck.

'Crescent Cove is on the coast where Daheed was … where Daheed …' Drake said, intervening on Joss's behalf before he, too, found himself lost for words.

Where Daheed was destroyed, Joss thought, the memory echoing in his head as he now sat on the roof of the inn where he had been staying with the others ever since their arrival in the tiny seaside town.

The narrow buildings were stacked in rows that ran down rolling hills towards the waterfront, clumped together like rotted teeth. From his poky little room, Joss could only see the townhouse opposite and the street down below. But up here, perched on the rooftop, he could see so much more. He could see the sky. He could see the horizon. He could see where his island home had once sat in the middle of the Silver Sea. And he could see the empty space it had left behind.

Haunted by its loss all his life, he felt utterly overwhelmed to now be directly faced with that absence. Especially as whatever grief he was feeling was tempered by the anticipation of beginning his training in earnest. The last survivor of Daheed. A prentice on his way to becoming a paladero. He was both these things, and now they were at war with each other. Should he be sad, or excited? Guilty, or nervous?

Down on the street, labourers were pounding hammers and rasping saws and chattering away to each other as they finished the last-minute preparations for the annual Sea Spirit Festival. Children ran from one end of the road to the other, laughing and screaming in excitement as they trailed a green kite in the shape of a manta ray behind them. Its tail corkscrewed around in the breeze as it climbed and dived through the sky, leaping with boundless joy, passing Joss as he watched from the roof. He smiled at the sight, nudging as it did distant memories of a similarly carefree youth.

As he rose to his feet, a gust of wind caught him off-balance. Reaching out to steady himself, he grabbed hold of a guy-wire that ran from the roof down to the street. Even with all his weight on it, the cable held firm.

To the pits with all this gloom, he told himself. *I'm a Bladebound prentice of Round Shield Ranch, mentored by Sur Verity Wolfsbane herself and on my way to becoming a paladero in my own right! Luck is muck. I make my own!*

Tightening his grip around the wire, a crazy notion overcame him. His favourite book as a child had been *Azof & the Pyrate King*, a Daheedi fable that he'd found tucked away in the library of the Orphan House where he'd grown up. Not only had it been an exciting story, which Joss had named his raptor after, but it had also helped to fill in some of the blanks in his memory about his lost homeland.

But for all the book's personal and cultural significance, Joss's favourite part had always been when Azof – the humble cabin boy aboard a merchant vessel that was under attack from a pyrate crew – had zipped from his ship down onto the enemy's deck via the marauders' own grappling lines. So, deciding to prove true to his word and make his own luck, Joss unhooked his sword-belt, flung it over the wire, and acted out his hero's defining moment.

One small leap and he was airborne. The leather coat that he'd been allowed to keep after running the Gauntlet caught the wind, blowing out behind him like a pair of pterosaur wings. For a second, he relished the daring image he struck – until another blast of wind knocked him askew. He dropped from the wire halfway up, the ground rushing towards him, and landed painfully on a riveted manhole cover in the middle of the street.

'*Argh!*' he grunted, rolling off the manhole cover and onto his back. His thigh was throbbing so much that he couldn't imagine trying to stand. Not even as the local kids ran back up the road, still trailing their kite, laughing at the sightseer from Thunder Realm who'd splatted like a seagull's dropping in the middle of the street.

'Just getting some fresh air,' he told them as he forced himself up and dusted off his hands.

'More like biting some fresh bitumen!' the biggest kid chortled, his friends joining in as they ran off together.

'Oh yeah? Come back here and say that to my face. I'd be happy to serve you up your own slice!' Joss shouted after them, sword-belt flapping in his grip. But they were already gone. Frowning, he buckled the Champion's Blade into place and started limping back to the inn. The sword's weight had become so familiar by his side that he often forgot it was there, but there was no chance of that now as it smacked against his bruised leg with every step.

Next time you decide to do something stupid like jump off a roof, he told himself as he trudged through the inn's front door, *don't!*

CHAPTER THREE

A Familiar and Friendly Face

JOSS found his brethren in the dining room, enjoying their breakfast. Hero had taken the chair in the far corner with her back against the wall, her hair even more unkempt than usual at this early hour. Beside her sat Drake, bundled up in his thick winter coat despite the roaring fireplace next to him.

'Joss!' he called out, waving his hand in an invitation to join them. The gesture struck Joss as a little unnecessary given that the dining room was empty but for the three of them, though he appreciated it all the same.

'How did you sleep?' Drake asked through a mouthful of buttery flapjacks as Joss took the seat next to him, his leg throbbing.

'Not well,' Joss replied, then reached, wincing, for the large jug of fig juice in the middle of the table.

'My brain wouldn't quit its thinking.'

Drake nodded. 'Brains are stubborn that way.'

'Our steward arrives today,' Hero said, cutting straight to business.

'I was planning on meeting him at the station,' replied Joss, before turning to Drake. 'Which reminds me … Would you mind if I took Pietro with me? Azof can't carry two.'

'Of course. I'm sure Pietro will appreciate the chance to shake off his fur. It's a shame, though. I imagine you'd be wanting to spend as much time with Azof as possible before we go.'

'If only thunder lizards could survive the cold of the Northern Tundra,' Joss said. The idea of leaving Azof in the care of the local stables while he and the others were away training had been gnawing at him for weeks now. Hero looked to be just as distressed about leaving her own loyal mount behind, despite her efforts to hide her every emotion.

'You'd think a sabretooth's fur coat would mean they'd fare a little better,' she muttered.

Joss eyed Drake with hesitant curiosity. 'Don't suppose you've had any luck in designing that thermal cloak we talked about …'

Drake shook his head. 'Couldn't conceive of anything that would survive a raptor's claws, unfortunately. Nor a sabretooth's fangs,' he added after he'd swallowed his last bite and took a sip of black coffee. 'You must be looking forward to seeing your friend again, though.'

'It'll be good to have him along. Not to mention helpful. But it still feels odd to think we'll have a steward. I know it's meant to teach us what it's like being responsible for a prentice of our own some day, but I'm not that much older than him. Being in charge is going to take some getting used to,' Joss said, though by now Drake looked to be only half-listening. His sea-green eyes were set on the window, his hand tapping against the discarded cutlery on his plate.

'Nervous?' Joss asked.

Drake furrowed his brow, confused. 'About having a steward?'

'About going home.'

The directness of the question forced Drake to pause. Turning his gaze from the window, he smiled awkwardly. 'Yes and no,' he replied. 'I suppose, if anything, it feels like I'm slipping on an old coat that doesn't quite fit any more.'

'Family concerns?' Joss ventured, based on the stories that Drake had told during their time on the Way. Drake prodded his empty plate again, pushing it back towards the centre of the table.

'Not really. They live too far from Starlight Fields.

But you never know who you'll run into, especially given how small all the Tundra settlements are.'

'What of your ascension then?' Hero asked. She was segmenting an orange, peeling back the skin to reveal the juicy innards. 'How do you plan to be a paladero in such uncomfortable surrounds?'

'Maybe I'll apply to a mainland order when the time comes. Somewhere I can live without the shadow of the past hanging over me.'

Hero, ever the diplomat, scoffed. 'Chance would be a fine thing,' she said, and popped a slice of orange into her mouth.

'Round Shield Ranch could always use another set of capable hands,' Joss said. 'Not that I have any say in that.'

'I appreciate the thought,' Drake said with a smile before his eyes drifted back to the window and the world outside.

Joss managed only a few bites of toast and half a glass of juice for his breakfast. He was too mindful of getting to the station in time to manage anything more. Bidding Drake and Hero a quick farewell, he left the inn.

Outside, the Kingsday morning was still bright and crisp. The whole town was now bustling with festival preparations. Bunting had been strung up in a zigzag pattern from one side of the street to the other, while streamers had been wrapped around every lamppost, transforming them into oversized candy canes. Shop-keepers were adorning their premises with brightly coloured banners, and townsfolk milled about, making last-minute purchases or simply chatting.

Joss ventured on, ill at ease but unable to explain why. Maybe it had something to do with the air. It didn't have the funk of Thunder Realm, the earthy aroma of sun-baked dirt, the tang of lizard muck. It smelt instead of wet sand and stinging salt, and the threat of frost on the wind. It felt both familiar and alien, leaving him with a creeping sense of déjà vu, which he only shook off upon arriving at the stables where their animals were being kept.

The stablekeeper was hunched on a stool out the front, flipping through that day's edition of *The Crescent Cove Crier*. He nodded as Joss passed by, then returned his attention to the page before him. The innkeeper had recommended this place to Joss and his brethren, and there was enough of a family resemblance between the two proprietors to guess why.

Inside, heat lamps ran the length of the walkway, keeping each of the stable's occupants warm and dry. Not that there were that many of them. Every stall that Joss passed was empty, perhaps a sign of how the people of Crescent Cove had come to favour their autowagons over living, breathing mounts. It was another stark reminder of just how far from Thunder Realm he was.

At the rear of the stables, Joss passed by Hero's sabretooth tigress, Callie, to find Azof waiting for him. The raptor trilled happily as Joss rubbed his snout.

'Good boy, Azof,' Joss said, running his fingers through the spiky feathers that adorned the animal's brow. 'I'm going to miss you, you know.'

Azof made a chuffing noise, possibly in confusion. They hadn't spent a single day apart since Joss had first received the raptor as a hatchling, feeding him liquefied mouse guts to ensure he'd grow up big and strong. Now they were going to be separated for a whole season. The notion made Joss queasy. Well, *queasier*.

Giving the thunder lizard one last pat, Joss continued on to the next stall. What waited for him there was a boulder of dirty white fur, its breathing loud and rumbling.

'Pietro? You awake, boy?'

The boulder stirred. The tundra bear looked at Joss from over his broad shoulder, then scrunched his eyes shut and yawned. The sound was enough like a growl that Joss steadied himself, trying not to cower at the flash of Pietro's hand-length fangs, which were dripping with drool.

Smacking his lips together, Pietro pulled himself up

onto all fours and waited patiently for Joss to open the stall. After bridling and saddling the furry beast, Joss took him by the reins and led him out, offering one last farewell to Azof before guiding Pietro onto the streets of Crescent Cove.

If Joss had been in any other town, he might have received more than a few bewildered stares about his choice of mount, but the people of Crescent Cove seemed well accustomed to the sight of tundra bears. No one so much as glanced at him as he walked up the hill of Main Street, Pietro grunting beside him.

At the top, Joss took a moment to look over the township and the ocean that lay beyond. Again he gazed at the horizon and imagined what it would be like to see Daheed out there, with ships sailing to and from its shores. He'd read, and even half-remembered, that the city-island had resembled a floating crown, its shining tower peaks earning it the name 'the Gleaming Isle'.

But Daheed gleamed no longer. It had been sucked beneath the waves when Joss was only five years old by an unknown force, his mother sacrificing her life to ensure that he made it to the mainland safely. It was strange to think how haunted he was by a place he'd hardly known. Though truth be told, it haunted the world as well. Nobody had ever been able to fully explain what calamity had befallen the city or its people.

There were theories, of course, and Joss had heard all of them. Those prone to rationality believed an earthquake or an underwater volcano caused the Destruction. The superstitious claimed that an ancient and unimaginably large kraken had awoken to drag the island down into the depths with it. And to the paranoid it was a conspiracy orchestrated by Regent Greel, the ruler of the Kingdom of Ai, to ensure his grip on power.

None of those theories matched with the story that Lord Malkus had told Joss of what he'd witnessed of Daheed's fall from the shore of Crescent Cove. Nor did they fit with what Joss remembered of that black day. The longer the mystery remained, however, the more it seemed to slip from the memory of the world. What had once been a burning question throughout the Kingdom of Ai had cooled over the years, until finally the Destruction was nothing more than a curious tale of interest to only a small few, leaving Joss to doubt that he would ever learn the truth.

But that was a concern for another time, and he hurried on. The last thing he wanted today was to fall into the same dark mood as before. Not when he had so much to be excited about, including the arrival of a familiar and friendly face that would be waiting for him now at the train station.

One of the finest buildings in all of Crescent Cove, the station was constructed of granite blocks that had been painted a perfect white. He could see it now, shining like a whetted blade, its grand staircase leading to a portico of marble columns and an archway entrance. At the base of the stairs, a hitching post had been fixed to the wall, small and discreet among all the architectural splendour.

'Stay here, boy,' Joss said as he knotted Pietro's reins to the iron bar. 'And try not to maim anyone while I'm gone.'

Pietro huffed as if insulted, and sat down. Starting up the stairs, Joss manoeuvred his way through the crowd, passed the city wardens at their guardhouse, pushed through the turnstile and arrived at the serpentrain platform. A few moments later a horn sounded from further up the line, signalling the arrival of one of the greatest pieces of engineering that had ever been accomplished in the Kingdom of Ai.

This was the first time that Joss had seen the serpentrain in person, and it didn't disappoint. Clad in shining silver scales, it hissed steam from the multiple exhaust ports scored along its carriages. Its movement was speedy and fluid, slowing to a stop at the platform with agile precision. The engine ticked loudly at the head of the procession as it whirred down, while the stationmaster blew his whistle to signal the all clear for disembarking.

The carriage doors slid open and all the passengers poured past Joss, thundering down the platform and out into the cobbled streets. Searching through the dozens of unfamiliar faces, Joss spotted a small figure with a brown hood drawn up over his head.

'Edgar!' Joss called out, but the hooded figure failed to hear him. *'Edgar!'*

The figure stopped, turned. A pink face gazed out from beneath the hood. Broke into a wide smile. And then Edgar was running towards him.

'Josiah!'

—

CHAPTER FOUR

A QUESTION, UNCOMFORTABLE AND RESTLESS

THE two Round Shield Ranch prentices met each other in a hug, laughing as they slapped each other on the back. The last of Edgar's fellow passengers scowled as he walked around them, prompting them both to shuffle out of the way.

'It's good to see you!' Joss said. 'How was your trip?'

'A bit of a bumpy ride, but fine all the same,' replied Edgar, struggling to heft his bags.

'Let me take those.' Joss stooped to grab the largest case, which Edgar quickly pulled out of his reach.

'No, that's OK, I wouldn't want to be a bother –'

'I insist,' said Joss.

'But it's the steward's job to take care of the luggage,' Edgar said, still grappling with his scuffed and tatty bags as the nearby station porters rolled their eyes at him.

'I think we can do without tradition for at least one day.'

Joss grabbed the bulk of the luggage and lifted it, leaving the smaller bags for Edgar.

'So. How are things back home?' Joss asked as they walked from the platform and down the staircase.

'Much the same,' Edgar said with what would have been a shrug if he could have managed it. 'Though Sur Verity has been assessing candidates to be her new prentice.'

Joss missed a step, stumbling to keep himself upright. 'She has?'

'The list has been whittled down, but there's one girl in particular she seems to have taken a shine to: Eliza Wildsmith. Do you know her?'

'Can't say I do.'

'Her uncle was a paladero with Fort Ironfang, till he broke his bonds and became Nameless …'

Edgar went on, speculating on what life must be like without lord or land, as it was for the Nameless paladeros who had forsaken their vows. Joss didn't hear much more than that; his mind was churning with the idea of Sur Verity replacing him. Of course, he'd known

it would happen eventually, but this felt all too soon. Joss wasn't even a paladero yet. What if he failed in his training? Would it even be possible for him to return to being a prentice now?

'What about Sur Wallace?' he asked, making an effort to turn his attention back to Edgar as they came to the bottom of the stairs. 'Has anyone been tasked with him in your absence?'

'Not by the time I'd left.' Edgar pulled his hood back, his silvery locks glowing brighter than the serpentrain's scales despite the clouds gathering overhead. 'I worry for him, truth be told. He doesn't cope well on his own.'

'You show him more loyalty than he's worth,' Joss said.

'And what worth would I have if I showed him anything less?' Edgar replied, stumping Joss into silence. Back home, Edgar was often dismissed for his size, but Joss had seen for himself often enough that what his friend lacked in muscle he more than made up for in character. He was looking for a way to express that admiration when Edgar emitted a noise that could only be described as a high-pitched squeal.

'Is that a *tundra bear?*'

They had come to the hitching post where Pietro was tethered. The bear hunched his shoulders and blew a puff of air at the boy standing before him.

'I didn't think Azof could make the trip, what with your luggage and all, so I brought along Drake's mount,' explained Joss. 'This is Pietro.'

'*Pietro*.' There was a hushed wonder in Edgar's voice. 'Can I … can I pat him?'

'I, uh, don't see why not,' Joss said.

On tiptoe, Edgar offered his trembling hand to Pietro's snout. The bear leant forward and sniffed the boy's fingers. Taking this as an invitation, Edgar rubbed the animal's muzzle. Pietro let out a grunt of satisfaction, then ran a big pink tongue over his bulbous black nose. Edgar yelped with delight.

With both Edgar and Pietro otherwise occupied, Joss focused on getting the luggage mounted on Pietro's back and strapped in place. When that was done, he gave Edgar a boost up into the saddle before climbing up himself and taking the bear by the reins.

'Hyah, boy!' Joss said, mushing Pietro up the hill. Though the bear's gait was lumbering, his strength was undeniable. Joss couldn't imagine having to wrestle all of Edgar's luggage back to the inn without his help. As they ambled past idling autowagons and were overtaken by rattling trams, Joss worked up the nerve to ask Edgar the one question that had been sitting uncomfortable and restless in the back of his mind for weeks now.

'I don't suppose you've heard any more about the Zadkille prentice?' he asked, making sure to look and sound as nonchalant as he could.

'Not since setting off from Round Shield Ranch,' Edgar replied, taking a pack of sunflower seeds from his pocket and sprinkling them into his palm. He offered the pack to Joss, who politely refused. Edgar chewed heartily. 'Last I heard, he'd left his order for parts unknown.'

'Of his own choosing? Or was he forced?'

'Can't say,' Edgar said, swallowing. 'Both, I heard. You know how scuttlebutt is; it's all the end of the world or the start of a whole new one, and never anything in between.'

They rode on in silence, with Joss stewing over what Edgar had told him. If things had worked out differently, Zeke would have been here with them as the fourth prentice bound for training in the Northern Tundra. But because of the disloyalty he'd shown while on the Way – and because of how Joss had handled that betrayal – he was now out there somewhere, lost in the world. Had Joss been right in turning his back on Zeke? The question haunted him almost as much as Daheed did.

'I've been meaning to thank you, by the way. For the opportunity,' Edgar said, cutting through the haze of Joss's thoughts for the second time in as many minutes.

'It's the Grandmaster Council who picks the stewards for the Bladebound,' Joss replied.

'And from what I hear, it was you who recommended me.'

'All I did was make a suggestion.'

'Well, however you want to put it, I owe you. Even more than I already did.'

Joss resisted the urge to brush off Edgar's gratitude again, thanking him for his kind words. Mercifully, the young prentice went back to munching his sunflower seeds, finishing the whole packet by the time they'd reached the stables.

Once they'd unloaded Edgar's luggage, returned Pietro to his pen and given Azof another quick pat, they crossed over to the inn. Drake and Hero were on the front step, on their way out. Joss introduced everyone, with Drake proving as friendly as ever and Hero just as reserved.

'We thought we'd take a look around the town before the festival starts,' Drake said while Hero remained silent beside him, her scarf pulled up to hide what little of her face hadn't already been obscured by her hat, hair and goggles. 'You're welcome to join us.'

'I would love that,' Edgar said, his big grin framing his chipped tooth. 'Though I think I should probably unpack first.'

'Maybe we can meet you later?' Joss suggested.

'Sounds like a fine idea,' replied Drake, following Hero as she slipped out onto the street. 'See you then.'

'Looking forward to it, Mister Drake!' Edgar called out. Joss was sure he heard Drake chortle at Edgar's 'Mister', while Hero continued on ahead without breaking stride.

'What a nice fella,' Edgar said, heaving his bags onto his shoulder as he and Joss entered the inn. 'Though have I done something to offend Miss Hero?'

Joss caught the front door with the tip of his boot and swung it shut behind him. 'Don't worry. She's like that with everyone,' he said. 'You'll learn soon enough.'

'I hope so.' The stairs squeaked as Edgar climbed them, luggage banging against the balustrade. 'I've had my fill of bumpy rides today.'

Quietly agreeing with him, Joss followed.

—

CHAPTER FIVE

AN EVEN DARKER SHADE OF RED

THE celebrations officially began just after sundown, first with a pronouncement from the lord mayor and then with an explosion of firecrackers and flaming pinwheels. Music filled the night as dancers in traditional dress took to the town square, their faces painted silver and blue, their arms and legs wrapped with green streamers. They hopped and bobbed and twirled in time with the drums that *pounded, pounded, pounded,* from the main stage.

Each of the dancers carried an oar, and they added to the ceaseless percussion by bashing the wooden shafts against one another in a tightly choreographed display that had been performed by the people of Crescent Cove for hundreds of years. They skipped back and forth in time with the drums, edging closer and closer to each other until they crashed together, wood smacking against wood with the intensity of blades drawn in battle.

The watching crowd clapped merrily along, save for some small children who screamed in distress. Even Joss had to plug his ears, the noise proving too much for him.

'When does the band stop playing?' Joss shouted over the din.

Drake laughed. 'They don't,' he shouted back. 'They play every minute of every day of the festival, switching band members in and out as they tire.'

'And how long does the festival last?' Hero's words were almost inaudible.

'A week from beginning to end,' said Drake. 'Why do you think the inn's so empty? Nobody else is foolish enough to take a room right above the orchestra.'

'Thank the liege we're leaving tomorrow,' Joss moaned.

Hero harrumphed, 'All we have to do is sleep in the meantime.'

The prentices were quick to escape, passing by spinning carousels, puppet shows and a petting farm that had been set up near the shore, on their way to browse the market stalls. While Hero stopped to buy a hand-etched castes deck, Edgar upgraded his worn cotton mittens for a pair of fur-lined gloves.

'What do you think?' Edgar asked as he slipped them on, the leather squeaking with the flexing of his fingers.

'They're green,' said Joss, trying not to make a face.

'They're real plesiosaur.' Edgar grinned. 'They're unique!'

'They certainly are,' Joss agreed, which Edgar luckily interpreted as a compliment.

After Edgar had paid, the four prentices drifted to a food stand that served steaming hot chowder with prawns, potatoes and chunks of grilled platecarpus. Coupled with fresh-baked bread, it was a warm and nourishing meal. No sooner had Joss and the others finished their supper than they noticed the flaming torches that were being passed out among the crowd.

'What's going on?' Edgar asked as a torch was thrust into his gloved hand, the fire flickering at his knuckles.

'Time for the ceremony!' said the warden who'd handed it to him, one of many city officials who were lighting the torches and passing them to the crowd. He didn't stay to elaborate, rushing off to light another as the people of Crescent Cove began marching down Main Street towards the waterfront. Curious to see what was happening, the prentices followed.

The procession led out onto the beach, where a pile of wood had been stacked as tall as a triceratops's horns. The lord mayor stood beside it, his crushed velvet robes eddying around him. Behind him, a skiff had been laden with jugs of oil, flowers and fabrics, swords and silver pieces. Two hulking men held the boat steady in the sway of the outgoing tide, while a willowy woman stood not far from them, with a longbow in her hands and a single arrow in her quiver.

'We come here tonight to pay our respects and to show our deference,' the lord mayor called out over the sound of crashing waves.

The townsfolk formed a line on the sand in front of him, each throwing a torch onto the wood pile. It caught alight quickly, soon becoming a raging bonfire. Edgar was one of the last to offer his torch to the flames and, when he'd thrown it on the pyre, the mayor began to speak again.

'We make this offering to the spirits of the sea!' He gestured to the two men who now pushed the skiff out into the ocean. The tide showed no hesitation in taking it, and it was soon far from shore.

'Praise be,' the crowd murmured.

'To the wraiths that stalk us, we give this tribute! To the sprites that guide us, we give this thanks! And to the changelings that steal the faces of our fellow men, we give this warning! Spirits all, grant us clear skies and calm seas, and let there be peace between us another year!'

'Praise be!' the crowd answered with greater strength.

'Archer – *light your flame!*'

The woman with the longbow stepped forward. Pulling the arrow from her quiver, she held the head to the fire and watched as it caught alight. She then spun on her heel, notched her arrow, and drew a line on the skiff. It was just faintly visible now, the lantern dangling from its prow a dull glint in the darkness.

The archer loosed the arrow and the crowd held its breath. Joss looked around – everyone was transfixed by the flaming arc.

'If it doesn't land on the first shot, the ceremony won't work,' Drake whispered to him as the arrow climbed higher and higher, peaked, then began its descent. With a jolt it met its target, and the skiff was consumed in a ball of flame. The crowd whooped and cheered as the lord mayor grabbed the archer's hand and held it aloft.

'*Her aim is true!*' he shouted, and the crowd cheered again. Their excitement only grew louder and more boisterous as the sky was filled with the first burst of fireworks. Dozens of rockets exploded in dazzling clouds of sparkling light, their colours reflected on the water below. And still burning at the centre of it all was the skiff and the tributes it offered.

All this time the band had been playing in the distance; now the music grew louder to call everyone back to the town centre. Gradually the crowd broke apart as people started filing back up Main Street, leaving only small clusters of onlookers staring out at the tiny boat blazing offshore. That included Joss and the others, who watched the skiff's passage under the rising moon.

'Strange to think we'll be standing on the other side of this sea soon enough, ready to begin the first part of our training,' said Joss, captivated by the blues and blacks and blazing reds before him, and the silver ripples that the moon scattered among them all.

'It's not going to be easy, you know,' Drake said as the flames in front of them began to die down.

'We survived the Way. What could be harder than that?' Hero asked.

'Drudgery,' Drake said. 'Eighteen-, maybe even twenty-hour days, seven days a week, herding mammoths from one paddock to another and back again.'

'We've herded livestock before,' Joss said, trying to stave off a creeping sense of disquiet.

'Not mammoths. There's a reason they get us to work with them as part of our training. Not quite as big as a brontosaur but ten times as wilful. They don't respond to song swords the way thunder lizards do – not that we'll have song swords to use, of course. It's going to come down to our riding and our teamwork. One false move and we get crushed underfoot or killed in a stampede. It's going to be hard work. Long, hard, gruelling work.'

The prentices fell silent.

'And here I thought you were the cheery type,' Hero remarked.

'The cheeriest you'll ever meet beyond the Veil of Frost.' Drake flashed a smile.

Out on the water, there was no more flame – the skiff had sunk beneath the waves. Joss shuddered as he imagined it surrendering to the ocean, anticipating the cold to come.

'How about a quick drink beside a hot fire before calling it a night?' he suggested to the others, and they heartily agreed. Leaving the shore behind, the prentices retired to a tavern halfway up Main Street, where they squeezed in with all the other patrons. They started with a couple of rounds of sarsaparilla, followed by Hero's recommendation of dreamflower tea.

'We drink it all the time back home,' she said. 'It helps settle the mind before bed.'

Joss wasn't sure what to make of drinking crushed-up weeds, but the taste was pleasant enough and it sat soothingly in his stomach as he and the others told stories from their time in the saddle. Edgar earned the biggest laugh of the night with his tale of Sur Wallace's ill-fated nap beneath a hive of territorial tiger wasps.

'The poor man!' Drake guffawed through his last mouthful of tea.

'Poor man?' Edgar said. 'I was the one applying ointment to his backside for more than half a season afterward!'

The prentices erupted with hilarity, so immersed in their conversation they hadn't noticed that half the tavern had emptied out until the owner shuffled past pushing a broom. They began the uphill walk back to their inn, with Edgar keeping everyone entertained with more stories of misadventure from back home. Joss was glad to see how well his friend was already fitting in, having been unsure what the others would make of him. Not that he had the energy to fret over any of that now.

'I'm exhausted,' he yawned. 'All I want is a warm bed and a soft pillow and a good night's sleep.'

'Don't know how likely any of us are to get it with all that noise going on,' Hero said as they neared the bandstand, her fingers brushing her bandolier full of throwing weapons. 'You know, all it would take is one quick zamaraq strike to the bandleader's neck …'

'I'm sure the cells in the local gaol are *very* peaceful,' Joss said, shaking his head.

'I wouldn't kill him. Just graze him a bit.'

The bandleader was grinning broadly at the crowd, waving his arms around in the air, baton in hand, keeping time with the music – inviting everyone before him to join in the dance. But then a black blur tore through the air. His smile disappeared. The crowd gasped as the bandleader looked down. A barbed bolt jutted from his breastbone, his crimson coat growing an even darker shade of red.

Joss searched the crowd, saw Drake doing the same. Edgar's mouth had dropped wide open, while Hero remarked, 'That wasn't me, I swear.'

The bandleader fell to his knees, swayed there a moment, then tumbled from the stage. The music died away, instrument by instrument.

'*Pyrates!*' came the cry from somewhere in the crowd, and the town's warning bells began to ring, far too late.

CHAPTER SIX

A Job to Do

S HADOWY figures cleaved their way through the town square, felling villagers left and right with blades as sharp as butchers' knives. Flames erupted overhead. Cries of terror curdled the air as people tried desperately to flee.

'What do we do?' Edgar asked, his voice cracking with fear, the crowd pushing and shoving him.

'You need to get back to the inn,' Joss told him. 'Now!'

'But –'

'Don't argue with me, steward!' Joss gave him a quick shove to get him started, and though the boy still hesitated he eventually nodded, calling out, 'Good luck,' as he ran off in the direction of the inn. Then Joss turned to Drake and Hero. 'We need to get to the stables! We'll have a better chance at fending them off if we're mounted up.'

'Agreed,' Hero said as she hurled her bladed zamaraqs with lethal precision, felling two pyrates who were trying to herd a crying family down the street. 'Let's go!'

Pulling the Champion's Blade from its scabbard and unhooking his whip, Joss led the way. People were running down alleys and crowding through any open door in their attempts to escape, while flames continued to burst all around them.

It was impossible to tell where exactly the attackers were within the crush of the crowd. Even the wardens looked to be having trouble, charging blindly with their weapons drawn at no discernible target, the chief warden himself at the head of the pack.

He was so focused on the crowd that he failed to see what was two only steps in front of him and crashed into Joss at full speed, the steel epaulettes of his chestplate smacking painfully against Joss's shoulder.

'*Muck!*' Joss cried out as he was sent spinning to the ground.

'Watchit!' the chief warden grunted, rushing past. His shoulder throbbing in agony, Joss quickly gathered himself together while muttering to the others, 'It's not enough to be attacked by pyrates, we have to watch out for wardens too?'

But neither responded. Looking about, he couldn't see Hero or Drake. A chill ran through him, spiking his skin. Could they have been grabbed off the street while he hurried ahead, none the wiser? Could they be lying in a gutter, dead or injured? He swayed in place, unsure of what to do or where to go, even as the crowd continued to scream, even as the pyrates continued to slash and pillage, even as he saw for the first time a red-bearded man standing where the bandleader had fallen, barking orders and growling dire threats.

Behind him, he might find Hero and Drake. Ahead of him awaited his only advantage. He called their names, heard nothing but panic and terror and chaos. He was numb, shocked, unsure. And then, in an instant, he wasn't. He had to go on. He had to make it to the stables. There was nothing else he could do. Not if he wanted to be of any help. Not if he wanted to save anyone.

He took a step. Another. Gathered speed. Began to run. With sword in one hand and whip in the other, he bolted down the side street to the stables.

'Grab everything you can! *The Shadow God must have his tribute!*' the red-bearded leader roared from the bandstand as Joss pressed on. He was almost at the stables when a figure leapt from the shadows with a flamecannon in hand.

'Drop your weapons! *Now!*' the pyrate ordered, firing his weapon at the sky in a fearsome display.

'I don't think so,' Joss replied, raising his sword.

The pyrate cocked his head, seemingly stunned that Joss was defying him. And if he were to be honest, Joss was just as surprised himself. His battlefield experience was limited, to say the least. Skirmishes with bullies surely didn't count, and the clashes he'd had while on the Way were won more through evasion than attack. His training as a paladero would involve sword-fighting lessons when the time came, but that did him no good here and now.

So he improvised. Cracking his whip, he kept the pyrate at bay and his finger from the trigger. Every time his attacker tried to draw close, Joss lashed at his face. Every time he tried to squeeze off a burst of fire, Joss snapped at his hands. It was enough to make the pyrate stumble backward until he was pressed against the wall of the laneway.

'Joss!' Drake's voice at the end of the laneway broke his concentration. He looked to see his friend rushing towards him, and that's all it took for the pyrate to aim and fire.

The burst of flame was so hot it felt like his flesh was melting off his face. Moving fast, Joss rolled out of the cannon's sweeping path. He cursed as he lost his grip on the Champion's Blade, the sword clattering on the pebbly street, while the flamecannon roared over his head and then went suddenly quiet.

He could hear Drake calling out in alarm, his cries echoing off the surrounding buildings. But he could also hear the hiss of the pyrate's flamecannon refilling its tank, the clicking of its filament as it prepared to spark. He had only a second to act before the pyrate launched another sizzling jet of fire at him, and this time there was no way he could avoid it.

'Any last words, ya pox-plagued bilge rat?' the pyrate asked, aiming the cannon right at Joss's face.

Crouching low, Joss coiled his hand against metal. 'Just one,' he replied, gripping tightly. '*Duck!*'

The pyrate didn't have a chance to react beyond a confused tilt of the head as Joss wrenched open the manhole cover and sent it flying. It landed with teeth-shattering force, the impact knocking the pyrate off his feet and out cold. Joss was still panting from the fight when Drake joined him, similarly breathless.

'Joss, I'm so sorry! I didn't mean to distract you.'

'No harm done.' Joss turned from the pyrate. 'What about you? Are you all right?'

'As well as can be expected.'

'And Hero?'

'We were swept back by the crowd to the tavern we

visited earlier. A dozen or more villagers have taken shelter there and Hero's holding off a regiment of pyrates outside it. She sent me to find you.'

'I don't know how much help I can be. Just one of these thugs was hard enough to deal with ...'

'Unless you had a ferocious raptor with you who's been begging to be cut loose,' Drake reminded him, prompting a grin to spread across Joss's face.

'Not to mention a great big tundra bear with a bad temper!'

Drake shook his head. 'It'll take too much time to saddle them both right now, especially if Pietro's feeling stubborn. Because, if you haven't noticed' – Drake turned his attention to the far end of the street – 'we've got company.'

Joss looked to see a whole gang of pyrates stalking down the laneway, scraping their cutlasses along the cobblestone. Drake drew his spear and stepped in front of Joss without hesitation.

'You get to the stables,' he said. 'I'll hold them off.'

Joss would have protested, would have drawn his sword alongside his fellow prentice, but he knew if anyone could handle themselves it was Drake. So instead he plucked the Champion's Blade from the ground and rushed for the stables, finding them as quiet as they'd been that morning.

'Come on, boy,' Joss said, hopping the gate to Azof's stable. 'We have a job to do.'

The thunder lizard growled its approval as Joss quickly saddled and harnessed him. All that was left to do was throw open the pen and ride out.

'Let's go cause some grief. *Hyah!*' He cracked Azof's reins, driving the beast into the burning night.

—

CHAPTER SEVEN

A WILD PANIC

DRAKE was fending off the pyrates with all he had, his spear flashing like the firing of a bolt gun. Every blow his attackers tried to land was swatted away, each riposte quickly coupled with a jab to the gut, a crack to the knees, a smack across the knuckles. The pyrates were growing increasingly frustrated, circling him with weapons at the ready, looking for the first chance to run him through. But Joss wasn't about to let that happen. He urged Azof forward, and the raptor proved as nimble as ever.

'*Look yonder!*' the nearest pyrate yelled as he caught sight of the advancing thunder lizard, only to be slashed across the chest with Azof's talons. He fell messily to the ground, his companion next to him faring no better. Azof snapped his jaws around the helmeted man's arm, using his tail at the same time to lash the pyrate behind him.

'What demon scourge is this?!' the largest of the pyrates growled, trying his best to keep Azof back with his blade.

'No demon!' Joss said, his hold on Azof's reins as loose as could be. 'Just pure raptor!'

The pyrates were in a wild panic, their urgency only growing as a horn sounded from the distant shore, its bellow low and booming.

'Back to the boats! *Now!*' the largest pyrate shouted, and those who could still stand turned and ran from the laneway. They showed no concern in abandoning their fallen comrades, who were groaning in agony beneath Azof's clawed feet. The raptor snarled and kicked at them, forcing Joss to take a firm grip of his bridle to keep him under control.

'What in the Ever After are they doing?' Drake said as he drew alongside Joss, watching the pyrates flee.

'Retreating,' Joss replied with just as much confusion. 'They must have got all they came for, I guess.'

'That doesn't mean Hero won't still be in trouble,' Drake said. 'Joss, you need to get to her.'

'But what about you?'

'I'll keep an eye on this lot, make sure they don't escape before the wardens can arrest them. Then I'll saddle up Pietro and join you as soon as I can.'

As much as Joss wanted to argue the point, he knew Drake was right.

'Take care,' he told his friend. 'These streets aren't safe, even with all these thugs on the run.'

'Likewise,' Drake said.

With no further words, Joss bolted in the direction of the tavern. Azof seemed to appreciate the chance to stretch his legs, weaving between burning buildings as if he were running an obstacle course. In no time at all they were at their destination, where Hero was standing in the doorframe with her hat pushed back from her face. Her cheek was bruised and her lip bloodied, but otherwise she looked no worse for wear.

'There you are!' she called out. 'I've been waiting.'

'Drake said you were under siege and that you needed help,' Joss replied as he guided Azof over to her, then slipped from the saddle. When he landed he saw several terrified faces pressed against the frosted glass of the tavern's window, checking to see if their attackers had returned.

'True for the former. Less so the latter,' Hero said as she sheathed her humming knife. 'As it happened, the pyrates turned tail the moment they heard that horn.'

'But ... why? Is this what they do? Cause some chaos, inflict as much violence as they can, just to pilfer some valuables and run off again?'

'More than just *some* chaos, I reckon.' Hero pointed down the avenue.

Joss turned to see villagers doing all they could to contain the blaze that had engulfed their town. They were forming lines to douse the flames with buckets of water while the fire brigade set up its hoses. The fearsome orange glow was reflected in the shattered glass from all the ransacked shopfronts, heaped in the gutters and half-burying the fragments of a trampled manta kite. Joss stared at its broken wings and ripped streamers, hoping its owner had made it to safety.

Following the path of destruction, Joss and Hero found that it led all the way to the shore, where the pyrates were retreating in waves. Many of them were carrying stolen loot, whisking it away to the fleet of copper submersibles that awaited them in the harbour. But it wasn't just stolen goods that they were taking with them.

'They have hostages!' Joss exclaimed, watching in horror as villagers were hauled down the pier and into the idling vessels. The town wardens, desperate to rescue the civilians, were blocked by the livestock the pyrates had let loose from the petting farm on their way through. Megatheria, glyptodons and dodos all charged up Main Street, the perfect barricade to the pyrates' escape.

'We have to do something!' Joss said, jumping back up into Azof's saddle. And that's when he heard someone screaming his name.

'*Josiah!*'

It was Edgar, his voice faint at the other end of the avenue. Two pyrates had him by the arms and were dragging him away, towards the pier. '*Help!*'

Joss's eyes went wide, his mouth dropped open. '*Edgar!*' he cried out as Azof reared beneath him. 'Hold on!'

Spurring his mount onward, Joss raced down the street. Firefighters and townsfolk alike blocked his path but Azof proved as agile as ever, dodging every hurdle thrown at him. Until they came to the stampede of animals charging up the road. Azof screeched at the beasts, but they wouldn't be deterred. They kept surging forward, gripped entirely by their hysteria.

'*Joss!*' Edgar called out again. The pyrates had a better hold of him, carrying him off like a baby brachiosaur to the butcher while he wriggled and kicked as hard as he could. It did him no good. They were loading him onto the submersible now, its hatch wide open and waiting.

'Edgar!' Joss shouted, his voice swallowed by all the surrounding discord. '*EDGAR!*'

Azof bucked beneath him and was forced to retreat. Joss lost sight of the harbour. Only when the street had cleared of the animals could he look again, searching for his friend. But there was no sign of the pyrates, or the submersible, or Edgar.

He was gone. And it was all Joss's fault.

—

CHAPTER EIGHT

A MAN ON THE EDGE OF A CLIFF

'EVERYONE, please! Remain calm!' the chief warden shouted over the demands of the crowd gathered before him. 'We'll answer all the questions we can, but we can only answer them one at a time!'

The early morning sun was masked by plumes of black smoke, with dozens of charred buildings still smouldering all these hours after the pyrates' attack. Only a few figures stood among the blackened wreckage, salvaging or clearing away what they could. Everyone else was at the steps of the serpentrain station. With the town square in ruins, this was the only place large enough to accommodate everyone who had gathered to demand answers of their officials.

Watching the chief warden from the outer edge of the crowd, Joss ran a hand across his soot-stained face and rubbed at his bloodshot eyes. He was exhausted, but there had been far too much happening for him to sleep. In the immediate wake of Edgar's abduction, he and the others had run for the docks to find a boat and give chase. But the pyrates had set torch to almost all the vessels moored there. Of the few that remained, none were swift enough to catch up to the escaping submersibles.

All Joss wanted to do was pursue them, to rescue Edgar and the rest of the townsfolk, but instead he and Drake and Hero had dedicated themselves to doing what good they could in the meantime, putting out fires and pulling people from the wreckage of their homes and reuniting lost children with their families, all the while waiting for some official word as to how those who'd been taken were to be returned. But now, as he stared into the face of the chief warden, the lord mayor and all the other officials, the suspicion that he'd been clinging to a false hope crept over him.

'I assure you,' the chief warden began, eyes darting across the crowd, 'we're doing everything we can to –'

'*They took my boy!*' someone cried out, urging the crowd into another frenzy.

'*Where did they take everybody?*'

'*They burned down my house! Who's going to pay for that?*'

'*Are they coming back? Are they going to attack again?*'

The chief warden stood for the longest time, like a man at the edge of a cliff. Then he drew a deep breath and bellowed, *'Listen to me!'* This time, the crowd fell absolutely silent. 'Thank you. Now, we have little information at hand, but I can tell you that we're not the only town to have been raided. Reports have been coming in from Paleshore and Selkie's Rest of similar attacks, all in the last few days, all of them ending in abductions. We're doing what we can to organise a united rescue party, but we're still awaiting word from the capital ...'

A murmur rippled through the crowd, giving voice to Joss's own sense of shock. So many people taken, for what nefarious purpose nobody could say, and the authorities were content to just sit on their hands? Surely the situation was far too urgent to delay. Too much time had already been wasted.

The chief warden continued: 'In the meantime, we're recommending that all vessels remain at port. This includes the Byfrost barge, which has been redirected back to Stormport and will remain there until we can be sure that it won't be at risk of attack. I understand this may affect those whose accommodation was only booked through to the barge's arrival. We're currently setting up cots in the warden's barracks for anyone left without a roof for the night ...'

'I've heard enough.' Joss turned away from the gathering to stalk his way back up the street.

'Joss! Where are you going?' Drake called out.

Joss didn't stop to answer. The problem was that he had no idea where he was going, or what to do. He just knew he couldn't stand around listening any more. 'I'm going to get Azof,' he decided out loud. If there was one thing he could rely on when everything else was falling apart, it was his raptor. 'And then I'm going to ride for as long as it takes to find a boat that will take me wherever those cowardly cussing pyrates have fled.'

'You're not thinking straight,' Hero told him, hot on his heels with Drake not far behind. 'We have no way of knowing when the barge is going to show up for us, and if we're not on it we can kiss the rest of our training goodbye.'

'You honestly think I care about training now?'

'Maybe not. But consider this. There's a lot of ocean out there. A lot of places to hide. Even if you could find a ship willing to sail, even if you walked away from your training just as it's about to truly begin, you'd still have no idea where to even start looking for the pyrates. This isn't the Tournament, Joss. There's no regent here to keep your saddle fastened and your hand in the game. And just because we completed the Way, we're no more invincible for it. You'd be forfeiting your future – and maybe even your life – on a fool's errand.'

The longer Hero talked, the more Joss slowed his pace. She was right, he knew. But that didn't mean he had to like it. Frustrated, he spun to face her, lost his balance, took a faltering step. The ground beneath his boot squelched, and he looked down to see that his foot had landed in a thick puddle of mud. And in the middle of it, half-buried, he saw a flash of green. He picked it up.

A fur-lined, green leather glove.

'You're right,' Joss said to Hero. 'This isn't the Tournament. Or the Way. All those people will die – *Edgar* will die – if somebody doesn't do something.' He shook the glove in her face. 'So, if you're telling me the choice is between searching for my friend and reporting for duty like a proper little prentice, then that doesn't sound like any choice at all.'

Hero had no answer for that. Though Drake did. 'Maybe we can do both,' he said.

Both Joss and Hero looked at him, his narrow face perfectly earnest.

'I know a tracker. Name of Salt. He lives just outside of Starlight Fields and he could find a snow leopard in a blizzard at midnight,' he explained. 'If we can get to the Northern Tundra ahead of the barge, then Hero and I can report for duty while you go with Salt to rescue Edgar.'

Hero jerked with shock. 'Are you suggesting we leave Joss to be expelled?'

Even with all that was going on, Joss found himself as surprised by the intensity of her reaction as he was touched. Given how much of herself she hid from the world, the occasions when she let down her guard were so much more significant. Not that Drake was any less concerned.

'Of course not!' he said, sounding offended. 'We can say he was injured in the raid. That he's recuperating in Crescent Cove. That he's tending to Edgar's family. Or any other excuse we can think of during the voyage. With luck they'll believe us, and it'll give Joss time to at least try tracking down Edgar and the other hostages.'

Both Hero and Joss stood silent, mulling over Drake's proposition. Joss had to admit it sounded like it could work. And Hero's scowl had softened, though she still couldn't resist pointing out their first obstacle.

'So all we have to do is find a ship that's sailing when nobody in their right mind would even attempt it.'

'Not easy, I know. But the harbourmaster might be able to point us in the direction of a madman or two,' Drake suggested, then turned his attention to Joss.

Looking again at the mud-stained glove, Joss curled his hand into a fist. 'Then let's start there,' he said.

—

CHAPTER NINE

A SLUMBERING BEAST

THE harbourmaster looked over his desk at the three young prentices as if they'd just burst into his office asking to be booked on a pleasure cruise straight into the gaping maw of a ravenous kraken. Which, for all intents and purposes, was exactly what they'd done.

'You'll be wanting yer heads examined,' he huffed, then turned back to the stack of insurance claims he was signing, handing them one sheet at a time to the meek deputy standing beside him.

'Maybe after we're back from our voyage,' Hero replied. 'If you know anyone who's sailing, that is.'

The harbourmaster sucked his teeth as he considered her question. 'I hear the *Behemoth* is preparing to set off in the next day or so,' he said. 'Not surprising.

The captain's as mad as a saltwater drunk. No doubt you'll have a lot in common.'

'What's his name?' asked Joss.

The harbourmaster's deputy snickered, stopping at a look from his boss. The deputy shuffled his stack of papers and went back to his business.

'Gyver. Captain *Joan* Gyver,' the harbourmaster said. 'And you'd best be remembering the "captain" part, if'n you want to stay on her good side. You'll find her at the dock. Now, if that's all, I already had more than enough work to do before that mob of marauders swept into town. Not that you'll find Regent Greel doing anything about it, or even so much as shifting his fat ar–'

'Thank you,' Drake said, grabbing the harbour-master's ink-stained hand and giving it a firm shake. 'But we should probably get going if we're to catch the captain in time.'

The prentices found the *Behemoth* moored at the very end of the pier. It lolled in the water like a slumbering beast, as big and nasty as its name would suggest, built of curving black iron with blood red runes inscribed on its hull, a spine of masts and smokestacks running the length of it.

All the other ships surrounding it lay empty and quiet. Not the *Behemoth*. Its crew was busy readying the steamship for its voyage, while dockworkers loaded in supplies up the gangplanks. In among all the activity, a lone figure stood high upon the ship's upper deck. Her coppery hair was slicked back and braided in a tail that fell between her shoulderblades, brushing the oilskin coat that she wore over a ruffled red blouse.

'Bernard! Alonso!' she shouted at two of the crew who were idling beside a stack of crates. 'Quit your blathering and get back to work! I have no need for jesters or washerwomen on my boat, and don't either of you forget it!'

'Is that her?' Joss asked. 'Captain Gyver?'

'Who else would it be?' Hero groused beside him. Even with everything that was happening, it was comforting to know that she hadn't lost her sense of good humour.

'Well met there, captain!' Drake called out, waving his hand to capture the woman's attention. 'May we speak with you for a moment?'

The captain said nothing, but turned her steely gaze to the three prentices huddled together beside her ship. The intensity of her stare was keen, as piercing as the point of an arrowhead. But then a smile found her face.

'And what business would I have with a couple of lizardfolk and their mammoth-herding companion, dare I ask?' she said, her grin shrouding the sharpness of her words.

'We're seeking passage to the Northern Tundra,' Drake explained. The surrounding sailors shared a range of dubious glances. 'We were told you might be able to help us.'

'Ha!' Captain Gyver said. 'I'm sorry, friend, but this isn't a charter cruise.'

'We're not looking for charity. We'd pay our way,' Hero told her.

'Even so. I'm a merchant captain, not a tour guide.'

'What about a kind soul in a time of need, then?' Joss asked. 'Our friend was taken, along with half the town. We're going to the Northern Tundra to find them and bring them home.'

Gyver only snorted. 'You'd be best off leaving the heroics to the proper authorities, boy. Those noble intentions of yours are likely to get you all killed. Or worse. And the last thing I need on my ship is a gang of unsalted, unblooded laggards suffering from delusions of grandeur.'

A voice rang out from further up the dock. 'Joan Millicent Gyver! I never knew you to be such a blackheart!'

Joss and the others turned to see a woman walking towards them. She was wearing the same oilskin as Gyver, her head shaved so close that it made her skin shine. A pair of gold-rimmed glasses framed eyes of burnt amber, and her complexion was the darkest shade that Joss had ever seen – darker even than his own. It marked her as hailing from distant Mraba, far beyond the western shores of Ai.

'Qorza! Button that lip lest I sew it shut for you!' the captain shouted, though the lightness of her tone betrayed her.

The woman, Qorza, merely grinned. 'Yes, captain,' she said, offering a mock salute.

Captain Gyver went on, 'I expected you back hours ago! The ship's not going to sanctify itself, y'know.'

'You can thank the township of Crescent Cove for that. Everything's shut up tighter than a clamshell after the raid. I had to bang on the apothecary's door near on half an hour before he'd serve me.' Qorza hefted the bulging satchel she was carrying up into the air. 'And ships don't get sanctified without proper supplies.'

'Never mind all that.' Gyver raised her hand in a dismissive wave. 'Just get to work already, will you? I won't be setting off late on account of your procrastination.'

But Qorza ignored the captain's orders in favour of staring at Joss, Hero and Drake, scrutinising them from behind her lenses.

'Who are our friends here?' she asked.

'Just a bunch of wayward timewasters,' the captain said.

A wave of anger rushed through Joss. 'Clearly we're

not going to find any help here. We'll have to make our own way to the Northern Tundra,' he said to Drake and Hero, before shooting one last scornful look at Captain Gyver. 'I'm sure we can find *someone* with a heart beating inside them. Let's go.'

He was a little way down the pier when he heard Qorza call out to him. 'Tell me, boy – did you perchance have any kin from Daheed?'

Joss stopped. It wasn't unusual for people to ask him about Daheed, but there was something in the tone of her voice …

'My father and mother. But they died in the Destruction,' he said, facing her. 'Why?'

Qorza walked towards him, studying him so closely he took a small step backward. 'I don't mean to be presumptuous,' she said. 'But you have the most familiar look about you. Your family name. It's not Sarif, is it?'

Joss blinked. 'How did you know that?'

A single, barking laugh erupted from Qorza's mouth. She grinned up at the captain. 'Joanie! Can you believe it – this is Naveer's boy!'

'Naveer Sarif?' the captain asked, clearly taken aback. 'Your old mentor?'

'The very same!' Qorza beamed, looking Joss over as Captain Gyver took hold of a mooring rope that stretched up onto the deck and used it to zip down onto the pier. Striding to Qorza's side, she stared at Joss with the same intensity as her shipmate did.

'Do you know this Naveer?' Hero whispered to Joss.

Before he had the chance to shake his head, Qorza was answering on his behalf. 'I'd safely say he would know his own father, though the memory may be dim. You were quite young when tragedy came to the Gleaming Isle. Weren't you, Josiah?'

'You know my name?' Joss asked, stunned.

'Of course,' replied Qorza. 'After all, I was there on the day it was bestowed upon you, a guest among all your family, along with the fishing boat captain after whom you were named. The ceremony was held upon Daheed's First Step, on the Thousand Sacred Stairs that led into the Silver Sea. I still remember how tightly your parents held you as they soaked your head in the foaming water. When it was all done we withdrew to Consular Plaza – they'd set up a marquee there. We ate and drank and laughed in celebration of you and your family's happiness. It's that shining memory I keep of them all these years later, long after they were lost to us all.'

Joss didn't know what to say. Ten years since their passing and all he remembered of his parents were fragments, precious and few. Now, here stood a stranger who spoke of them with fond familiarity. Joss would never have dared dream that such a thing was possible.

'Josiah, you don't know me,' Qorza said, her tone growing serious. 'If you did, you'd know that even with all the games that she and I might play, I would never seek to undermine my captain. But in light of the ties you and I share, and of the tremendous work of fate that brought us together here and now, I am confident she might show some of the compassion of which you spoke and reconsider having you travel with us.'

Qorza fixed Captain Gyver with a bewitching smile. The captain chewed the inside of her cheek, gave a tetchy grunt, then finally relented. 'We leave tomorrow at dawn,' she sighed, before stomping over to the ship's gangplank. 'Be here in time and there'll be a place for you. And don't make me regret it.'

Qorza's smile widened into a grin as she gave a small and courteous bow. 'Until tomorrow then, Josiah,' she said, pulling her satchel onto her shoulder and following the captain. As Joss watched her go, a lifetime's worth of questions cascaded through his head, all of them so tantalisingly close to being answered. And with them came also a sliver of hope, tiny but undeniable, that their journey would lead them to Edgar.

———

The hull echoed with the sounds of despair. Men, women and children all wept and shook with misery.

And to his shame, Edgar was one of the loudest of them all. His face ached where he'd been struck, his lip was swollen and he could taste blood. Through the pain he shed bitter tears. His nose was running and his chin wobbling, just like a frightened little boy who'd lost his mother. He felt disgusted with himself, but the emotion would not be held back.

He still couldn't quite understand how it had all happened. One moment he'd been running for the inn, its front door in sight, the next he'd been snatched up and carried away. The more he'd tried to resist, the angrier the pyrates had grown. Eventually, one of them had used the pommel of his machete to subdue him, smashing him so hard that he'd seen sparkly pterosaurs fluttering in the air before him. Everything had gone black after that. And then he'd woken up here, in chains. It was enough to make anyone get a little watery.

'Are you hurt?' someone gently asked him.

Edgar looked to see a slender woman opposite him, her face lined with age and concern.

'I'm sorry, I – yes, I'm – no, I mean …'

'Shush now,' she said, her manacles rattling as she placed a comforting hand on his knee. 'Take a moment. Breathe. Everything is OK.'

'But it's not!' Edgar replied, the words bursting from him. 'We're somewhere only the Sleeping King can say!

Held captive by monsters who want to do with us what only the Sleeping King can know!'

'Don't you see, though,' the woman said, 'if they wanted us dead, we would be by now. Which can only mean we're being held for ransom. All we need to do is keep calm and wait for rescue.'

She said it with such certainty that Edgar believed her. Or at least he knew how much he wanted to believe her.

'Wait for rescue …' He tried to ignore the doubt that was not only flickering in the woman's eyes, but clutching at his own heart as well. 'Right.'

The woman drew closer to him, inspected his lip. 'My name is Lilia, by the way. I'm a physician.' Edgar flinched at her touch as she ran her fingers lightly across the swelling, then he relaxed into it. 'And the good news is that I don't think you'll be needing stitches.'

'I'm Edgar.'

'Pleasure to meet you,' she said, gripping his one gloved hand, 'despite the circumstances.' She surprised him again with a warm smile, before a sudden clang from the front of the ship made them both jolt.

'Keep quiet back there, lest I rip you from ear to rear!' bellowed one of the pyrates, smashing his fist against the cabin wall. 'We've a ways to our destination and I won't be tolerating any racket!'

The hostages cowered and fell into a tortured silence. Edgar could only offer Lilia a look of gratitude by way of thanks. She nodded, then settled back against the wall and closed her eyes as if in meditation. With nothing else to do, Edgar tried to follow her example. Pressing his back against the cold steel hull, he scrunched up his face and concentrated on the same few words, over and over again.

Keep calm. Wait for rescue. Keep calm. Wait for rescue.

If only such a thing seemed possible.

CHAPTER TEN

A RUMBLING STORM

T HE sun was only just creeping up into the sky as the *Behemoth* set sail with Joss and his brethren aboard. Their arrival at the dock had not been without its challenges. First there was Joss's protracted farewell with Azof at the stables, with the raptor somehow sensing what was happening.

'Shush now, you silly creature,' Joss told him as he smoothed down the thunder lizard's feathers. 'I'll be back before you know it, and they'll take good care of you here in the meantime.'

Still the raptor chittered nervously, nuzzling his snout into his master's ear. It was enough to make Joss wish that he'd pushed Drake harder to fashion that thermal cloak. He wiped a tear from his eye. Ordinarily he might have baulked at such a show of sentimentality in front of the others, but Drake had been too busy saddling up Pietro to take any notice, while Hero proved just as syrupy in comforting Callie.

Their farewells said and their stable fees paid up, their next complication came as they reached the docks with Pietro in tow. Captain Gyver was standing at the ship's gangplank with a clipboard in hand. Upon seeing the massive tundra bear, her face told a tale that was short and sharp, with a dark and violent ending.

'Nobody mentioned anything about any animals.'

'He's clean, tidy and well behaved. And he's made this voyage before without incident,' Drake quickly replied.

'We'll pay extra,' Hero added.

Captain Gyver eyed them with suspicion, but nevertheless relented. 'Get him into the hold, quick as you can. I won't have my crew tending to him. He's your responsibility – understood?'

'Yes, ma'am,' Drake said, wasting no time in guiding Pietro up the gangplank and onto the ship. As they led the bear across the deck and down into the cargo hold, Joss kept an eye open for Qorza. There was no sign of her.

They found Pietro's accommodation alongside their own – three hammocks strung up in a dank corner. Deciding it was best to stay out of the way, Joss and his brethren settled in among the stacks of barrels to play a game of castes, using a crate for a table. Hero plucked the deck of cards she'd bought at the festival from her jacket pocket, shuffled them, then dealt.

'Normal thunderfolk rules,' she announced as she threw everyone their hand of six cards, one at a time. 'One swap each and points as printed. Dealer shifts with each hand. We have no coin to wager so we'll be playing for bragging rights instead.'

Picking up his cards, Joss examined his hand. Castes was played with a deck that included three suits: red, blue and gold. Each suit consisted of one King, two Messengers, four Attendants, six Paladeros, eight Wardens and ten Servants. The Kings were worth ten points, the Messengers eight points, and so on down the line until all that was left were the Servants with one point each.

Joss had only Servants.

'So,' Drake said as he sifted through his cards, 'here we are.'

'Mm,' Hero grunted.

'I wouldn't have thought it was possible, finding a ship willing to sail under these conditions. But you did it,' Drake said to Joss, getting to the point. 'Edgar must mean a lot to you.'

Joss tossed the card he wanted to exchange into the centre of the makeshift table.

'Friends are as rare as kings,' he said as Hero dealt the

replacement cards. 'Which makes them very valuable. And I always believed that you fight for what you value.'

Drake glanced up from his cards and smiled ever so slightly, touched by what he'd heard or perhaps pleased with the hand he held. That left Joss to examine the new card that had landed in front of him. A Warden. He frowned. Perhaps he could still bluff his way through. He tried to concentrate.

What am I even doing here? he asked himself as Hero went on to win the round and Drake gathered the cards to deal the next one. Somewhere out in the world, Edgar and all the people taken from Crescent Cove were in mortal peril. But even more immediately, somewhere on this ship was a woman who held answers to questions that had haunted Joss his entire life. His mind reverberated with everything he wanted to ask her, everything he wanted to know. And between those two earth-shattering concerns, here he was playing cards.

And losing.

'Attention, Prentice Sarif!' Hero blurted in his ear, imitating a loudspeaker. 'It's your turn to deal.'

'Oh.' Joss collected the deck, tapping it on the crate to make sure the cards were flush. He tapped and tapped, until the deck was a perfect brick between his fingertips. And then he tapped again.

'Please don't take this the wrong way, Joss, but is there

somewhere else you'd prefer to be?' asked Drake, his eyes shifting from the cards to Joss's face.

'Actually.' Joss set the deck down. 'There *is* something –'

'Go,' Hero said. She picked up the cards to shuffle them and then start dealing them between Drake and herself. 'We can look after ourselves.'

'Are you sure?' Joss asked.

'I'm surprised you haven't gone already, to be honest,' Drake replied, smiling at him. Even Hero managed a smirk as Joss hopped up and rushed for the stairs.

Emerging onto the ship's deck, he saw the crew hard at work, but still no sign of Qorza. 'Excuse me.' Joss addressed the sailor who looked the least busy. He was an older man, with leathery skin and shock white hair, his chest as round as a rum barrel. 'Can you tell me where I could find Miss Qorza?'

'*Miss* Qorza?' the sailor repeated, then snorted with laughter. 'Alonso! Did you hear that! This wee spurt is looking for *Miss* Qorza!'

A second sailor dropped from the overhead rigging to join the first. '*Miss* Qorza, don't you please! Will wonders never cease, Bernard!'

The two sailors slapped each other on the back as they enjoyed a good laugh at Joss's expense. Joss glowered but held his tongue. This was too short a journey to go about making enemies.

'I'm sorry, lad. We don't mean to test you none. It's just been a leviathan's age since anyone exchanged customs of the like around here,' said Bernard, the first sailor, as he wiped a tear from his eye. 'You'll find Qorza's quarters at the aft of the ship, right by the captain's.'

'And the aft of the ship would be …'

Bernard stifled a chuckle and gestured to the rear deck. 'That way, lad, that way.'

'Thank you,' Joss said, his face burning bright red. He hadn't gone more than ten steps before he heard the two sailors burst out in another round of laughter. He turned to see them bowing and curtseying as they called each other *Mister* Bernard and *Mister* Alonso.

Joss was relieved to disappear back inside the ship. The interiors at this end couldn't be more different from the hold. Instead of iron struts, the walls were panelled with rich oak that had been shellacked to a blinding sheen. The passageway led to a pair of ornate doors, which featured a pair of curved, brass tentacles as their handles.

Beside that, tucked away like an old broom cupboard, was a small room from which a warm light emanated. Approaching the open door, Joss saw a tiny cabin overstuffed with leather tomes, bottled herbs and countless toolkits and, at a table in the centre, a woman with a shaved head and her back to the door.

'I was wondering how long it would take you to come find me,' Qorza said as she filled out a large journal, the scratching of her pen sounding like a raptor with a nasty itch.

'I thought maybe you'd search me out yourself,' Joss replied, lingering in the passageway.

'It can be hard, grappling with questions you've wanted answered your whole life. I didn't wish to rush you,' Qorza replied, still focused on her work. 'What would you like to know?'

'My father. You said his name was Naveer ...' Joss began, poking at the tentacle doorhandles of the cabin beside Qorza's. 'What was my mother's name?'

Qorza stopped writing. She put down the pen. Her chair creaked as she turned around. 'You mean you don't know?'

Joss bit his lips together and shook his head.

'Isra,' Qorza said, eyes sparkling beneath her cabin light. 'Isra and Naveer Sarif. And they were fine people. Perhaps the finest I've ever known.'

'How did you know them?'

'Your father trained me. I was a deckhand aboard his vessel, the *Seeker*. He must have seen some potential in me as he took me under his wing and showed me his ways.'

'*His* vessel?' Joss said, seizing on what might prove something he'd always believed. 'So he was a captain then?'

'No, no,' Qorza chortled. 'Though to be fair, the crew respected him so much that he may as well have been. Even old Captain Melchior would more than likely have admitted to that. No, he was like me. He was the ship's ethereon.'

'*Ethereon?*' Joss repeated uncertainly.

Qorza's face fell in what looked to be shock. But, perhaps not wanting to embarrass Joss, she simply explained: 'Much like a wizard, though specialising in the repelling of spirits and the removal of hexes. You may have seen the runes engraved on the ship's hull. I put those there, just as your father showed me how to when he did the same for the *Seeker*.'

'Why would a ship need a wizard?' Joss drifted closer to Qorza's cabin.

'The ocean is a treacherous place. I'm right in thinking that you've spent some time in Thunder Realm, yes?'

'All my life. Ever since ...' Joss faltered. 'Ever since that day.'

Qorza nodded solemnly. 'Well, much as Thunder Realm is riddled with ancient spriggan bindings, so too is the Silver Sea snared with hexcraft. To say nothing of the wraiths and wisps and sirens and changelings that haunt its waters, looking to ensorcel unsuspecting seafarers. It's an ethereon's duty to safeguard their ship and keep it from falling prey to such influences. And your father was one of the finest ethereons on the Silver Sea.'

'I never knew …' Joss said, venturing all the way into the cabin until he was standing by Qorza's side. 'I mean, I always knew he was a sailor. A captain, I thought. I remember sailing with him once when I was very young. And I remember the strange instruments he kept at home, gold and glass objects that he polished every day. I took them to be navigational tools or something like that.'

'The devices of an ethereon,' Qorza said, and reached for a nearby bag. Unbuttoned, it fell open to reveal an array of gleaming tools, each of them searingly familiar. Joss gaped as he grazed the tools with his fingertips.

'Is this aurum?'

'You have a keen eye,' Qorza told him, sounding both impressed and delighted. 'Not many people can distinguish aurum from regular gold.'

'Neither could I when I first saw it,' he replied, and reached for his sword-belt. Unsheathing the Champion's Blade, he presented it to Qorza for inspection. 'But others have shown enough interest that I quickly learned.'

'What a remarkable weapon!' Qorza said. 'May I?'

Joss nodded, offering it to her.

'How tremendous!' she breathed as she took the sword in hand. 'I've heard of the weapons that paladeros offer as prizes in their ceremonial competitions, but I never realised their true significance ...'

As Qorza examined the blade, Joss cast a curious eye over her cabin. There was no bed to be seen, which left him wondering where she laid her head at night. But of more interest were the various items she'd collected. Among the wands and the bottles of blessed water, there were also needles, scalpels and what looked to be a filtered muzzle for the applying of anaesthetic.

'What are all these for?' he asked.

Qorza looked up from the Champion's Blade to see what Joss was enquiring about. 'An ethereon's role is multifaceted,' she explained. 'Once, a ship would have employed both an ethereon and a physician. But that was a long time ago. Now an ethereon must be as adept at setting bones and sewing wounds as they are at exorcisms and incantations. It's demanding work, but rewarding.'

Qorza handed back the sword. 'I imagine you have a thousand more questions and no idea where to start,' she said. 'But I'm afraid I have a number of duties which I must attend to right now. If you're curious to see exactly what an ethereon does, I'll be performing a warding ritual on the main deck tonight. You'd be most welcome to observe.'

'I'd like that,' Joss replied as he slipped the Champion's Blade back into its scabbard. 'Thank you.'

Qorza beamed happily at him. 'Then I'll see you after dinner,' she said. 'Though before you go, I have a question of my own.'

'Yes?' Joss said, unsure of what someone so knowledgeable could possibly have to ask him.

'Your friend and the other missing townsfolk – are you really planning to rescue them? Or were you just spinning a story that you thought the captain wanted to hear?'

Joss didn't have to consider his answer. 'I've bent the truth a time or two. But I've never believed in filling people's ears with false promises because I hoped they'd like the sound of them,' he said, and Qorza's eyes shimmered even brighter.

'I see,' she said. 'I hope then that you find them.'

'So do I.'

They bade each other farewell, and Qorza turned her attention back to her papers. As he left her cabin, Joss felt the first rumblings of a storm in the pit of his stomach. Their conversation had brought with it a profound sense of shame.

To someone who'd known his parents as well as Qorza had, it must have seemed that their own son couldn't care less about them, given how little he knew of the lives they'd led. Of course, nothing could be further from the truth. And if Qorza had any doubts, then tonight would be his chance to dispel them, even as the storm clouds lingered inside him, twitching with thunder and threatening a downpour.

CHAPTER ELEVEN

A CURIOUS AND UNSETTLING SIGHT

THE morning crawled. Joss lost count of how many rounds of castes they played, and when they finally tired of that they swapped to a game of whipcrack. By then it was well past midday, Pietro was snoring in the corner, and Drake suggested having lunch up on deck.

'You go ahead without me,' Joss said. 'I think I'll take a nap instead.'

'A nap?' Hero repeated, totally confused by the idea. After all, naps weren't exactly favoured in Thunder Realm. There was always far too much work to be done.

'Qorza invited me to watch her perform her ethereon duties later. I don't want to be too weary when the time comes,' he explained.

'But still' – Hero wrinkled her nose – 'a nap?'

'Come on,' Drake said, shooting Joss a wink and

steering Hero to the steps. 'Let's get some fresh air and leave Joss to have some shut-eye with Pietro.'

As grateful as Joss was for the peace and quiet, he was unsure if he'd actually be able to sleep. He just had too much going on in his head. Nevertheless, he crawled into his hammock and made himself comfortable. The tundra bear's breathing proved hypnotic, and soon Joss was drifting off.

When he woke, the cabin was almost in total darkness, his mind foggy. With no idea of how long he'd been asleep, he scrambled to his feet and went in search of the others. He found Drake on the main deck, leaning out over the railings, watching the waves crashing against the hull. The sound was so great he didn't hear Joss approaching until they were standing next to each other, elbow to elbow.

'Where's Hero?' asked Joss, joining Drake in admiring the view.

'She was fretting about the effect the salt air would be having on her weapons, so she's gone to find the quartermaster to barter for some blade oil. Though honestly, I think she's feeling a touch seasick. Safe to say a sailor's life is not for her.' Drake levelled a concerned gaze at Joss. 'How are you feeling?'

'Fine,' Joss replied with some puzzlement. 'Though why wouldn't I be?'

Drake grimaced and turned his attention to the water. The sun was bleeding across the horizon, drowning the sky with scarlet and gold. But strangely enough, amid all the burning colour, there stirred a shadow in the distance. While all the sea around it raged, the waves that broke where the shadow rested were little more than ripples. It was a curious and unsettling sight.

Joss shuddered. 'That's not – is it?' He couldn't give voice to the thought that throbbed as painfully as a wound.

'Daheed. Or where it used to stand, at least,' Drake said. 'I'm sorry, Joss. I didn't mean to draw your attention to it.'

'No. I'd prefer to see – I've always wondered …'

The words still wouldn't come. A lifetime's worth of wondering was now unfolding before him so rapidly that he felt unbalanced, as tossed about as the *Behemoth* as it crashed onward through the waves. Joss flinched as he felt Drake touch his shoulder. It seemed as if he was considering saying something, before deciding that perhaps silence was best.

They dined that evening beneath the stars. Onion soup was ladled out from a massive pot, which the crew mopped up with bread slathered in mammoth cheese and washed down with mulled wine. Figgy pudding was served for dessert, wrapped in cloth and still steaming.

The food was simple but filling, and not at all what Joss had expected. It reminded him of the meals served back at Round Shield Ranch, and the thought was enough to start him worrying about Edgar again. Would his captors be feeding him or leaving him to starve?

The sailors joked and laughed and told tall tales as they sat together, just as thunderfolk would do around a campfire. Even the captain joined in, seemingly happy to be dining with her crew rather than alone in her quarters. The only person missing was Qorza.

'She's a busy woman,' the captain said when Joss asked her where the ship's ethereon might be. 'And she has a busy night ahead.'

When everyone had finished their dinner, a few members of the crew fetched their instruments and began to play. Drums, accordion and fiddle whirled together in a jig, to which the rest of the crew clapped and stomped along.

Drake offered his hand to Hero. 'Care to dance?' he asked.

Joss couldn't have been more shocked than if he'd asked her if she wanted to fly to the moon with him. Until she accepted.

'But only if I lead,' she told him as they took each other arm-in-arm and joined the jig, moving with such confidence that they could have been secretly practising this routine for weeks. Joss had never seen either of them look so happy and carefree, both of them seeming to find a moment's reprieve from the hardships of the past few days. Even the ship's crew looked impressed, cheering his brethren on with gusto. Ordinarily Joss would have been happy to do the same. But he was far too distracted for that.

'Not in a mood for merriment, lad?' Captain Gyver asked him, refilling her cup from the wine barrel.

'Feels strange, after everything that just happened in Crescent Cove,' he admitted.

The captain cocked her head. 'We dance because we live another day,' she said. 'It's in dire times that you make sure to celebrate the simple things.' She raised her cup to him in salute, then wandered off into the crowd.

She was right, he knew. Even so, the most he could bring himself to do was tap his toe and smile vacantly. He watched the crowd as much as the dancers, hoping to spot a pair of gold glasses framing a set of amber eyes. But they remained frustratingly absent.

Gradually, the party grew thin. Those who weren't on duty retired below deck to sleep. Sweaty and exhausted, Drake and Hero joined Joss by the railing.

'Well, I'm done for tonight,' Drake said, draining what little liquid remained in his cup. 'Think I'll turn in.'

'I'll join you,' said Hero.

'What about you, Joss?' Drake asked.

'I'll stay. Qorza will be along any moment now, I'm sure.'

'Don't wait up too long,' Drake said, roughing up his hair the way an older brother might. 'We still have a lot of travel ahead of us.'

They all bade each other a good night, then left Joss to his own company. Patting down his hair, he settled in to wait. On deck, the crew went about their duties, including the lookout, who climbed up into the crow's nest. He looked no older than Joss himself. If life had turned out differently, it could have just as easily been Joss up in that nest, watching for whatever threats the night held.

'Well met by moonlight, Josiah,' Qorza called out, startling him from his musings. She stepped from the shadows that had gathered across the deck.

'You can call me Joss,' he replied as he stood and approached her. 'You didn't come up for dinner?'

'Too much to be done, unfortunately. I took a light meal in my cabin. Besides, I could never have worked around all that carousing. I'd have ruined the crew's good time.'

After seeing Qorza's collection of instruments earlier, Joss had expected her arms to be laden with obscure and exotic tools. Instead, she wore a simple satchel over the shoulder of her oilskin coat, in which Joss glimpsed a heap of charcoal.

'So.' Her boots clicked on the timber deck as she crossed to the starboard side. 'Let's get started, shall we?'

CHAPTER TWELVE

A HUNDRED MILLION KNIVES IN THE NIGHT

DROPPING to her knees, Qorza used the coal to trace arcane symbols on the deck's wooden planks. First she drew a large circle, cutting across it here and there with thin little dashes, before surrounding the circle with all manner of rune marks. It looked a lot like spriggan script, until she began to add wavy lines that flowed around the other symbols like water.

'I learned how to do all this from your father,' she said, standing up long enough to reposition herself, before starting to etch out a whole new symbol. 'But in thinking back on it today, I realised he was still quite a young man himself so, really, we were learning together. I was learning how to be an ethereon and he was learning how to be a teacher.'

'Really?' Joss said, strangely surprised by the idea of his father having been young. He'd always loomed so large in Joss's memory, it was hard to think of him as anything but a mythical and ageless being. Yet here was someone who'd called him friend. Already it was turning him into a mortal man of flesh and blood.

'You mentioned something about my parents naming me after a fishing boat captain,' Joss said as Qorza stood to start tracing another sigil, this one surrounded by stars.

'Josiah Eichmore,' she replied. 'He saved your father's life, you know. Before the *Seeker*, your father crewed on a different ship. During a voyage it was hit by a severe storm and was smashed to pieces. Naveer was one of the few survivors. He and the others clung to driftwood through the night, finally swimming ashore on a tiny patch of sand that would be too generously described as a desert island. They survived there for three days, catching what fish they could with what little supplies they had at hand, until the flash of your father's thunderbolt pendant caught the eye of a passing fishing boat captain. When Josiah Eichmore finally delivered your father home to safety, your mother was so overwhelmed with relief that she pledged there and then to name their firstborn child after him.'

'Even if I was a girl?' asked Joss, one eyebrow raised.

'You'd have made a fine Josie, no doubt,' Qorza said with a wink. Having begun her work on the starboard side of the ship, she was already halfway across the deck with almost every inch covered in markings. Even with all the questions Joss was asking her, she was impressively efficient.

'What did my mother do?' he asked her now, his curiosity growing hungrier the more it was fed. 'If my father was an ethereon and always away at sea ...'

'She worked in Daheed's Imperial Library, one of the greatest repositories of wisdom and culture that ever existed, now lost to the world.' Qorza stopped what she was doing long enough to sigh sadly. Grabbing a new piece of coal, she continued: 'And she was one of the smartest people I've ever known. I remember an article she authored on the history of Kahnrani poetry. Her words were as enchanting as the writings she sought to praise.'

'It was my mother who escaped with me when Daheed ... when what happened to Daheed happened,' said Joss. 'We shared a leaky old rowboat that was missing its oars. I remember the blood she had on her dress. We reached the shore in Crescent Cove with only enough time for her to tell those gathered there my name. And then she was gone ...'

Qorza had again stopped what she was doing, staring

up at Joss with a wellspring of sorrow in her eyes. 'I'm so sorry to hear that,' she said.

Joss shrugged awkwardly. 'Nothing you did.'

Perhaps sensing that he'd prefer not to have her staring at him, Qorza returned to her efforts. 'I have to admit,' she said, drawing a complex web of intersecting triangles, 'I had been wondering what had happened, what miracle had brought you here to stand before me. I should have known that your mother's resolve would have something to do with it. I just wish that miracle could have included her with it, and your father too if I was being greedy.'

'I thought I saw them once,' Joss said after clearing his throat of the emotion that had choked it. 'Just recently. In Vaal. Have you heard of it?'

'The Ghost City. Where the paladeros send their hopeful prentices to prove themselves,' Qorza said. 'A strange and vexing place is Vaal. Notoriously so.'

Joss thought back on his time in the Ghost City, fleeting as it was, where restless spectres had stalked him through the labyrinthine streets. He thought of the confrontation he'd had with the Stitched Witch, of the arcane blood ritual she'd hoped to perform by sacrificing his life. He thought of the Witch's menacing emissary, the masked figure known only as Thrall, who seemed to be able to shift between the shadows as if passing through an open window. That peculiar ability had allowed him to escape, and now he haunted Joss's dreams along with the spectres of Vaal.

Joss thought of all these things, these encounters with the unexplainable, and a chill ran up his spine. 'We don't talk much of the supernatural in Thunder Realm,' he told Qorza, holding his arms tightly around his chest. 'If it don't eat, bite, make muck or earn a buck, it's not worth the trouble. At least that's what the old fieldservs say.'

Qorza chuckled. 'I've not heard that one before. Don't know if I'll ever get the chance to use it myself.' Her laughter petered out to be replaced by a look of seriousness. 'You know, the world's a big place, Josiah. Bigger than the boundaries of Thunder Realm.'

'I'm coming to see that,' Joss replied, before his attention was diverted by a curious sight glinting on the horizon. 'What is that?'

He pointed out to the water, where a shimmering curtain of crystal flakes filled the sky. The curtain stretched on beyond the ocean's darkest edges, sparkling like a hundred million knives in the night.

'That's the Veil of Frost,' Qorza said, pulling the hood of her coat up over her head. 'I'd steel myself, if I were you.'

The *Behemoth* ploughed onward, bouncing over the choppy waters. Mesmerised, Joss watched the ship's prow pierce the curtain, the grasping tentacles of its kraken figurehead quickly engulfed by the frost. Then the rest of the ship quickly followed and the cold struck Joss like a slap across the face. It froze every exposed hair, thickened his blood, turned his teeth to chattering.

'Here, take this,' said Qorza, offering Joss a blanket. 'I should have given you fuller warning. But then there's nothing quite like your first time passing through the Veil. Bracing, isn't it?'

The only response Joss could offer was a trembling nod and a murmured thanks as he drew the blanket tight around his shoulders. It offered him little comfort at first, though gradually the heavy material warmed him and he found himself able to feel his limbs again.

He was staggered by how different things were on this side of the Veil. Where before the sky had been a flat black slab studded with stars, it was now rippled with a dense fog. Even the surface of the water was affected, with great clouds of mist whirling about the waves.

'I ne-ne-never realised …' he stuttered. He'd heard of the Veil of Frost, of course. Knew that it divided the Northern Tundra's eternal winter from the rest of the world. But reading about a phenomenon and experiencing it firsthand were two wildly different things.

'Mainlanders rarely do,' Qorza replied, looking entirely unbothered by the cold as she kept at her work, her coal fragmented to fine crumbs. She had almost filled the deck with her markings, which stretched from port to starboard.

'Do you do this every night?' Joss asked when he'd finally stopped shivering enough to be able to speak coherently.

'Every night that we're at sea.' Qorza discarded the remains of her coal and replaced it with a new piece. 'Depending on how worn away the sigils have become over the course of day, that is. Sometimes I can get away with just filling in the blanks. But not often.'

'Seems exhausting.'

'I prefer to think of it as absorbing,' she said. She was just about to press the tip of her coal against the deck when she stopped and looked at Joss. 'Would you like to do the honours and finish off the last sigil?'

'What, me?' Joss asked. 'But I wouldn't know what to do.'

'I can guide you.'

'But if I get it wrong, won't that leave the ship unguarded?'

'The longer you stand here arguing, the longer that continues to be the case. Don't worry so much. Spellcraft runs in your blood. And if you mess it up, I'll just start over.'

'You mean the entire deck?'

'That's right. So don't mess up,' she said with a devilish grin. 'Begin by drawing a circle, as round as you can make it.'

Hesitantly, Joss took the coal from her. He had just stooped down to make his first stroke when Qorza touched her fingertips to his shoulder.

'Wait,' she said. 'Do you hear that?'

Joss tilted his ear to the wind. There was a sound like fireworks fizzing through the air, far off at first but growing closer. He looked up to see what resembled a swarm of falling stars speeding across the surface of the water, crisscrossing each other as they leapt and flew from wave to wave. Joss was reminded of the fireflies in the ruins of the Forgotten Order, but these lights – whatever they were – burned both brighter and colder, the sparks they cast as sharp as icicles. He was about to ask if they had anything to do with the Veil of Frost when Qorza shouted, *'Joss! Take cover!'*

The warning came too late. One of the spheres of cold light shot up over the ship's railings, blinding Joss in a burst of luminescence. Then a sudden blow to the chest knocked him off his feet and into the quiet dark of nothingness.

CHAPTER THIRTEEN

A Parting Gift

A DARK sky stained with blood. A hole torn in the fabric of all things. A crimson fire burning fast and far, an unquenchable blaze. A stone mask watching with disinterest as a great black shadow ripped the world in two. All these things Joss saw, and they filled his heart with icy dread.

'Joss, can you hear me?' someone asked through the darkness. 'Joss, are you all right?'

He felt something tap at his face, making him wince. With great effort, he wrenched open his eyes. Qorza was crouched before him, her face full of concern.

'What happened?' Joss asked.

'You were struck by a wisp,' she said. 'But don't worry. They're mostly harmless –'

'*Mostly* harmless?' he repeated, rubbing his chest

where this *wisp* had hit him. His skin felt bruised and burnt, and that burning sensation now spread to his fingers.

'Compared with any of the other supernatural entities that you could have been attacked by out here,' Qorza replied.

'I saw … something,' Joss said, unsure of how to put into words the rush of sights and sounds that had flooded his head.

'A wisp's touch will often trigger visions,' Qorza replied. 'In fact, for as long as you bear its mark you'll be more susceptible to the supernatural as a whole.'

'Its mark?' Joss looked down as Qorza pointed at his chest. She must have unbuttoned his shirtfront, exposing the silver starburst that now scarred the skin above his heart. '*Muck!* It's not permanent, is it?'

'It should fade. But in the meantime it would be best to wear this.' Qorza reached into her jacket and removed a leather wristband with four small gold discs attached to it, each of them etched with the same sort of mystic symbols that she had inscribed across the deck.

Joss looked at it dubiously. 'Jewellery?' he said as Qorza thrust the bracelet into his hands. 'I'm not really the type –'

'It's not jewellery. It's a protective charm. With that scar on your chest you might as well be bleeding in megalodon-infested waters. This will help ward off any entities attracted by its presence. Consider it a pocket-size version of all the work we've done here tonight.'

With that endorsement, Joss slid the bracelet around his wrist. 'Thank you,' he said, buttoning his shirt. The wisp scar had warmed him up, but even so he retrieved the blanket and wrapped it around his shoulders again.

'Come on.' Qorza offered her hand. 'You're going to need to rest after a shock like that.'

She helped him up, and once she'd put the final touches on the last protective sigil she walked him below deck. Feeling like a paladero who'd suffered an ankylosaur-strike to the head, he collapsed into his hammock, so shaken that he couldn't recall Qorza leaving the room, nor did he remember thanking her on her way out. All he heard was the snoring of his brethren, the crashing of waves against the hull, and the breathing of the ship as it carried them on into tomorrow.

———

Joss awoke drenched in sweat. As bad as the visions had been after first getting struck by the wisp, his dreams had been even worse. They were filled with monstrous faces baring mirrored fangs, valleys of dead thunder lizards rotting beneath a black sun, and the final sensation of plummeting helplessly through a burning sky towards a scorched earth.

His chest throbbing, he tumbled out of his hammock and took in his surroundings. Both Pietro and Hero were still fast asleep, the tundra bear luxuriating in all the rest he'd caught up on while aboard the ship. Drake, however, was awake and fully alert. He was sitting, rigid, on the other side of the hold, peering out the only porthole. Shaking off his troubled night as best he could, Joss joined his friend.

'You look worse than I feel,' Drake said, glancing over.

'I had the strangest dream … It was –' Joss stopped. 'Wait. What do you mean?'

Drake turned back to the porthole. 'We're docking at Snowbridge,' he said, his voice edgy.

'Is that a problem?'

'I thought we'd be arriving at Stormport and going straight on to Starlight Fields from there. I never thought we'd be coming to Snowbridge.'

'What's wrong with Snowbridge?' Hero asked through a yawn, her hat still pulled down over her face.

'My father,' said Drake gravely. 'He's the harbourmaster here.'

Joss raised his eyebrows while Hero slowly pushed back the brim of her hat and sat up. 'Your father?' she said, sliding from her hammock to join them. 'But you don't speak to your father.'

'I don't.'

'You haven't spoken to him in years,' she went on.

'I haven't.'

'So this –' she stopped, leaving Drake to finish the thought for her.

'Is a complete disaster!' he said as he slumped against the wall.

———

As the *Behemoth* docked, its crew immediately set to unloading. While crates and barrels were winched from the hull to be safely deposited onto the wharf, Joss, Drake and Hero were left to fend for themselves. Unwilling to abandon the warmth of the ship for the cold outside, Pietro was proving stubborn in leaving. And, to make matters worse, they had to coax him out under the watchful eye of Captain Gyver.

'Thank you again for your hospitality, captain,' Joss said as he hunkered into the fur-lined coat Drake had lent him for the trip. It didn't fit quite right given how much taller his Bladebound brethren was, but he was more than grateful for its warmth.

'If you really want to thank me, you'll get that animal

off my boat before it mauls someone,' she replied, eyeing Pietro warily as Drake tried to cajole the bear into moving. 'And you'll find the person who really warrants your gratitude waiting by the gangplank.'

Looking over, Joss saw Qorza there, a red bandana wrapped around her head and a faint smile on her lips.

'Feeling any better?' she asked.

'A little,' he admitted, rubbing at the wisp scar.

'Try not to touch it too much. Let it heal.'

Joss nodded. 'I can't tell you how much it's meant, getting the chance to talk to you and hear your stories,' he told her. 'I hope we can stay in touch.'

'Of course! In fact, I have something for you. Consider it a parting gift.' Qorza handed him a disc made of copper and glass.

'A Scryer?' Joss asked, running his thumb over the device's crystal projector, its seams and screws. It was thicker than the one he remembered Zeke having on the Way, its construction a little more crude. Obviously an older model.

'I've loaded it with the call sign for our transmitter, should you ever need to reach me,' Qorza said. 'But that's not all. Press the red button there on the side.'

Curious, Joss did so, and the disc exploded with light. Images swirled all around him, a pair of faces that, until now, had only hovered at the edges of his memory.

'My parents ...' Joss said, the words struggling out of his throat as he stared in awe at the people who gave him life. They looked ghostly to him, translucent and serene. Both of them were dressed in what looked to be ceremonial robes of pale silk, and each was holding a beaded necklace, his mother's white and decorated with a golden sun pendant, his father's black with a silver lightning bolt. Smiling warmly, they each slipped their necklace over the other's head, settling it in place.

'Is this –?'

'Their wedding,' Qorza explained. 'It's Daheedi tradition for the bride and groom to bestow necklaces upon each other. Each pair is unique, made by the jeweller for that couple so that they mirror one another, though always with the female symbol of the sun and the male symbol of the thunderbolt. I had to hunt through my records to find the footage I recorded that day. I added a few other images, too ...'

The projection flickered, and what had been Naveer and Isra's wedding ceremony now jumped to their young son's naming day. Joss watched as the couple knelt together on a stone step worn smooth by the sea, to dip their baby in the salt water.

'That's me!' Joss's voice was soft and wavering. He watched with rapt fascination as the waves lapped over his infant self's forehead, his parents delighted at how calm he was. They each cooed and laughed as they raised him back up, offering a view of him to the crowd. Everyone applauded.

'They look so happy,' Joss said.

'They were,' Qorza replied as the image faded.

Tears streaked Joss's face. They clouded his eyes and warmed his cheeks. His hands shaking, he wiped them away. 'I don't know what to say,' he told Qorza, who was watching him with concern. 'Thank you. So much. For everything.'

'I was serious, you know. Should you need anything, we're only a push of a button away.'

'And Captain Gyver? She'd say the same?'

'Oh, trust me. She can put up a tough front, but –'

'I understand,' Joss said with a wave. 'I have my fair share of people who put up tough fronts …'

Qorza grinned, then gestured to the pile-up that was growing behind Joss's back. 'I think your help may be appreciated over there,' she said. 'So let's call this goodbye for now. And good luck with finding your friend.'

Joss offered her his hand, but Qorza pulled him into a hug instead. When they parted, he tucked the Scryer safely away in his coat pocket, then rushed over to help Drake and Hero get Pietro down the gangplank, paw by paw, disregarding the comments of the frustrated crew held up behind them.

The harbour was deathly quiet. With the *Behemoth* the only ship berthed, there was no shortage of dockworkers ready and waiting to unload the cargo in hope of a day's pay. Their efforts were overseen by the harbour officials, who strode around the wharf to ensure that everything was done according to regulations. It was easy enough to distinguish the two parties. While the workers were dressed in greasy overalls and rugged jackets, the officials all wore black leather gloves and impeccably tailored coats of dark navy, their brass buttons flashed in the frosty light.

'We can hire a couple of snowskimmers for you both from Efram's Garage and be on our way within the hour,' Drake said as kept his head down and marched towards the harbour gates as fast as he could without breaking into a gallop.

'Is that wise at this time of day?' Hero asked, she and Joss both struggling to keep pace as they lugged the belongings that couldn't be strapped to Pietro's harness. 'Doesn't the sun set early here?'

'I've lived here all my life. A little dark won't be any trouble. We can navigate by the stars if it comes to that.'

'Drake,' Joss said to silence. '*Ganymede!* Stop. Wait. You're not thinking things through. We need to talk about this, come up with some sort of plan –'

'I *have* a plan,' Drake shot back without slowing, Pietro huffing at his side. 'The plan is to leave this merciless patch of ice before anyone has a chance to even know we've been here.'

He threw the barest of looks over his shoulder, and that one moment of ill-attention was all he needed to walk straight into one of the navy-coated officials. Both of them tumbled to the ground, Drake landing painfully on his rear while the official sprawled out on his shirtfront.

'Ganymede!' Hero exclaimed as she rushed over to him, helping him up while Joss tended to the official.

'Sorry about that, sir. My friend didn't see you.'

'Then he should have been looking where he was damn well going!' the official barked.

At the sound of his voice, Joss noticed Drake freeze. Brushing himself off, the official rose to his full height, his moustache twitching irritably as he spun around to confront the person who'd knocked him over. They both went pale with shock.

'Gwendoline!' the official exclaimed, his eyes wide beneath a bushy brow. 'What are you doing here?'

Drake clenched his jaw, clenched his fists, clenched his entire being. 'Hello, father,' he said. 'Fancy running into you here.'

CHAPTER FOURTEEN

A HAPPY HOME

D RAKE stared blankly at Joss, looking entirely unlike himself. Though his hair was cut almost as short, his face was much younger. And his expression was pure misery. Perhaps it had something to do with the clothes he was wearing, the dress a frilly concoction of lace and ribbons.

'I remember that day,' the real Drake said as he joined Joss by the fireplace, perusing the collection of family portraits that were arranged on the mantelpiece. 'There was a two-hour war of words getting me into that outfit.'

'You had something else in mind?'

'My grandfather's old dinner suit,' Drake said, picking up the framed picture to stare at it. 'I'd had it tailored and everything. But my parents didn't take too kindly to that idea.'

Drake's smile was a small, fragile thing. The same smile he'd forced back at the wharf, when his father had coerced him into bringing his friends home for the evening following their brief and awkward reunion.

'Your mother and sister would both be heartbroken to know you'd been in town and didn't bother to see them,' his father had said over Drake's many protests. It was that argument that had finally clinched it. Before they'd even really known what was happening, all three prentices had been escorted to the outskirts of town, to have dinner and stay the night in the Drake family household.

As the smile faded from Drake's face, Joss peeked over his shoulder to scrutinise the portrait more closely. Drake's father was at the centre of the picture, stoic and sober, with the rest of the family assembled around him. Drake's mother looked almost as upset as Drake, with strands of hair falling loose from her bun to dangle in his sister's face. While his sister had her mother's arm around her, Drake was standing all on his own, isolated from the rest of his family.

'You look so …' Joss searched for the right word. 'Different.'

Drake scoffed. 'You say different. I say strange. And I felt even stranger. It wasn't long after that photo was taken that I set off for Starlight Fields to become a prentice.'

'And to become "Ganymede"?'

Drake's smile turned bittersweet. 'Remember when we talked in the Barbed Forest?' he asked, and Joss cast his mind back to the night that Drake had shared the story of his life: though he had been born a girl, he had never seen himself that way, never felt that reflected who he truly was. 'I've always been Ganymede. Even when nobody else called me that. Even when the world saw me elsewise.'

Joss flushed with embarrassment to have made such a mistake. Not that Drake seemed offended. He was far too preoccupied for that.

'This really is going to be hard. Isn't it?' Joss said, the gravity of the situation weighing heavily on him. Drake merely ran a thumb over his former visage, then placed the portrait back on the mantle. Pivoting, he spotted a half-assembled metal cylinder sitting atop an oily rag on a nearby sideboard.

'What's a gyrothruster doing in here?' he mumbled, picking it up. While he scrutinised the device and fiddled with the mess of wires that hung from one end, Joss turned his attention to the family home.

It was a unique structure, shaped like the circular dome of a High Chamber. All of the individual rooms were clustered around the central parlour, much as the Drake clan itself had clustered around their patriarch in that picture taken all those years ago. The room was decorated with a suite of wooden furniture and stone tables, mammoth-skin rugs and embroidered tapestries, with brass lamps hanging high overhead from the timber rafters. They shed a buttery light that was complemented by the crackling fireplace, turning what could have been a large and draughty space into a cosy den.

It certainly wasn't what Joss had expected while on the way here. On the rare occasions that Drake had spoken of his family, Joss had imagined his home to be something more like a military barracks or a boarding school. Formal and austere and, most of all, cold.

This was the complete opposite of that, and it made Joss long for his own place in the world to which he could return, a place where his memories were kept safe and the people closest to him lived in comfort and contentment. Of course he knew it was more complicated than that for Drake. A handsome home didn't make for a happy one. But surely even an unhappy home was better than no home at all.

It didn't look like Hero would agree. She was leaning against the doorframe at the opposite end of the room, arms folded across her chest as she stared resolutely at her own reflection in the polished floorboards. Not even the chiming of the grandfather clock stirred her, though its ticking served as a constant reminder for Joss that every moment they lingered here was another moment lost in tracking down Edgar. As restless as that prospect left him, he knew this reunion wouldn't be rushed. Still, he couldn't help counting the passing seconds as Drake's father entered from the adjoining study, having excused himself earlier to go use the illumivox machine.

'I spoke with your Aunt Glynis. Beatrix and your mother left some time ago. They shouldn't be far off now.' Spotting the gyrothruster Drake was holding, he nodded at it. 'From one of the old snowskimmers. Haven't been able to get the damn thing running.'

'Probably just a filtration issue,' Drake replied, still facing the sideboard as he tapped the instrument between his fingers.

'Can't be,' his father said. 'I cleaned out the housing unit.'

'What about the secondary housing unit? Where the starter circuit's kept?'

His father's eyes flickered as he looked away, turning his attention to Joss and Hero. 'Would, uh … would anyone like some coffee?'

'I'm fine,' Hero said.

'Some hot cocoa would be nice, if you have it,' said Joss.

Drake's father grimaced. 'I, uh … don't really …'

'It's usually mother who takes care of all that,' Drake said on his father's behalf.

'Oh,' Joss replied. 'Well. Coffee would be just as good. Thanks.'

Drake's father nodded, then turned to his son. 'And you, Gwendo–' He caught himself as Drake winced in much the same way his father had. 'And you?'

'Thank you.' Drake again mirrored his father, offering him the same formal nod.

His father retreated into the kitchen as fast as his feet would carry him and Drake shot Joss a consolatory look. 'Sorry. He doesn't know how to be … well, he doesn't know how to *be*, really.'

Joss waved away the concern. 'What about you? How are you feeling?'

'We don't have to stay here, you know,' Hero piped up from across the room. 'We can go whenever you feel the need.'

'Thank you. Both of you,' said Drake. 'But now that we're here, I suppose I should at least try to –'

The doorhandle beside Hero clicked and rotated. She moved out of the way just as it sprang open and a young girl with honey-coloured hair came rushing into the room.

'Ganymede!' she cried out, rushing straight for Drake. He almost dropped the gyrothruster as she crashed into him, her arms wrapping around him in a tight embrace.

'*Oof!*' he said, the wind knocked from him. 'Hey, kid! How's Trix?'

'Did you get all my letters?' the girl asked, too excited to take in his question.

'The ones you sent to Starlight Fields I did, but I've been on the road since then. Did you get mine?'

'I did! Was the Ghost City as scary as it sounded?'

'Scarier.'

'And is this Joss? And Hero?' The girl let go of Drake long enough to stare excitedly at them both.

'That's right,' Drake replied. 'Josiah Sarif of Round Shield Ranch, Hero of Blade's Edge Acres – allow me to introduce my sister, Beatrix Drake. Trix for short.'

'Pleasure to meet you,' Joss said, offering his hand.

Trix ignored it in favour of grabbing him in a hug that was just as intense as the one she'd given her brother. Then she flung her arms around Hero, who patted her shoulder so uncertainly that Joss couldn't help but smile.

'Ganymede has told me so much about you both!' she said, then, when Joss and Hero shared a look of apprehension, she added, 'Only good things, I promise!'

'I didn't realise you were in such close contact,' said Hero, addressing Drake.

'Not as close as I would like!' Trix replied. 'Ganymede, are you staying long? Please say you are!'

'Beatrix, don't be a bother now.' A woman's voice

floated from the doorway. Everyone looked to see Drake's mother standing beside Hero. The flaxen hair of the photo was now smoothed back and sprinkled with snowflakes. While Drake's mother hovered on the threshold, cold was rushing in from the mudroom, where their boots and coats had been left lined up on the racks. A guarded little smile flittered upon her lips, while worry pooled in her eyes. 'No doubt it's been a long journey here for your sister and her – for *his* – for *our* guests.'

'Mother, I –' Drake began with a weary sigh, but his mother immediately shooed away her own words as she took a tentative step inside.

'I'm sorry, I didn't mean to – it's just been so long since … And it's hard to know the right thing to say …' Her hands were trembling.

Drake's father returned at that moment from the kitchen, with enamel coffee mugs in his grasp. His face fell as he looked at his wife, and he set the coffee mugs aside. 'Eudora. You're upset.'

'No, Torvald, I just –'

Drake's father turned on his son. 'What did you say?'

Drake glared. 'Nothing.' He slammed the broken gyrothruster back on the sideboard, making the family pictures over on the mantelpiece shake. Even Trix jumped at the noise. 'But it's good to know that you regard me as charitably as you ever did.'

'You run off in the middle of the night, break your mother's heart, shame your family, and you seek to lecture me on charity?'

'*Shame* my family? I didn't realise my existence was so shameful to you.'

'Yes, it was shameful!' Drake's father exploded.

'Torvald, please,' Drake's mother said, taking him by the arm in an attempt to calm him. But he would not be so easily appeased.

'It was shameful having to explain to all our friends and neighbours why you had fled in the night without a word, as if we were monsters who kept you locked away!' he shouted. 'For years we carried that burden, and not once did you seek to talk to us, to let us know you were safe and well.'

'I sent letters.'

'To your sister. Never to us. Not one word of contact! Do you have any idea what that did to your mother?'

Again, Drake's mother took hold of her husband. 'Torvald, we don't need to go into all that now. Please calm down.'

Her second attempt worked better than the first, helped as it was by Trix wedging herself between her parents to gaze pleadingly up at her father. When he spoke again, his tone was quieter, almost conciliatory.

'I don't mean to lash out. Especially not when we've

only just come back together.' He took a shuffling step forward, his brow wrinkled. 'But I need you to understand, Gw—'

Drake bristled, not allowing his father to again address him by a name he'd long ago left behind. 'My name is *Ganymede,*' he said, striding across the room. 'But don't worry, after tonight I won't ever bother you again. And then you can call me whatever you damned well please.'

Brushing past Hero, Drake flung open the mudroom door and then slammed it shut behind him. Hero's dark locks were whipped across her face by the sudden gust of air. Unfolding her arms and standing upright, she smoothed back her hair, adjusted her hat, then opened the door and left.

Drake's parents looked from the door to each other, and then to Joss. Joss took one step away from the mantelpiece, then another. He was halfway across the room when he thought to speak. 'You have a lovely home.'

No one answered as he grabbed his coat from the rack, sidestepped the melting piles of slush on the floor, and followed Drake and Hero out into the cold of the night.

CHAPTER FIFTEEN

A FAMILY HEIRLOOM

J OSS trudged through the thick bank of snow towards two figures breathing clouds of steam out by the bluestone barn, their backs to the house. They looked to be staring up at the aurora rippling in the sky above them, its radiance only really striking Joss as he cleared the corner of the barn.

Stretched across the full canvas of the sky, the aurora's flames were as green as absinthe and as red as phoenix feathers, churning like waves one moment and then flowing like ribbons the next. It was hard to believe its colours could have been caused by anything but magic as it swirled and danced, wrapping up the stars themselves in its luminous fabric. It would have been a wholly spectacular sight if not for the heartache that Drake was suffering in its glow.

Crunching through the ice, Joss approached his Bladebound brethren.

'How're you holding up?' he asked Drake.

'Fine,' he said, his eyes set on the sky. 'I was just apologising to Hero for my melodramatic exit. I didn't mean to make a scene.'

'And I was telling him that he needn't worry. We all know how family can be.'

Though of course she didn't mean anything by it, Hero's words stung Joss. They served as a stark reminder of everything he'd lost so early in life, as well as of an unspoken bond between his brethren that he could never share. Not that any of that mattered right now. Not with the hurt that Drake was feeling.

Tentatively, Joss sat down next to Hero, with Drake on her other side. Drake's hand was at his face, tracing his high cheekbones with his fingers, prodding at his dimpled chin. It was as if he were examining his own flesh and bone, testing to see it was real, making sure it hadn't turned to sponge.

'Do you remember that night on the Way? When we talked about the dreams we'd had of becoming paladeros?' he asked.

'I remember arguing about it,' Hero replied.

'Not one of our finer moments,' Joss admitted. The cold was so bitter that his whole body was trembling.

Looping his arms around his knees, he hunkered tightly to himself. Drake, meanwhile, looked untouched by the chill. Stretching his legs out before him, he turned his gaze to the aurora, though his fingers still explored the details of his face.

'I've been thinking about it a lot on the way here. I remember saying that it was all I'd ever wanted. But that isn't true. Before I dreamed of being a paladero, I dreamed of being nothing.'

Joss and Hero both stared at Drake with concern, listening intently as he continued.

'I would come out here and watch the aurora, and I would imagine it growing so bright that it reached out and absorbed me. Or I'd imagine myself at the bottom of the ocean, deep beneath the waves, where piece by piece I would dissolve as easily as an ice floe, never to be seen again, never to be heard, never to be ridiculed or judged. The idea of it comforted me ...'

'I don't know if I like the sound of all that,' Hero said, brow scrunched over her goggles, her mouth drawn tight. Drake smiled softly, his hand drifting away from his face to thread his fingers together with hers. To Joss's surprise, she didn't pull away.

'Not like that,' he said. 'Not really. Maybe in my darkest moments, I suppose ... but never for very long. There was too much going on in the world. Too much possibility. And I didn't want to sacrifice the chance that things could change. That *I* could change.'

Joss watched as the aurora shifted tones. What had been green and red now warmed to pink and gold, the colours lighting up Drake's face.

'That feeling became so much stronger the day I found an old photograph of my grandfather,' he said, looking almost like a stranger to Joss in this rosy glow. 'He was dressed in his finest furs, saddled on the back of his bear, Wagner, and he'd just been named the winner of the Tundra Games. His face, the resemblance – it was like discovering a version of myself that I'd never met but had always known, deep inside. That one image was everything I'd ever wanted to be and had never had the language to express. I wanted to be a paladero. I wanted to be me. The *real* me. I wanted to be Ganymede Drake.'

'Because being Gwendoline Drake – that was too painful for you?' A voice came from behind them. They turned to see Drake's father. He was standing by the barn wall, holding something longer than he was tall. It was wrapped up in a fur pelt and fastened with leather straps, and while there was no way of knowing how much he'd heard, he'd clearly been listening for a while.

'What do you want?' Drake asked him, pulling his hand from Hero's.

'To talk,' his father replied. He glanced at Joss and Hero. 'May we have a moment?'

Joss moved to stand, but Drake would have none of it. 'Hero and Joss are my brethren. Whatever you have to say to me, you can say in front of them.'

Drake's father swayed on the heel of his boot, uncertain. His jaw was clamped tight, as if he had a flood of words in his mouth threatening to burst loose. If only he would let them. 'Very well,' he relented, loosening the straps on the pelt. 'For what I said just now, and for all I said in the days and weeks and years before you took off for Starlight Fields ... I apologise.'

Drake blinked, Joss saw, clearly taken aback.

His father continued, his eyes on the knotted straps of his bundle as he worked them loose. 'I never meant to turn you away or make you feel like you were worth less than you are. Sometimes it can be hard to know the best path to take. It's your mother who reminds me that it should more often be the path of compassion. Understanding. Love. And she reminded me of that again, now. Which made me think. There's something that I've been meaning to share with you. Something I've wanted to pass on.'

Drake's father undid the last of the straps and pulled loose the pelt, revealing a gleaming spear of what looked to be platinum and bronze, its grip wrapped in finely embossed leather. Drake stared at it, stunned, as the aurora's rays leapt from its pointed tip.

'Grandfather's spear?' he said with quiet awe.

Drake's father nodded solemnly. 'The Icefire spear,' he said, setting the pelt down before walking forward. Joss and Hero also rose as Drake stood up to meet him. 'The prize he won that day at the Games – the last Tundra Games that would ever be held, as it turned out. You recall, I know. There was talk of him being sent to compete in the Tournament, if only his order had the funds to pay for it.'

'I remember. Well … I remember him talking about it.'

Drake's father chuckled. Somehow it managed to sound both affectionate and bitter. 'He did like to talk about it, didn't he?'

Examining the spear and the way the light played upon its surface, Drake's father went on. 'I was never really the son he wanted. Couldn't ride, couldn't fight, couldn't muster. I had a head for numbers and procedures, and dreams that stretched only as far as hearth and home. It was a disappointment for him, I know. He liked you, though. You've proven to be everything he could have ever wanted in his own son. And perhaps that's what I've struggled with so much – beyond any name that you may have wanted to be called or any identity you wished to claim for yourself. I'm ashamed to think of how I've acted. I hope that you can accept my apology, along with everything else that is yours by right.'

Raising his arms, Drake's father offered his son the Icefire spear.

'I – couldn't possibly …' Drake said.

'Yes. You can. The spear is yours. It always has been,' his father told him. 'Ganymede.'

Drake's eyes widened. Shaking, he raised his hands and accepted the spear. It seemed then to shine even brighter, as if it was exalting in being united with its true owner. Joss watched as Drake took a moment to look the blade over, to appreciate its weight in his grasp, before looking up again.

'Father …'

Neither Hero nor Joss knew what to do with themselves as Drake and his father embraced. They shifted awkwardly aside, Hero's feelings as impossible to read as ever, while Joss tried to focus only on his happiness for his friend, to not let the seed of jealousy he could feel sprouting inside him grow into something even uglier.

Casting his gaze elsewhere, Joss noticed two silhouettes at the window of the family home. He could just make out the tearful smile of Drake's mother, then the second silhouette dropped away, only to reappear again as the front door was thrown open. Trix's grin was twice the size of her mother's, tinged by the tears rolling down her cheeks.

Drake and his father parted. They looked at each other now with a new and shared understanding. But while Hero drew close to Drake again, Joss remained distant, full of contradictory emotions.

'I never intended any harm. You should know that,' Drake said to his father, hefting the spear so that its end rested in the snow. 'I just needed to live the only way I could.'

'I know,' his father replied. 'But there'll be time for all that later. Come back inside. I'm sure your mother and your sister would appreciate it. And I think it's safe to say your friends would prefer a warm bed to sleep in tonight.'

Drake agreed and, with his father and his brethren, walked back to the house. The aurora was burning even brighter than the full moon now. Joss cast one last glance at its radiant hues, his heart full of joy for Drake and sorrow for himself. Making his own silent and selfish wish, he followed the others inside.

CHAPTER SIXTEEN

A Legacy to Inherit

THE snowskimmer kicked harder and growled louder than any raptor that Joss had ever ridden, and it took all he had to keep from being thrown off it. It wasn't like Zeke's jet-cycle, technologically advanced and built for comfort. In fact, it was little more than an engine with a seat soldered onto it, and a trio of bladed struts that carved the icy terrain with limited reliability. Every stone and fissure left Joss to bounce painfully in his seat. That would have been difficult enough without adding the sleet that was misting up his goggles, turning his vision into little more than white fog.

'How much further?' he called out, risking his safety in letting go of the handlebars to quickly polish his lenses with the inside crook of his elbow. His breath was hot against the scarf that hid his face, his only source of warmth other than the dull heat of the wisp's mark on his chest.

'Not long now!' Drake shouted from the back of his own skimmer. Joss grumbled at the response, not that his discontent could be heard. Drake had been saying the same thing for hours now, almost since they'd left Snowbridge. Their original plan had been to bring Pietro with them, but Drake's father had pointed out that there would be nobody to look after the bear where they were going.

'You can take the spare snowskimmers instead,' he'd offered, after Drake had fixed the broken gyrothruster and reattached it, making all three vehicles operational again. 'And we can look after Pietro while you're gone.'

Trix, sad to be losing her brother again so soon, looked buoyed by the prospect of having a tundra bear in his place. She was still brushing Pietro's coat and scratching him around the ears as the rest of the family were saying their goodbyes.

'Promise you'll visit again soon,' Drake's mother told him in no uncertain terms.

'I promise,' he said. 'And I'm sorry I didn't come home sooner.'

'There's nothing to apologise for,' she replied, and kissed him on the cheek as his father stepped forward.

'You're a brave man, son,' Drake's father told him. 'Don't ever doubt that.'

Drake had responded with a wholehearted hug that was swiftly returned. Joss watched them, as happy for his friend as he had been the previous night, and still just as envious. Family, home, a sense of belonging, a legacy to inherit. Everything that Drake had reclaimed for himself. Everything that Joss would never truly have. The Icefire spear was the most conspicuous symbol of all that, and it glinted in the frosty sunlight as they exchanged their final farewells.

And so the prentices had set off on the Freezeway, an unpaved stretch of compacted snow that ran from Drake's hometown all the way to Stormport, with dozens of smaller paths branching off it. Every intersection was marked by a wooden pole as tall as the *Behemoth*'s mainsail, each of them adorned with colourful flags in lieu of street signs. The signposts grew increasingly rare the further the Bladebound travelled, with a whole league passing before they finally encountered the tallest and grandest signpost of them all. It had a large blue banner attached to it, swirling and snapping in the wind, which was emblazoned with a swooping white star.

Drake skidded to a stop beside the pole, pulling his scarf and goggles off as Joss and Hero ambled alongside him. Joss did the same as Drake, feeling the sunshine on his skin for the first time in hours. He let out a shaky breath and saw it escape from him in a thick mist.

'There it is,' said Drake, pointing down an icy track. It curved through a wide valley towards a cluster of domed buildings on the horizon. 'Starlight Fields.'

Joss gazed out towards the distant structures. Brown masses were slowly moving among them, no doubt the mammoth herds that he and his brethren would be expected to muster as part of their training. It felt odd to be within such a short distance of his future and only having a chance to glimpse it. He wondered for a moment if he was making the right decision to head off in pursuit of Edgar, but that doubt lasted for only a split second. After all, if he didn't try, then who else would?

Still, it was daunting to have come to the moment that he would be setting off on his own. He had grown to depend on his brethren in a way that he never had with anyone else. He didn't want to part with them now, not when he needed them most.

'Salt lives less than a league further up the road, off a track marked by a narwhal skull,' Drake said, pointing the way. 'It shouldn't be hard to find.'

Joss squeezed the rubber grip of his brake handle, off and on and off again, unable to bring himself to look at either Drake or Hero. 'So – this is it, then.' Loath to betray just how nervous he felt, he cleared his throat and hunkered back on his seat.

'Well … better get started,' he said. 'I hope the training isn't too tough. With any luck, I'll see you both again. Soon.'

A thought leapt uninvited into Joss's mind. No, not a thought. A doubt. This would be the first time since his days in the Orphan House – or ever, really – that he would be truly, totally, hopelessly, on his own. What chance did he have of finding this Salt – a total stranger – in such an unfamiliar landscape, let alone winning him to his side? More importantly, what chance did he have of finding, and then overcoming, an army of marauding pyrates that had disappeared somewhere into the blue?

Joss felt himself tremble, ever so slightly. He hoped neither Drake nor Hero spotted it. The last thing he needed now was their pity. His palm was stiff from where Sur Verity had crossed it with her sword as part of their binding ceremony, all the way back in Tower Town, but still he wrapped it around the accelerator and revved the engine. The sooner he was on his way again, the better his chances would be of keeping himself from completely falling apart. Before he could get going, however, Drake gestured for him to stop.

'Joss – wait …' Drake's green eyes were glistening much as they had back at his family homestead. 'I can't take my grandfather's spear and my father's praise about being a brave man and then send you off into the unknown all by yourself,' he said. 'What would that make me?'

'The owner of a priceless heirloom that could easily fetch a small fortune,' Hero said, staring so intently at the Icefire spear that at first she didn't notice Drake and Joss staring at her with disbelief. 'Oh,' she said, when she saw their expressions. 'But now's probably not the time for that.'

Drake turned back to Joss. 'What I'm saying is – I'm with you. We'll find Salt together. And then we'll save Edgar. Together.'

Joss felt his trembling subside. 'You mean it?' he asked, shifting on his seat.

'I swear it,' Drake said.

Beside him, Hero grunted and shook her head. 'You two are going to be the death of me.'

The faint smile on Joss's face grew brighter. 'Can I take it by that grumpy little observation that you're coming too?'

Hero kicked a pile of snow off her boot. 'Well, I'm not exactly going to let you both ride off without me, am I? That would be the surest way to never see either of you alive again.'

'But what about our training?' asked Joss, still having

trouble accepting their offer of help. 'You'd be risking everything we've worked for.'

'We'd be risking a lot more than that,' Drake soberly pointed out. 'Though with a little luck we can make it back before anybody notices we're gone. Besides which, it's not like it's the first time we've put our training at risk.'

'And who'd want to break with tradition now?' Hero agreed.

Joss wanted to hug them both, wanted to thank them, wanted to leave them behind to keep them from making a grave mistake. He settled for something in between.

'Then let's ride.'

With engines roaring they set off again across the tundra, leaving the Starlight Fields banner blowing in the wind behind them. And Joss felt a surge of renewed hope. Together they would find Edgar. Together they would rescue him, as well as all the other hostages. Together, they'd be unstoppable.

———

The submersible slammed to a stop, knocking around the hostages and throwing Edgar from his seat. He landed with a gasp of pain, his knees smacking on the riveted steel flooring. He had little time to recover.

The hatch beside him screeched open, and through it flooded a whole regiment of armed guards.

'Move!' the largest of them ordered, droplets of water tracing the contours of his spiked helmet, and like a herd of startled hadrosaurs the hostages were driven from the vessel. They were shoved and cudgelled and threatened at knifepoint down a narrow gangplank onto a rickety pier, where the rest of the fleet was moored.

Gangs of pyrates mustered the remaining hostages, and once everyone was unloaded they were marched along the creaking planks towards the main wharf at the end of the pier. As dark as it had been in the submersible's hull, it was somehow even darker here. Having trouble adjusting to the dim light, Edgar searched the sky only to see craggy rocks overhead.

'Where are we?' he asked in a whisper.

Lilia, shuffling along beside him, surveyed their surroundings. 'A cavern, from the looks of it. Though beyond that I have no idea.'

'Quiet!' shouted one of the guards.

Edgar and Lilia obeyed, falling quickly into silence. But as the group filed onto the main wharf, one of their fellow hostages proved far less submissive.

'You can't do this!' he shouted from further up the line at the pyrate pushing at him. 'We're people – *good* people! You can't just –'

Whatever the man intended to say next, he was swiftly silenced when the pyrate smashed him in the mouth with his sword handle. A cry of shock and fear surged through the crowd as the man fell to his knees, clutching his bloodied face. Edgar watched helplessly with the other hostages as the guards pushed in and grabbed the man, dragging him away down the wharf.

But the man wouldn't be taken away quite so easily, shoving away his captors and moving to run. For one dazzling moment, Edgar thought he might actually have a chance at getting free. Then a bolt of lightning scorched the air and tore a hole straight through the man's chest. With a gasp, he dropped to the ground a second time. This time he didn't get back up.

'Gentlefolk! Your attention please!'

In silent horror, Edgar and the others looked to see a man standing at the far end of the wharf, halfway up a set of stone steps that had been carved into the cavern wall. He had a smoking bolt gun in his fist, which he now tucked into the holster strapped to his leg. His frockcoat was ripped and frayed, embroidered with dozens of staring eyes, and the grin he wore could only just be seen through his great red beard.

'Welcome all, to the city of night neverending!' he barked at them. 'From now until your dying day, this is your home. And if that thought scares you, if it fills you

with dread that you'll be here forever, then take heart!'

The bearded man's grin darkened into something far more sinister. Something demonic.

'It won't be long at all.'

CHAPTER SEVENTEEN

—

A FIGURE NEITHER ANIMAL NOR MAN

THE road grew ever more treacherous, strewn with stones and frozen over with patches of ice that made for even harder riding. Joss was just beginning to despair of ever finding the place they were looking for when finally they came to the narwhal skull that Drake had spoken of, and the tiny track that led from it.

Turning onto the track, they soon approached a squat but sprawling barge anchored in the middle of an icy river, its hull frosted white. A stovepipe chimney stuck out from under a tarp in the middle of the barge's deck, from which a thin trail of smoke curled into the sky.

'He's home!' Drake said, guiding his skimmer towards the small wooden ramp that led from the barge onto the snowy riverbank. Joss and Hero dismounted alongside him, their bones cracking and joints popping.

'Muuck!' Joss moaned as he stretched his arms, his legs, his back and shoulders. 'Give me a raptor and a well-worn saddle over that contraption any day.'

'Remind me to give Callie an extra helping of sardines when I see her next,' Hero added with a grunt.

Drake was too busy to listen to their complaints. With his skimmer still whirring down, he tramped through the snow to the barge's ramp.

'*Salt!* Salt, are you there? It's me – Ganymede!' he called out.

No noise came from within the barge. No movement. All that stirred was the smoke from the chimney.

'Doesn't seem like anyone's about,' Joss said, just as the water beside the barge erupted, and from its frozen depths there burst a figure that was neither animal nor man. It leapt up onto the riverbank as fluid as the stream itself.

Turned away from them as it was, all Joss could see was a broad back and a pair of powerful arms that ended in clawed flippers. Instead of legs it had a long tail, its flesh covered in a sleek sable fur, while tangled locks of algae-brown hair hung between its shoulders.

'Salt …?' Drake asked uncertainly, and the creature flinched. It turned its head towards them, though only slightly, giving Joss the barest impression of its large dark eyes and wiry whiskers. And then it flexed its muscles, and the fur that covered it from snout to tail began to recede into its skin, revealing a mass of tattoos that resembled the runes that Qorza had inscribed across the *Behemoth*'s decks.

Steam poured off its flesh as tendons snapped and bones reset themselves. The tail that had been draped in the water split in two and formed legs, while what had been flippers now became hands. Reaching out, the figure took hold of a rough-spun brown robe that hung from the barge's anchor chain and threw it around himself. His modesty covered, the man turned fully.

'Ganymede. It's been too long. And I see you've brought company with you.' His words were flavoured with an accent Joss didn't recognise.

'I have, and I'm sorry to intrude, Salt. But this isn't a social visit. We need your help.'

'That may be, but first I require introductions. Preferably over a warm mug and a cosy fire. Care to join me?'

Turning on his heel, Salt strode up the ramp and into the barge without waiting for them. As the prentices followed, Joss took the opportunity to ask Drake a hushed question.

'Remind me – how do you know this …?' He hesitated in calling Salt a man. He surely wasn't a mortal. But then who was to say when magic was involved?

'Friend of mine?' Drake finished for him, while Hero tilted her head to listen along with Joss. 'He's exactly that. A good friend made during a long and often lonely time at Starlight Fields. Lord Oric hired him once, when we had a fieldserv run off with the paymaster's coffers. Sur Fabian and I were tasked with accompanying him and he must have saved our lives about a dozen times during the course of that misadventure. I only had the one occasion to repay the favour. But if you can't call someone a friend after that, chances are you'll never have any friends to name.' Drake stepped through the hatch into Salt's barge.

Following him, Joss waited for his eyes to adjust to the shift in light. When they did, he saw the nets that hung from the curved ceiling like giant spider's webs, holding pots, pans and enamel plates, as well as countless bottles and jars. The floor was covered in fur rugs, the likes of which would have no doubt warranted an angry growl from Pietro, while a cast-iron stove kept the space warm. Thin blades of light cut into the room through the shuttered windows, painting everything in glowing stripes.

Joss's memory was cast back to the Barbed Forest and the hut in which he and the others had sheltered while on the Way. He remembered Bittersweet, the healer who had tended to Drake's wounds, and the story she had told of all the races of fae who had fled when the mortals had come to dominate the land.

She had spoken of the spriggans, her own ancestors, as well as the other tribes of fae: the sylphs of the air, and the selkies of the water. Looking around at Salt's abode and all its trappings – the driftwood furniture, the blades carved from bone, the bottles of fermented kelp and fish hearts and heavy water – Joss knew immediately from which tribe Salt hailed. Of course, the fact that he'd also seen him shapeshift only a moment ago helped to dispel any doubts.

Even now, in the soft light that radiated from the stove's searing belly, Salt still had a wild look about him. His hair was a tangle of silvery grey and dull ochre waves, braided with seashells and small dark feathers. His eyes – black and bulging when Joss and his brethren had first arrived – had withdrawn into his face to become distant points of light at the bottom of two deep wells. And he was staring at them all with cold curiosity.

'Drinking chocolate?' he said as he placed a full kettle on top of the stove.

'Thank you very much,' Drake replied. 'Salt, may I introduce my Bladebound brethren: this is Hero of Blade's Edge Acres, and Josiah Sarif of Round Shield Ranch.'

'Pleased to meet you,' Joss said.

'Likewise,' Hero added.

But Salt had little interest in exchanging niceties. 'Brethren, eh? So you've completed the Way and you're off on your training. Congratulations, Ganymede. I know that's long been an ambition of yours.' Though Salt's words were nothing but courteous, his tone carried with it a note of judgement. If Drake picked up on it, he didn't seem to care.

'You're right. It has been. Though we've recently suffered a loss that threatens to overshadow all that.'

'Oh? Do tell.'

Drake went on to explain all that had occurred in Crescent Cove. He didn't mention Edgar by name, simply referring to him as 'Joss's fellow prentice from Round Shield Ranch who was to serve as our steward'. The impersonal description struck an off-note to Joss's ear, but he kept himself from saying anything. Drake was clearly choosing his words carefully.

By the time the kettle boiled, the story had been told in full. As Salt went about filling each of their mugs and handing them around, he kept his reaction closely guarded.

'That's quite a tale, and I'm sorry to hear it. But why is it that you've come to me?'

'You're the best tracker I know, Salt.'

'I'm the only tracker you know.'

'Even so, if anyone can find those hostages, it's you.'

'It's been a long time since we last saw each other, Ganymede. You should know, I don't do that kind of work any more.'

'You don't?' Drake asked, clearly surprised. 'But … why?'

Salt turned his gaze to the window and the cold, unforgiving landscape that howled outside. 'Not everyone who comes to my door does so with noble intentions. If anything, they come looking for an animal to hunt their prey. And I am not a beast to be unleashed. Not for you. Not for anyone.'

Salt punctuated his refusal with a long, slurping sip from his cup, and Joss felt himself flaring with an intensity that would have put the aurora itself to shame. When Captain Gyver had refused them, it was Qorza who'd intervened on their behalf. Now here they were in the middle of a frozen wasteland, with nowhere else to go and no one else to turn to for help, and they were being denied for a second and seemingly final time. There was no way Joss was simply going to accept Salt's words without a fight.

'What a load of muck!' he cursed.

'Joss!' Drake said, but Joss wouldn't hear it.

'We came looking for an ally, not a beast. Because I remember what it's like to be prey to beasts.' He ignored

Drake's and Hero's shared looks of confusion. 'When we were on the Way, Ganymede was nearly killed. And we would all have likely died right along with him if not for the intervention of a kindly stranger. Her name was Bittersweet. She saved his life and gave us food and shelter until we were ready to travel again. She said it was her people's way to offer help where it was needed. And yet, when innocent lives hang in the balance, you would flatly refuse us?'

Any hint of light had drained from Salt's eyes. He stared darkly at Joss as he replied, 'Your understanding of fae culture is confused at best. Ignorant at worst. This *Bittersweet* – she was spriggan, yes? I am selkie. Selkies do not rush to make lackeys of themselves for mortal gain. We are not so easily swayed. Certainly not by packs of callow pups seeking to goad us for their own purposes.'

Drake looked dismayed. 'Salt, please ...' he began, but Salt was unmoved.

Joss spoke again, his voice softer this time. 'I'm sorry. I spoke without thinking,' he said, winning back Salt's guarded attention. 'But the longer we travel, the more desperate our search becomes. And we've travelled very far to ask you for your help.'

Salt's lips twisted as if he'd just tasted something tart, but not altogether unpleasant. 'Ganymede – you call this boy here a friend of yours?' he asked.

'He's like you, Salt,' Drake replied. 'He's my brother.'

While Joss flushed red, Salt lowered his face in deliberation, the shadows knitting together to cast his features in darkness. When he turned back towards the lamplight, the shine of it caught his eyes.

'Do you have anything that belonged to the missing lad?' he asked.

Joss felt Drake's elbow in his side, prompting him to respond. 'Only this,' he said, pulling out the glove he'd saved from the streets of Crescent Cove.

'That will serve. Though if we're to do anything with it, we best move quickly.' Salt rose from where he was sitting and threw open a rosewood chest that was as long as a coffin. Contained within was an array of arcane objects, even more unusual than Qorza's collection.

'So, you'll help us find our steward?' asked Drake.

'I can't promise that, my brother,' Salt told him. 'But I will guide you.'

—

CHAPTER EIGHTEEN

A PRIMAL VOICE

ENEATH the wide and watchful eye of the full moon, upon the frozen fields that surrounded the river, Salt had performed his spell. He started by taking a driftwood staff and carving a circle between himself and the three prentices. He'd then asked Joss for Edgar's glove. Joss had watched with mounting disbelief as Salt whispered incantations over the glove before tossing it in the air, where it swam around of its own accord like a stitched and leathery fish. Joss found it difficult to accept that what he was seeing was not some elaborate trick, and it was made all the more surreal by the nonchalance with which Salt had performed the feat.

'We search for Edgar of the Greyson lineage, taken against his will by those who would do him harm,' he'd intoned, staring up into the burning rainbow of the aurora. 'We beseech those listening that they might whisper in Mother Mab's ear, seek her divine insight, impart unto us her wisdom. Bestow upon me sight and sense. Show me where he can be found!'

At this, the glove had begun whipping around faster and faster. The wind had shrieked, the cold had sharpened, and an unseen force swept through to strike Salt. Lurching backward, he'd managed to right himself before being jolted again by another invisible blow. Joss and Drake both stepped forward hesitantly, unsure if they should intervene.

'Don't break the circle!' Salt had warned them, just as a final rush of force knocked him off his feet. The wind died all at once. Edgar's glove fell to the ground. And Salt sat straight back up with insight flashing in his eyes.

'Wherever your friend is, it's a place rife with mystical energies. Something powerful resides there.' His shiver was slight but telling. 'Something dark ...'

'Can you take us there?' Joss asked, prompting Salt to stare out across the tundra. Clouds had pushed in to cloak the moon, the darkness swallowing the horizon.

'We'll set out for the Bay of Crossing at dawn, past the glaciers. It's about a day's travel, dependent on the weather.' Salt picked himself up off the frozen ground. 'With some luck, Bhashvirak will be in a charitable mood.'

Distressed that they'd be losing yet another day since Edgar's abduction, Joss had asked who Bhashvirak was. If they could make the trip without him, then surely it would be better to set off as soon as possible. But Salt would not be drawn on the subject. He had simply told them to rest, and that any questions they had would be answered soon enough. Now the sun had risen and peaked and was starting its gradual descent, and still they hiked on through the bleak chill of the tundra, none the wiser.

Though with every step the glaciers grew closer. More than that, it felt as if they grew *larger*. Their crystal blue peaks would be beautiful if not for how daunting they were. Joss could hardly imagine trying to climb them. They were as jagged as the Spires of Ai, and they looked to be weeping ice under the afternoon sun. It would be impossible to scale them without any equipment at hand, even with Salt's skills in the occult. Would they have to? The prospect weighed heavy on Joss. Opening his mouth to give voice to his concerns, he caught sight of something set in the foot of the frozen mountains.

'There,' said Salt, pointing at a circular, ironbound hatch. The metalwork was wrought with the same style of runes that mapped Salt's skin, leading in a circle towards a lock twice the size of Joss's head.

Drawing closer, Joss found that what he'd taken to be

a hatch was, in fact, more like a bank vault, tall enough for a mammoth to walk through comfortably, even with his twin brother balancing on his back. Though whether the door was meant to keep the world out, or whatever was inside locked within, Joss didn't dare to guess.

'A moment, if you will,' Salt now said, lowering himself to sit cross-legged in the snow, his driftwood staff lying across his lap. With eyes closed, he began to chant. And with every word, the runes glowed, dimly at first, then more intensely, until they beamed so brilliantly they blinded Joss and his brethren. They were forced to look away as the vault door unlocked itself and swung open.

His chanting at an end, Salt stood. 'Shall we?' he said, and together the group entered the vault.

A perfectly rounded tunnel lay within, carved white from the ice and veined with thick swathes of watery blue. It reached deep into the mountain, bending this way and that, but remained level throughout. It offered an easy path through the glaciers, for which Joss was silently but profoundly grateful. After the challenges of traversing the tundra, this felt as easy as bounding through a sunny field on a summer's day.

'A pathway built by my ancestors, impenetrable to unaccompanied mortals,' explained Salt, his voice soft and melodious in the serene space. Though Joss hadn't known him all that long, this unsolicited information seemed highly out of character. But then Salt coupled it with a warning. 'Grave consequences would follow for any who spoke indiscreetly of its nature or location.'

The tunnel wound on like a serpent's belly, its walls growing ever darker. What had originally been as clear and brilliant as crystal was now as black and rippled as slate. Even the air felt different, the cold having taken on a ghostly chill. It prickled Joss's flesh and gripped his heart tight, squeezing the breath from his lungs.

In this funereal darkness, his mind wandered. They had been travelling for days now, chasing dragon tails and phantom footprints in their quest for Edgar and, no matter the assurances that Salt made, Joss felt no closer to finding his friend. There was every chance he was already dead. How could Joss possibly live with himself if that was true? The thought ate at him, as did the cold and the all-consuming darkness.

But then, mercifully, the tunnel began to lighten again. Before long they came to a second vault door, which Salt again opened, and together they stepped out into the dazzling light of day and onto the stony shore that waited there for them.

The bay was small, shaped like a sickle, and surrounded by the impervious glacial ranges. A rocky reef guarded the only outlet into the limitless expanse of the ocean beyond, in front of which sat a stone platform. Joss could just make out the footbridge that stretched from the bay's distant curving shoreline to connect to the platform. Though there were no waves, the water still churned so restlessly it looked to be a living thing, dark and wild.

'There's nobody here,' Joss said, searching for a hut, a cave, a bolthole, anything. But the entire area looked to be long abandoned.

'Why should there be? We've not made our invitation yet,' Salt replied, walking down to the water's edge. An immense landing had been set there, same as the stone platform that obstructed the outlet. It was covered in mounds of dry seaweed and inscribed with all manner of sigils – some fae, others more feral in style.

Bending to one knee, Salt bowed his head and began muttering under his breath. By now, Joss, Drake and Hero had become accustomed to this sight, though what purpose it served this time was a mystery. Who was this Bhashvirak whom Salt had spoken of? Where was he? And what help could he possibly offer in tracking down Edgar?

'Be honest,' Joss addressed Drake in a hushed tone. 'Do you have any clue what's going on here?'

'Not a one,' Drake admitted. 'But I've learned to trust Salt, no matter how cryptic he may be at times.'

'At times?' Hero asked. 'He treats evasiveness like a competitive sport.'

'And you should know,' Joss said, quickly receiving a thump to the shoulder. 'Ow.'

'Even so,' Drake said while Joss nursed his injury, 'if anyone can find Edgar and the other hostages, it's Salt.'

'If you're all quite done ...' Salt interjected, having turned from the stone landing to stand before them. 'The entreaty is made and time is now of the essence. Bhashvirak and his kind have no taste for patience.'

Salt hurried them along the curve of the shore towards the bridge, a creaky old thing that was as spiky and knotted as a spinal cord. It swayed with worrying abandon, forcing Joss to watch his every step as the group edged its way out across the water. The gaps between the boards seemed to widen beneath him, demanding that he drop something precious through their cracks and lose it forever. Keeping a tight hold of the Champion's Blade, he continued with the others towards the great granite disc of the platform.

Treacherous as the bridge was, the platform was doubly so, slick with moss and studded with the same sigils as the landing had been. Salt leapt onto it with the confidence of a captain taking to his ship, while Joss, Drake and Hero stepped nervously across, their boots skidding around of their own accord.

Here, stuck between the shore and the open water, it would take only one wave to reach up and pull them away, never to be seen again. If Joss had been uncertain before, he was utterly mystified now. This Bhashvirak had to be a submersible captain or something similar, though Joss was damned if he could see how incantations performed on a rocky landing could have any hope of contacting him. And there was simply too much at stake to remain silent about it.

'Where exactly is this friend of yours?' Joss asked Salt, who had moved to the edge of the platform to search the horizon. There was a swift rush of motion out in the depths.

'I wouldn't call him a *friend*,' was all Salt said, not taking his eyes from the shadow that glided beneath the surface of the water. The closer it came, the larger it seemed to grow. As it approached the platform, a small part of its being broke through the churning water, making Joss and his brethren gasp in shock.

'That's not – is it?' said Drake, his half-asked question going unanswered. After all, there was no mistaking what was growing nearer by the second. It was a fin, curved and serrated and tall enough to block out the sky, only hinting at the scope of the creature to which it was attached. Picking up speed, it looked as if it was preparing to ram them all, before it quickly dived away and disappeared from sight.

Water lapped at the edge of the platform. The Bladebound, each of them braced for impact, looked at each other in confusion and alarm. And then, in an explosion of white water, the creature revealed itself.

Jagged teeth. Depthless eyes. A mouth big enough to swallow them all whole, and a form that lay somewhere between monster and god. Joss had heard tell of megalodons, but tales were one thing. The reality was something else entirely.

And then, in a primal voice that entered the listener's mind without any need for sound, the creature spoke.

'*I AM ARRIVED!*' the monstrous shark declared, falling back into the water to fix them with its fearsome gaze. '*WHO BECKONS MIGHTY BHASHVIRAK?*'

—

CHAPTER NINETEEN

A SCRATCHING AT THE EDGE OF SANITY

EVERY word pierced Joss's brain. They beat on his eardrums and set his teeth to grinding. There was a pressure in his skull like a dam on the verge of bursting. It felt as if blood would come spurting from his nose at any moment.

'Joss! What's wrong?' Drake said, taking hold of Joss's shoulders to keep him from crumpling.

'That voice! Can't you hear that voice?!' Joss clamped his hands around his head while the mark on his chest burned as painfully as it had when the wisp first struck him.

'What do you mean? What voice?' Drake asked, splitting Salt's attention between Joss and the massive megalodon before them.

'You can hear him, boy? Yes?' Salt hissed through clenched teeth. 'Then be still and silent and let me handle this.'

'Mighty Bhashvirak!' Salt said, turning back to the creature. He knelt down and bowed his head even lower than he had on the shore. 'We have come because we have no other recourse. Innocent lives are threatened and we need your help to save them.'

'*WHAT CARES MIGHTY BHASHVIRAK FOR MORTAL LIVES?*' the creature demanded. Having made its dramatic entrance, it had now slid back beneath the waves and was circling the stone platform, leaving only its fin and part of its upper back exposed. In doing so, it revealed a curious device that looked to be somehow fused with its flesh: a bubble of hand-blown glass, caged in oxidised copper and large enough to accommodate a group of passengers. Joss gaped in astonishment. Surely this wasn't what Salt had in mind.

'Our two races once lived in harmony,' Salt continued. 'Together we hunted and we prospered. My mother would sing songs that told of the glories we accomplished when we worked as one. I see you still carry a lifechamber on your back …'

'*A RELIC!*' Bhashvirak growled, and Joss's head threatened to burst. '*A FORGOTTEN THING!*'

'And yet you came when called. Mighty Bhashvirak's memory is more stone than sand, I say. But what of his oaths? From what are they made?'

'*A PLEDGE TO YOUR ANCESTORS IS NOT A PLEDGE TO YOU, SELKIE!*' the megalodon countered as he circled the platform. '*WHAT OFFERING DO YOU MAKE?*'

Salt hesitated. 'I can offer only the opportunity to perform a just act. An act of mercy.'

'*HA!*' Bhashvirak boomed, cold and unfeeling.

'An act of courage, then!'

The megalodon grew silent at that, his fin disappearing beneath the water. Desperation taking hold, Joss stepped to the edge of the platform. Though he did not know exactly what to say, he knew enough about a great beast's pride to hazard a guess.

'Mighty Bhashvirak, my name is Josiah Sarif!' he shouted, doing his best to sound as formal and servile as he could. 'Once my family hailed from Daheed! And as the last survivor of my people, I've come to warn you! The legend of your race has grown dim in the mortal world. People have forgotten your grandeur. There are even those who seek to snatch your glory for themselves!'

'*HERESY!*' Bhashvirak snapped, his fin slicing back up out of the water's depths.

'Joss – have you gone mad?' Hero asked in a hushed voice while Salt stared at him aghast. 'You're hurling insults at a shark the size of a siege engine.'

'Trust me, I know what I'm doing,' Joss whispered in reply, adding silently to himself, *I think.*

Turning back, he called out to the great shark. 'They call themselves *pyrates*! And they control the high seas with submersible vessels that they've crafted in mockery of your kind!'

'*BLASPHEMY!*' Bhashvirak's tail lashed out to smack the water's surface, sending a powerful wave rippling towards the shore. The pain in Joss's head was so intense it felt as if he'd chomped down on an iron dagger. Fighting through the agony, he pressed his argument to the great shark. The bait had been taken. All he needed to do was reel in the hook.

'If the great megalodons still ruled the seas, these pyrates would never have tried anything so brazen! But for too long you've shied away from the world, so now they seek to reign over the ocean unchallenged and unafraid. To prove their dominance, they stole away with our friend and our fellow mortals. They consider themselves invincible –'

'*MIGHTY BHASHVIRAK WILL PROVE OTHER-WISE!*'

'So you'll help us then?' Joss asked.

'IF IT IS MIGHTY BHASHVIRAK'S AID YOU REQUIRE, MORTAL BOY, THEN HAVE IT YOU SHALL!'

The quiet admiration on Salt's face was enough to tip off Drake and Hero as to what had just happened. They both looked at Joss with amazement.

'WHERE HIDE THESE CRAVENLY CREATURES?'

'Salt can lead us there,' Joss said, venturing one last request. 'Should you allow us to ride in your lifechamber ...'

'The boy is right,' said Salt, before a moment of loaded silence as the megalodon considered the deal.

'VERY WELL,' it finally replied, the agony of its soundless voice finally easing for Joss. *'BUT QUICKLY, LEST MIGHTY BHASHVIRAK'S FAVOUR RUN RED!'*

Moving quickly, the prentices took their leaps of faith one by one onto the back of the enormous creature as it circled the platform, first Drake and then Hero. That left only Joss. Pushing away the pain that still clouded his mind, he ran for the edge of the platform. Jumped.

'Gotcha!' Drake said as he grabbed hold of Joss's arm. Hero was already at the lifechamber's hatch, wrenching it open with one quick yank.

'This is going to be a nightmare of a ride,' she said, eyeing the wooden handholds and leather straps within the glass bubble, before climbing inside. 'And I've ridden through a hailstorm on the back of a pterosaur who was suffering from vertigo.'

'Well, that's reassuring,' Joss muttered as he followed her, and received another whack to the arm. '*Ouch.*'

'Salt! Are you coming?' Drake called out to the platform, where their guide was slipping off his boots.

'To lead you, I can't be confined to the lifechamber,' he said, and turned away to shed himself of the rest of his clothing. The shifting of his flesh then began, as natural as the flowing of water: his legs fusing together to form his tail, his hands sprouting into clawed flippers, his skin bristling with fur, the curve of his neck growing gills.

When he turned back, he was a creature of the sea, and he took to it now with the ease of drawing breath. The water accepted him without a splash, ripples forming only when he re-emerged to cock his head at the mortals gathered on the megalodon's back.

'*Follow …*' he snarled, and dived away again. Joss, Drake and Hero had precious little time to secure the glass lifechamber before Bhashvirak plunged down into the dark waters to trail him.

As the water cascaded against the glass, the three prentices each settled into place. Crude though the set-up was, Joss found himself grateful for the wooden handholds scattered throughout the chamber. Lying on his belly to grip them, he was kept from violently bumping and rolling as Bhashvirak swam with the power of a jet-cycle through a clear sky.

Water rushed by them, foam and bubbles fizzing off the surface of the glass. Beneath them was the flesh of the gargantuan creature that bore them, pure muscle sheathed in skin as smooth as marble. Every shake of Bhashvirak's tail was like an earthquake in its power.

'How did you do that back there?' Drake asked. His face looked pale green, and Joss couldn't tell if it was from seasickness or a trick of the light. 'Speak to the shark, I mean. Is that some sort of Daheedi trait?'

'Can you talk to other animals too?' asked Hero, just as intrigued.

'I don't think so,' Joss said, rubbing at his chest. The wisp scar had eased to a dull ache, twinging beneath his shirt as he told the others what had happened aboard the *Behemoth*, as well as the advice that Qorza had given him. 'She wasn't sure how long it would last, but she said that the wisp's touch would draw the supernatural like blood in shark-infested waters. All I can think is that's why I could hear Bhashvirak, because of the wisp. Not that I have any real idea how this magic muck works.'

'Blood in the water, huh?' Hero said, adjusting her grip on the handholds. 'That's even less comforting than the fact that there's no commode in here ...'

Drake looked around in alarm. 'She's right. Not even a bucket!'

Hero snorted. 'If you think being hit by a wisp is something, then I strongly advise against any attempts to relieve yourself. The first one of you to expel anything from anywhere gets a zamaraq plugged right in the offending hole. Got it?'

'And what if the first person is you?' Joss asked.

'Won't happen.' Hero shrugged. 'I have a will made of iron.'

'And a bladder made of aurum, apparently,' Joss added, making Drake chortle and earning yet another thump on the arm. He was still nursing the injury as they flew past the watery boneyard of over a dozen wrecked ships, their hulls torn wide open among the ocean bed's jagged rocks. It was one of the last things the Bladebound saw as the water surrounding them grew as black as night.

Joss wondered how Bhashvirak could possibly see Salt ahead of them, even with eyesight keener than that of a mortal's. It felt as if they were being blindly propelled through a limitless void, with only the odd flash of scales from a passing fish to serve as a reminder of where they were. *It was into water like this that Daheed would have sunk*, Joss thought. *Cold and black and bottomless.* The idea sent a shiver running down his spine.

Shaking it off, he settled in for the ride ahead, hoping against hope that they would find Edgar and the other townsfolk unharmed, that they could liberate them all without loss or injury, and that he had the willpower to avoid being plugged by any of Hero's zamaraqs.

———

All sense of time slid away. All sense of place. All sense of warmth. There was only the black ahead of them, the black behind them, the black all around. It was enough to scratch at the edges of one's sanity. No wonder Bhashvirak and his kind had turned away from the world – it was so easy to forget that it even existed down here. Where could Edgar possibly be that would warrant such a journey, Joss wondered. How far beyond the horizon had the pyrates travelled that they could vanish like this? It was as if they'd stepped off the edge of all things.

Trading one blackness for another, Drake and Hero both drifted off to sleep. Not Joss. He was too preoccupied and far too tense for that, scanning the water for whatever might lie just ahead of them, watching luminescent spores rushing by the lifechamber like stars streaking across the night's sky.

But for all his resolve to stay awake he could feel exhaustion settling over him like a blanket. He was just starting to drift off when the burning sensation of the wisp's mark flared so painfully that it startled him, forcing him bolt upright.

'Whazzit –' Drake moaned as he wiped a thin line of drool from his chin. Gazing all around him, Joss saw no sign of danger, no hint of supernatural threat. There was only Bhashvirak's rippling flesh beneath them and the water that engulfed them, which was now shifting from black to grey.

'Is that light outside?' asked Joss, rising to a crouched position so that he could edge over to the glass wall. What had been ceaseless, numbing black was now warming into a gentle wash of lilac and gold. Iridescent jellyfish swirled all around them, dancing on the gentle currents, while Salt swam on to guide them down towards the ocean floor.

There, a massive trench ripped the ground in two. Circling down into its depths, they found the source of light: a curving sheet of sparkling violet energy that blocked the bottom of the trench. As they neared it, they saw it was an enormous and translucent dome. And beneath that, even further down, dozens of small fires traced the outlines of what looked to be rooftops and towers.

Joss pressed a hand against the glass, the world spinning all around him.

'What is that?' Drake asked, rising to stand beside him.

'Some kind of hidden base. Or an underwater city,' Hero replied as she gazed with them at the collection of dark buildings clustered together beneath the dome of mystical energy.

'That's not just any city,' Joss said gravely. 'That's Daheed.'

—

CHAPTER TWENTY

A CITY LONG DESTROYED

DRAKE and Hero were gawking at him as if he'd gone suddenly and inexplicably mad, but Joss knew the truth. He'd never been so certain of anything in all his life. And the truth of it was that the city where he'd been born, the city he'd lost, the city he'd spent his entire life mourning, was whole and intact here at the bottom of the world.

'It can't be,' Drake said. 'Daheed was destroyed. This place – it has to be …'

But Joss wouldn't hear it. 'It's Daheed, Ganymede,' he said. 'I know it is.'

'How?' asked Hero, blunt as ever.

Joss stared down at the city, where a central spire loomed taller than everything that surrounded it. He would have known that golden needle anywhere, even without it having been so brilliantly illustrated on the cover of *Azof & the Pyrate King*.

'See that?' he said, pointing to the spire. 'That's the Tower Memoria. The Daheedi version of a High Chamber.'

'I thought you didn't remember much about living there,' Drake said, stubbornly sceptical.

Joss couldn't help but fume. 'Would you forget your home, Ganymede?' he asked. 'I may have been young when I left, but being here now brings the memories back. Even if I hadn't been told stories about it, even if I hadn't read every book I could ever find about it, I would still remember.'

He pointed again to the golden spire. 'I remember the Tower Memoria. I remember how brightly it shone. I remember going there for Tribute, to give thanks to our forebears. I remember the Sworn Sisters and the Blessed Brothers who led the services, I remember their singing as it echoed around the chamber.' The more Joss spoke, the more choked up he became. His eyes were filled with tears, though he refused to let any fall. 'And I can hear the sound of my family lending their voices to the choir …'

When it felt as if he was about to lose all control, he clenched his mouth shut and hid his face in the crook of his arm. That was when he felt a warm hand squeezing his shoulder, and looked up to see Drake's reassuring face, with Hero standing right alongside him.

'So this is Daheed,' she said with conviction, then softened as she added, 'You don't need to be a baby about it.'

Her dry wit made Joss laugh. He looked up to see the ghost of a smile on Hero's face, which only grew as he wiped his watery eyes.

'It's a good thing we're friends,' he told her. 'I'd hate to think what you'd say if we weren't.'

'And I'd hate to tell you,' she replied, her smile widening into a spiky grin. 'What about you, Ganymede? Still unsure of where we are?'

Drake didn't seem to hear the question. He was staring at the city as if he'd been presented with a particularly challenging mathematic equation. He turned after a few moments. 'If Joss says this is Daheed, then it's Daheed,' he said with his steadfast manner. 'But how did it come to be at the bottom of the ocean? How is it that there are lights coming from within a sunken city? What's that field of energy that's sealing it off?'

'And, most importantly,' Hero added, 'is this really where the hostages are being held?'

'I don't know,' Joss said, staring again at his lost homeland. 'But we're going to find out.'

The moment was shot through by a blaring pain in Joss's head as Bhashvirak spoke again.

'*MORTAL BOY!*'

'Yes? Can you hear me?' Joss replied out loud through the throbbing agony and the pulling in his chest.

'*THE SELKIE LOOKS NOW FOR A WAY INSIDE,*' Bhashvirak said, answering Joss's question by ignoring it. '*WE AWAIT HIS RETURN – PROVIDED HE DOES NOT PERISH.*'

Joss could just see Salt as he delved deeper into the trench, disappearing into its dark recesses with one last flick of his tail. It occurred to him that they were now stranded on the back of a colossal shark at the bottom of the ocean, thousands of leagues from any safe harbour, circling a city long thought destroyed but now seemingly populated by a band of vicious marauders. Eighteen-hour days of herding mammoths back at Starlight Fields suddenly sounded like a far more appealing prospect.

'The shark – did it say something?' asked Drake.

'Salt's gone to look for a way in,' he explained.

'A way in? Is that even possible?' Hero asked.

'Clearly, if people are living in there …' Drake told her.

'*Clearly* I meant without being detected,' she replied.

'We'll have to wait and see,' Joss said, and slid down into a sitting position. The wisp mark was throbbing on his chest so powerfully it felt as if it was trying to rip itself free, making him wonder what else might be lurking in the city below.

There was a stirring in the murky distance as Salt re-emerged from the dark waters, the gills on his neck undulating heavily. Gesturing for them to follow him, he led the way to a craggy hole in the trench wall that hung over the city and its glowing barrier like a full moon wrapped in black clouds.

The gap was just big enough for Bhashvirak to squeeze through, bringing them into a tunnel that curved down and around, wide in some places and chokingly tight in others. It drew them deeper and deeper into the darkness, descending further than Joss thought it was possible to go.

But slowly they began to ascend again, emerging at last into what looked to be a subterranean lake. Looking around, Joss saw that a wharf had been built along the gravelly shoreline, transforming the cavern into a makeshift harbour. And on the lone pier that stretched out into the middle of the water, a whole fleet of submersibles clanked against one another.

They had made it through into the city. But even more amazingly than that, Salt had done exactly what he'd said he would. He had led them straight to the pyrates' hiding place. Still in his animal form, their guide climbed up onto the pier, beckoning with one outstretched flipper for them to join him.

'*MIGHTY BHASHVIRAK CAN GO NO FURTHER,*' the shark said with an edge of frustration. He circled the lake, keeping Joss and the others from the pier. '*HOW CAN THE PRETENDERS BE PUNISHED NOW?!*'

Joss thought quickly. 'If you allow us onto the land, Mighty Bhashvirak, we can find the pretenders and draw them down to you here ...'

Again, there was a moment of stony silence as the megalodon considered the proposal. '*VERY WELL.*'

The great shark drew close enough to the pier for the prentices to jump across, where they found that Salt had shifted back to his mortal-looking form. While waiting, he'd taken a tarp that had been strewn across one of the submersibles and crafted it into a makeshift cloak.

'Can you lead us to Edgar from here?' Joss asked him.

The selkie shook his head. 'This is as close as I can sense him,' he said, then lowered his voice. 'And Bhashvirak will grow restless if left on his own. He may not be here when we return.'

'Then we need someone to stay behind and guard the harbour,' said Drake. 'Salt ... this isn't your fight. We asked you to lead us here and that's exactly what you've done. Asking anything more than that would be too much. But –'

'You would like me to stand guard,' Salt finished his thought for him.

'I wouldn't ask you to do it unarmed,' Drake told him as he unslung the strap around his chest. Keeping hold of the Icefire spear, he presented Salt with his original blade, the spear that he'd forged himself.

'Don't fret, Ganymede,' Salt said as he took the weapon in hand and tested its weight. 'No living soul will pass while I have breath left in my body.'

Joss ventured forward to express his gratitude. 'Thank you. For everything,' he said. 'We would have been lost without you.'

Salt waved away the words, sincere though they were. 'There'll be time for all that later. Go. Save your friend and all those taken with him. Make this a day of warning to those who would seek to prey upon the innocent.'

Their mission set, the prentices unsheathed their blades and made for the wharf, following it to a stairwell that had been carved out of the rock. Joss had taken only a single upward step when a bolt of pain crashed through his head.

'AND FETCH ME FODDER, MORTAL BOY, THAT MIGHTY BHASHVIRAK MAY HAVE A TASTE OF JUSTICE!'

The great shark's words still throbbing between his temples, Joss pushed on into the looming darkness.

CHAPTER TWENTY-ONE

An Unpitying Age

THE stone stairwell curled upward like black smoke. Every breath, every step, every movement that the Bladebound made echoed through the confined space, betraying their presence no matter how cautious they tried to be. It slowed their ascent to a painful crawl, each corner they came to rife with the threat of ambush.

Finally, approaching a jagged crack in the wall that served as the tunnel's crude doorway, Joss and his brethren paused. Listened. If anyone was waiting for them, ready to attack, they were more silent than a knife slipped between the ribs. Still, the prentices took no chances. Signalling wordlessly to each other, they readied themselves and their weapons, then burst from the passageway ready for a fight. But nothing awaited them save a trail of phosphorescent fungi that led from the caverns to the remains of a long-abandoned campsite.

'This'd be where the pyrates would station their guards for the harbour below,' Hero said, investigating the site. She inspected one of the few weapons that had been left behind, its blade turned to rust. Then she looked over the ashy brazier set among a crop of boulders, the rocks no doubt having served as seating. 'But nobody's been here for weeks.'

'Not commanding the same numbers they once did, do you think?' asked Drake.

'I wouldn't say that,' Hero replied, dusting off her hands. 'Could be they see themselves as having the perfect hideaway. They've grown careless.'

'Which gives us the element of surprise,' Joss said. 'We'll need to be quick and quiet.'

The trail of glowing moss and mushrooms continued, leading out into an open field that practically hummed with otherworldly light. Above them, the water swirling around the protective energy dome gave the appearance of a sky rippling black and purple, while Daheed stretched out before them lit only by a bank of fires burning at its heart. Despite what he'd just said, Joss couldn't help but slow to a stop and stare in wonder. It wasn't just the play of light that mesmerised him. It was the city itself.

The buildings were dark and half-destroyed, but still he

recognised many of them. There was the old bakehouse, from which plumes of sweetly scented air would waft every morning, perfuming the world with sultanas and pistachios and rosewater. Further on was the toymaker's workshop, where Joss now recalled the puppets and wooden pterosaurs that used to hang in the windows. He remembered the painted sword he would beg his mother for whenever they passed, and her patient reply of not wanting him to play with weapons. His eyes turned to the Champion's Blade in his hands.

'Joss, what's wrong?' asked Drake, both him and Hero faceless black entities against the bright green glow of the moss.

'Nothing,' Joss replied. 'Being back here is just …' He frowned, unsure of what to say or how to say it.

'What?' asked Drake.

Joss shook his head to clear his thoughts. 'Never mind,' he said. 'Let's keep going.'

They were silent as they progressed into the city in an arrowhead formation, Joss leading the way. Even with Hero behind him at a distance, he could sense her eagerness to push ahead and take command. Perhaps that would have been the wiser course of action, given her superior stealth and tracking abilities. But there was no way he was going to be led like a tamed beast through his own city.

Not that he recognised it now. After the first rush of familiarity, he was having a hard time identifying anything else. It didn't help that for every building that had managed to survive, there were piles of rubble where its neighbours had once stood. What was left was a bewildering puzzle in need of solving.

The city wasn't laid out in a grid or in concentric circles or in any recognisable pattern. Instead it was like a coral reef, with undulating waves of buildings set along twisting streets, their balconies stacked on top of each other as if all the drawers in a cabinet had been left wide open. Even the roads were an exotic oddity, paved with crushed oyster shells to create a sleek, black surface veined with mottled silver. Joss's boots, newly bought for this expedition, slipped as he traversed the maze, growing less sure with every step of what direction to take.

And then they came to the golden needle of the Tower Memoria. Though it had been an awe-inspiring sight from Bhashvirak's back, all that remained impressive about it now was its stature. Otherwise the building was a wreck, tarnished and tumbling down, though not entirely abandoned. Flames could be seen flickering from within, through the glassless arched windows at the base of the building. Sneaking over with sword drawn, Joss peered inside.

Nothing. Tiered rows of marble benches led downward to a centre stage, where a metal barrel held a small crackling fire. Blankets were scattered nearby, a few helmets, a couple of hessian sacks. Graffiti soiled every surface: *Gnash was here!* read one wall. *Where be the mermaidens?* asked another, with impatient underlining to score the question. But, most ominously of all, one phrase, threaded like a spider web among all the others, was repeated over and over again.

Darkness take us all.

Joss couldn't help but shudder. Though, for all their seeming importance, the dire words had been abandoned here along with everything else. Seeing Drake and Hero approach, weapons at the ready, Joss shook his head. 'Nobody's here,' he said and both his brethren sagged.

He was wondering where they should go next when, from somewhere beyond the tower, there came the sound of chanting. 'Do you hear that?' Joss asked, tilting his ear upward.

'What?' Drake said.

Joss quickly shushed him, still trying to trace the sound. He needn't have worried, however, as it quickly grew louder. It was a throaty call, at first emitted by a lone voice and then by many. It had the resonance of an instrument carved from wood, tubular and winding, pulled straight from the gut. And then, over that, there came the hissing of incantations. Dark words. Strange but somehow familiar.

'This way,' he said, and sprinted in the direction of the noise, Hero and Drake following. Stalking their way through the ruins, Joss kept an eye out for any movement, for any sign of life. Nothing stirred, but he couldn't shake the feeling that they were being watched by some unseen force.

He tried not to check over his shoulder too much for fear of giving himself away, though every time he did he saw nothing suspicious. Maybe it was just the lingering effects of the wisp's touch playing tricks on his mind. Still, he remained keenly vigilant as the chanting grew ever clearer.

The words being recited were harsh things, spat from the back of the throat to befoul the ear. Though he had no hope of pronouncing them himself, nor any way of translating them, Joss knew the nature of them. He knew their dark origin, their malevolent intent. He knew it all from having heard them before, and he feared why he might be hearing them again.

Running through the shadows of Daheed, Joss slipped past a row of terrace homes, where he remembered staying once in the care of a distant relative. From there, he turned a corner into a wide avenue that he recalled leading to the waterfront, and it was here that he found all the fires blazing. It was here he found the well of voices.

'Hide!' he told the others as they caught up to him. Together they dived behind a fallen statue, the plaque on its base identifying the subject as Consul Tazh, the first independent leader of Daheed. Even in the midst of danger, Joss felt a pang of sorrow at discovering such a magnificent artefact destroyed.

The chanting continued. Only when he was sure they hadn't been spotted, Joss cautiously inched up to steal a glance. Over two hundred figures were gathered on the Thousand Sacred Stairs. Once, the rough-hewn limestone steps had led down the avenue into the sea, as if the steps were an amphitheatre with all the ocean its stage. Now they fell away into nothingness. The figures were lined up on the descending tiers, humming and chanting together, their spiked helmets muffling their voices but failing to silence them.

A large cage had been soldered into place on the walls that surrounded the stairs. It was full of hostages, arms reaching out from between the bars, faces pressed up against the cold black iron. As Joss scanned it, he hoped desperately to spot the one face he'd come all this way to find.

But Edgar was nowhere to be seen, leaving Joss as tense and fearful as the prisoners watching from their cage while a pair of armoured pyrates marched up and down before them. They seemed to be assessing the hostages as a buyer might judge a herd of stock at market, and when they'd made their decision they came to a stop in front of the cage's door. The hostages inside screamed.

'No! *Please no!*' one man, still dressed in his Sea Spirit Festival garb, cried as the pyrates unlocked the cage and pulled him out. Though he struggled against them, they kept a tight hold as they dragged him down the Thousand Sacred Stairs. There, on Daheed's First Step – where Joss had been blessed with sea water and given his name – stood two men.

The first was slender, with a brass apparatus that housed a glowing mechanoid eye sewn onto the top half of his face. The eye shifted and contracted as the pyrate surveyed the crowd, a cruel little smile playing on his lips.

The second figure sported a big red beard, streaked with silver and woven through with bird skulls and finger bones and thunder lizard fangs. He wore a long coat covered in ornate eye designs, its colours faded to a bruised purple. Joss recognised him as the captain who'd led the attack on Crescent Cove.

'Brothers!' the captain shouted, and the pyrates ceased their chanting to roar with full-throated zeal. 'You have toiled! You have plundered! You have wrought a tribute of agony and heartbreak, and now the hour of triumph is at hand! And here to lead us into our glorious new era, here to herald our master's fated coming, is the Shadow God's first true disciple!'

The pyrates roared even louder, their excitement growing into a frenzy. Joss wondered if all that enthusiasm was for the slender man with the mechanoid eye. His skulking demeanour betrayed him as an underling, however, not a leader. But there was nobody else near the First Step. Who could these fanatics possibly be awaiting?

The answer came all too soon.

A shadow glided along the ground. It swam between the captain and the pyrate with the mechanoid eye to gather in the centre of Daheed's First Step, forming a pool as dark and deep as a bottomless pit, from which there now arose a third figure. His stone mask, black hood and feather cloak made him a thing of nightmares – a malevolent unkindness that could materialise anywhere, at any time, that could not be struck down or evaded.

Constant.

Immortal.

'King's mercy!' Hero gasped.

'That's not …' hissed Drake, unable to finish the horror of his thought.

'It is,' Joss said. 'It's Thrall.'

The masked man stood with arms outstretched, basking in the pyrates' collective adulation. As the hostage was brought before him, kicking and thrashing, Thrall lowered a single hand to draw his curved blade from its scabbard, raising it as if were a holy object to be admired by all.

'With this sacrifice, we show our fealty,' he said, his voice low but as resonant as distant thunder. 'With this sacrifice, we demonstrate our devotion. And with this sacrifice, we usher forth a new and unpitying age, to be ruled over by our rightful master.'

The mob roared its approval. The hostages cowered in terror.

Desperate to see what was happening, Joss spotted a row of barrels that skirted the very edge of the stairs, just behind the crowd. Without saying anything, he darted from behind the fallen statue and to the hiding spot. He ran as fast and as low to the ground as he could, ignoring the alarmed protests that Drake and Hero hissed behind him. Peering over the rim, he now had a better view of the First Step. Once, sapphire waters would have lapped at its edges. Now those waves had been replaced by a strange black vortex, just like Lord Malkus had described, which swirled around and around the city's bedrock, gradually eroding it.

The damage would have been catastrophic if not for

the dome of purple energy that cut through the vortex, to cradle the underside of the island and keep it from slipping all the way into oblivion. It shocked Joss to see just how precarious the city's position was, teetering on the edge of destruction. Most of the vortex was outside of the dome, pooling at the bottom of the trench. But there was enough inside, swirling below the First Step, for the pyrates to do their worst. Joss watched as Thrall dragged his prisoner to its very edge.

'We give this sacrifice willingly, that we might please our master and hasten his arrival into this world,' Thrall said, clamping a hand on the prisoner's shoulder. 'Darkness take us!'

'Darkness take us all!' the crowd chanted in return.

The prisoner didn't cry. He didn't scream. Instead, a single gasp escaped his lips as Thrall thrust the blade into the man's heart, then pushed him into the vortex below. The body hadn't even hit the swirling black nothingness before the man's flesh gave way, disintegrating into a cloud of calcified particles swallowed quickly by the void.

The darkness had taken him.

And it was only a matter of time before it took everything else.

CHAPTER TWENTY-TWO

A Blade in Each Hand

JOSS gagged on the bile burning his throat, the wisp mark throbbing beside his heart, as the whole island rumbled beneath him. What was happening? Thrall looked unperturbed by the tremors. Instead, he stood calmly on the edge of the vortex cleaning the blood from his sword.

'Bring me another,' he ordered. And the two pyrates who had pulled the first prisoner from the cage stalked back to choose their next victim.

They're going to kill every single one of these people, Joss realised. *And when that's done, who knows what they'll unleash!*

Again he scanned the row of caged faces, panicked that Edgar might be offered to the vortex next. Or worse, that he'd already suffered that fate while Joss had been quizzing Qorza, or asking for hot cocoa in the Drake household, or sightseeing through the Northern Tundra. So, when Joss finally caught sight of him, it was with a profound relief that immediately turned to horror.

Edgar's mouth and chin were covered in dried blood, his pale pink skin stained brown and copper. He was towards the back of the cage, a small frightened face in the crowd. Joss gripped the hilt of the Champion's Blade. Without thinking, he raised it before him. He had no plan. No real hope. But he couldn't stand by and let more innocent people die. He wouldn't.

'*Whatareyoudoing?*' he heard Hero hissing at him, and looked back to see her glaring from behind the fallen statue. Beside her Drake was shaking his head, imploring him to stay still, to keep silent.

He looked back towards the cage. Edgar was staring at him. Stunned, he mouthed Joss's name.

'Admiral Ichor!' someone shouted, his voice echoing across the gathering below. '*Intruders!*'

Joss whipped around to see two pyrate guards to the left of the fallen statue, advancing on Hero and Drake.

'Impossible!' the bearded leader grunted, before catching sight of the two Bladebound prentices. Teeth bared in a furious snarl, he issued his orders. 'Catch 'em, kill them, whichever's easiest! They can't escape!'

Drawing their swords, the guards rushed for Hero and Drake. Hero palmed a zamaraq from her bandolier and launched it at the closest guard, striking him between the seams in his armour. He grunted through his helmet as he collapsed to the ground. This only spurred on his partner, who slashed at Hero with lethal fury. His attack was blocked by Drake wielding the Icefire spear, the sound of clanging metal enough to make everyone's eardrums throb.

Springing up from behind the barrels, Joss rushed to join the fray. But his path was blocked by a whole regiment of guards surging upward from the Thousand Sacred Stairs, each of them armed and ready for battle. They converged upon Hero and Drake on the landing at the top of the stairs, quickly outnumbering the pair but not overpowering them.

'Drake! Hero!' Joss called out, drawing the attention of a handful of the pyrates. They broke off their attack to converge on him, surrounding him like a pack of wild raptors. Drawing his humming knife, he stood with a blade in each hand, ducking the axe of the closest pyrate.

Joss raised the Champion's Blade just in time to deflect the swing of a rusty sword across his torso. Slashing with his humming knife, he backed away from his assailants towards the sandstone wall of the old clock tower, the clock itself long since silenced. Within moments they would have him cornered. And then what? He didn't dare to imagine.

All the while, Thrall watched on coldly. Even as Admiral Ichor's face reddened to the colour of a blood blister and his words rang out like cannon fire, the masked man beside him didn't move. He seemed spellbound by the chaos breaking out before him.

'I want to squeeze that runt's heart in my fist until it bursts! Do you hear me?!' Admiral Ichor screamed. 'None of them leaves here alive!'

'Joss!' he heard Drake shout, and looked over to see him and Hero overwhelmed. The pyrates had them by the arms and legs, wresting the weapons from their hands as they dragged them back towards the cage. Hero was kicking and biting at every helmeted thug that came within striking distance, though even with all her thrashing she was soon overcome by the sheer numbers. They had a firm hold of her now, just as they did Drake. There was no quarter left to fight, no chance left to escape.

'Joss, *go!* Save yourself!' Drake's voice was strained as he thrashed against the dozen pyrates who had him by each limb.

'I can't leave you!' Joss cried out, losing ground to his attackers with every step. He was only just holding them at bay now, but still he searched desperately for some way to break through them, to aid his brethren, to save Edgar, to keep them all alive. There must be some way out, some way to win, even if everything was screaming at him that it was impossible.

And then, from some unseen source, a clay pot flew through the air. Trailing sparks from a lit fuse, it sailed past Joss to shatter right in front of the pyrates. Blue flames erupted violently, spreading with just as much force. A second clay pot landed less than a foot away from the first, and was soon joined by a third. Joss could feel the fire licking his face, could see the pyrates scurrying back through the eerie blue light of its flame.

'There's no help for your friends now,' someone said behind him, and Joss spun around to see a hooded figure lurking in the shadows of a narrow alleyway. In one hand he held a last clay pot, while the other beckoned Joss to follow him. 'Come with me or stay and die. Choose!'

CHAPTER TWENTY-THREE

A Faded Majesty

JOSS hesitated, turning back to see Drake and Hero being pushed into the cage with the hostages. 'I can't just leave them,' he said, the flickering blue flames that separated him from the pyrates growing weaker by the moment.

'You also can't save them if you're imprisoned alongside them,' the hooded figure said.

'And I can't save them if they're thrown into that void!' Joss stood his ground.

'This interruption means the entire ceremony will need to start over from the beginning. It'll be some time before any other sacrifices are needed,' the stranger replied, growing impatient. The pyrates were now gathered just beyond the wall of fire, testing its heat with their blades. Any moment they would be leaping through, ready to renew their attack. 'Now follow me.'

The stranger disappeared down the alley. Uncertain, Joss gazed again at Hero and Drake as the cage was closed on them. Admiral Ichor was still screaming bloody murder from the First Step, while Thrall lingered beside him. But he didn't appear to be looking at any of them. Though his stone mask made it impossible to tell, Joss could have sworn that the cloaked man was staring straight at him through the flames. He shuddered at the thought.

And though he was reluctant to flee, he knew now that he had no other option. Taking one last look back, Joss followed the stranger. As he squeezed between the walls of the alley, he swore to himself that he would return.

His mysterious rescuer was waiting for Joss at the other end of the alley, hood drawn low to hide his eyes, scarf pulled up high to hide everything else. A leather satchel sat on his hip, while a crossbow had been slung across his shoulder along with a quiver full of short barbed bolts. His tunic was woven from fabrics of bright sky blue and deep ocean green, stitched with threads of sunrise red and decorated with foam-white braids around the cuffs and collar. It was a traditional form of Daheedi dress that Joss recognised not only from the books he'd read but also from the recordings that Qorza had shown him. Did it mean that this man had been an inhabitant of the Gleaming Isle before its fall? Or a false friend leading him into an even greater danger?

'This way,' the stranger said, crossbow thumping against his back as he darted around the corner of the alleyway. Joss followed him into another alley, this one twice as wide but littered with papers and refuse and broken bottles. While the stranger navigated all the obstacles with ease, Joss had to choose each step carefully. It was almost enough of a distraction to keep him from questioning the man.

'Who exactly are you? And what's going on here?' Joss asked.

The stranger just kept moving, approaching a rope that hung against the wall at the end of the alley. 'You can call me Darra,' he said. 'Any other questions you may have will be answered in time, but for now we need to keep moving.' He grabbed hold of the rope to pull it taut. 'Up this way, quicker than you think you can.'

Joss paused, eyeing both the rope and this Darra warily. But he took the rope and started to climb. When he was halfway up, the stranger followed him, and together they scaled their way to the ceramic tiles of the rooftop. Joss watched as Darra then untied the rope from the chimney around which it had been strung, gathering up its length in his fist.

'How long until the pyrates start sacrificing people again?' Joss asked.

Darra shrugged. 'Hard to say. We should have until tomorrow, at least. But time's like a jellyfish down here. Spongy. Prone to stinging. And it'll be particularly spiky if we're caught.'

Noises echoed from the alleyway. Joss glanced over the edge to see that the pyrates had followed them. They were barking in confusion, searching every inch of the alley and confounded as to how their quarry had eluded them. Joss stepped back out of sight, while behind him Darra was dashing across the roof.

'Wait for me!' Joss hissed, pursuing Darra, who doubled his speed and showed no signs of slowing even as he came to the other end of the rooftop. Tiles clacking beneath his sandals, he vaulted off, landing on the building opposite. Frowning, Joss ran faster to do the same.

But his last step was snagged by a loose tile, throwing off his balance just as he launched himself into the air. His jump became a wayward tumble to the paving below. Before he could scream, he felt an iron grip snatch him by the arm. He'd barely realised what was happening before Darra had yanked him up to safety.

'You need to take more care. Only a turtle can turn a century,' Darra said as Joss panted at his feet, unable to begin puzzling through the stranger's odd turn of phrase.

'Thank – thank you,' Joss gasped. His breath was coming in bursts, his heart pounding furiously, and the wisp mark hot on his chest.

'Control your breathing. Calm yourself,' Darra said, crossing his arms. Joss watched him closely, trying to glimpse the man beneath the hood. Whoever he may be he was fast and strong, though anything more than that was impossible to tell with his face so hidden. All Joss could see was a severe brow that topped a pair of piercing maroon eyes, pupils specked with distant stars. But even those small details proved deeply revealing.

'You really are Daheedi,' Joss said, knowing it was the truth. After a lifetime of thinking he was the last survivor of his people, it turned out he wasn't. It was as comforting a revelation as it was disquieting.

Darra looked at Joss, then turned away to gaze out across the city: black buildings edged in purple and green and flickering orange, fringed by palm fronds and fruit trees that were shrivelled and shedding dry leaves. Death had defaced this city. But still there was a dignity to it, a faded majesty.

'This was a paradise once,' Darra said, not looking away from the pavilions and pagodas and all Daheed's humble homes. 'A shining jewel. The heart of the

Silver Sea. Even its people seemed to glow in their rainbow refinery, their happiness as perfect as every sunny day that filled their lives. But the gentle breeze that drifted through these streets is now a stale and dreadful silence. I would weep at the loss of this place and its people, if there wasn't salt water enough serving as their tomb.'

'Did you know the Sarif family?' Joss asked. 'Isra and Naveer? She was a scholar at the Imperial Library and he was an ethereon aboard the *Seeker*. They lived in a small cottage in the northern district.'

The same stillness that filled the city streets now fell upon Darra, leaving Joss to wonder if his question had gone unheard. But then Darra twitched, and cast a firm glance from over his shoulder. 'Their memory remains,' he replied.

Joss, confused by the response, was about to ask what he meant when Darra started again across the rooftop. 'Come along. We're nearly to safety. Or as close to safety as can be found in this cursed place.'

Joss picked up his pace to follow.

———

The cage slammed shut with the force of an iguanodon snapping its jaws. The hostages regarded Drake and Hero warily, looking uncertain about what might happen to them if they too readily embraced these new arrivals.

'Y'think yer tough now, but you'll be crying out the other side of yer ruined faces when the admiral is done with ye,' growled one of the pyrate guards through the bars. 'And ya won't have any fancy weapons at hand to save yerselves.'

He shook Hero's bandolier at them as he spoke, before tossing it onto a pile of supplies that he carried away with him. His amputated leg, replaced with a rusted blade, hummed and swished as he hobbled off, leaving the prisoners to fend for themselves. The hostages stirred listlessly, their eyes at the ground.

'Glad we went to the effort of trying to save these people,' Hero muttered in Drake's ear, though before he had the chance to reply a voice called out from the back of the cage.

'Miss Hero! Mister Drake!' Edgar exclaimed. He pushed through the crush to be reunited with them, dragging a thin old woman along with him. 'Am I ever glad to see you!'

CHAPTER TWENTY-FOUR

A BRIGHT AND BURNING REALITY

THEIR flight across the roofs of Daheed took them past abandoned markets, empty haberdasheries, derelict galleries and silent coffee houses. At one stage they descended to street level, their only option to cross a fractured bridge that spanned a muddy river full of fish skeletons. On the other side they climbed over crates and up along scaffolding to return to the air, Darra's pace never slowing.

But as fast as they ran, Joss's mind raced even faster. It skipped from one thought to another and back again. Edgar and Hero and Drake. Admiral Ichor and his pyrates. He wondered about the Admiral – how he had come to lead his men down here, what his connection to Thrall could be. How Daheed could have possibly survived the Destruction, even if its people hadn't.

But most of all, he watched the Daheedi before him, trying to imagine what face might lie beneath his disguise and trying not to lose himself to hope.

'This way,' Darra said when Joss was lagging, and hopped across a break in the row of buildings to land on the lower tier of a massive domed structure. Joss followed without hesitation, and together they scaled the surface of the dome towards its apex. It was fashioned from solid bronze which had rusted green, and though it curved high into the air its surface was chalky enough to grip to, making it relatively easy to climb.

Before long Joss and the stranger were standing together at the top of the dome, looking at a hole in its surface where once a grand leadlight window might have been. Instead, a length of rope secured to its frame now dangled into the void below.

'Daunting, I know. I can go first if that makes it easier,' Darra offered, his voice softening into a tone Joss hadn't heard before. Joss nodded in response. Darra immediately grabbed the rope and slipped into the darkness. And again, Joss followed. Nothing could be seen inside. Nothing but limitless black, same as the deep ocean. It took all of Joss's faith to step over the side and inch down into its depths.

He had been descending the rope long enough for his biceps to start burning when he heard noise echoing from below, and saw sparks igniting. The entire chamber lit up as dozens of orbs flashed green and white. Bathed in emerald light, Joss could now see that he was only a few feet from the ground. He slid down the remaining distance, landing not that far from Darra, who was poised with his hand on the lever of a large generator. Cables ran from the thrumming metal box, stretching to each of the orbs that had been strewn and strung around the room. They illuminated all the pinewood desks that were assembled in hexagonal rows, as well as the vast bookshelves that lined the curving walls.

'I don't believe it,' Joss whispered, staring all around him. 'This … this is the library!'

'The Imperial Library, yes,' Darra said with a bare nod.

'I remember …' The floor screeched under the soles of Joss's boots as he pivoted to look at everything, the polished marble floor reflecting his expression of wonder. The light was severe, filtering everything in green and casting deep shadows. But still Joss recognised the room, dredging up memories that had long lain dormant. He recalled sitting at these very desks, drawing pictures of his family as he waited for his mother to take him home. Touching the tabletop, he came away with a thick layer of dust on his fingertips, though that was the least of the room's disrepair.

Spiders had fashioned cobweb castles in every corner. Piles of books were spotted like battlefield casualties throughout the walkways, likely scattered by the island's sinking. Barricades blocked all but one door, roughly assembled from crates and odd pieces of broken furniture. Eyeing them warily, Joss realised with mounting concern that he was now trapped in a confined space with an armed stranger. Adjusting his sword-belt, he glanced sideways at his companion.

'An effort I made to keep Admiral Ichor's men from breaking in,' said Darra, gesturing to the barricades as he unhooked his crossbow and placed it on the table before him. 'Not that it's ever occurred to them to search here. Those without thought rarely see the value of libraries.'

'How long have they been here? The pyrates?' Joss asked.

'They arrived not long after the Destruction. Though it's hard to say when exactly,' he replied. 'As I said, time has no real meaning here. The clocks have stopped. The sun never rises, the moon never shines. There is only stillness and insanity and death.'

'You've been here all this time, just yourself?'

Darra shuddered. 'Yes,' he said. 'When the pyrates first arrived, I spied on them from the shadows. I knew that they weren't to be trusted. Originally they saw this place as the perfect lair from which to launch their raids.

But as time passed, the vortex that stirs beneath us began to play on their minds. They became enthralled with it, prey to it, enslaved by it. They transformed into a ravenous cult, led by a deranged sadist prepared to go to any length to please his new-found master.'

'The master ... the one that Thrall referred to?' Joss asked.

'Thrall?' Darra asked, the name obviously unfamiliar to him.

'The man in the stone mask. The one leading the ceremony.'

'Ah. *Him*. He arrived shortly after they began artlessly worshipping the vortex. It was he who formalised their devotion, who filled their heads with the need for sacrifice. A preacher to their zealous disciples. It was also he who alerted them to my presence, though it was Admiral Ichor who ordered my execution should I be captured. It was then I knew that any semblance of the man I'd called friend was lost forever.'

'You knew Admiral Ichor?' Joss said in astonishment.

'In the days before his descent into madness and bloodshed, before his career of pyracy – when he was merely a fishing boat captain by the name of Josiah.'

'*Josiah?!*' said Joss, so stunned by the revelation that he had trouble grappling with it. 'This Admiral Ichor ... his name is Josiah Eichmore?'

'Indeed,' said Darra, raising his hands to pull back his hood. Black curls spilled out, long and wild, flecked with grey. 'In fact, it was Josiah whom your mother and I named you after.'

The stranger pulled loose the scarf to reveal a face of haunting familiarity. Tears welled behind Joss's eyes, a rising tide that threatened to drown him any moment, while his heart bulged as if trying to escape his body. The faint hope he'd had before, the glimmering suspicion, now exploded into a bright and burning reality.

'Father!'

'Yes, Josiah,' Naveer Sarif said, maroon eyes glistening black in the green light of the library. 'It's me.'

—

CHAPTER TWENTY-FIVE

A FIERY DAWN

JOSS felt himself trembling. His father – ten years dead but now miraculously returned – stood before him with the stiff posture of someone greeting a visiting official. Despite his long curls and unkempt beard, he had a dignity to him that reflected the city outside. Beaten but unbroken.

All his life, Joss had imagined what he would talk about with his parents if he were somehow inexplicably reunited with them. Of course, these conversations had never been anything but a passing fantasy. Until now.

'The first thing I should do is apologise,' his father said, still rigidly formal. 'I didn't wish to deceive you, but I also knew we couldn't afford to linger out in the open. Not with Ichor's men hunting us. And this wasn't the kind of reunion that could take place while on the run.

Better to be somewhere safe first.'

'How … ' Joss began to speak, then found himself with just one word. *'How?'*

'How am I alive?' his father said. 'That's the question I've been asking myself ever since the day you and your mother were torn from me.'

'How did you recognise me?'

His father, Naveer Sarif, this stranger, this man called Darra – whoever he was – stared at Joss with unwavering certainty. 'How could I not?' he said.

Joss was silent. He turned his gaze to the floor, before looking about at the chamber. He began a slow walk, wandering in circles, lost in a daze.

'Why "Darra"?' he asked without looking up.

'It's an old Kahnrani word. It means "Father".'

Joss faltered mid-step, then continued. Here he was, in a sunken city surrounded by ruthless enemies, with his only friends in the world held hostage, and yet he had so many questions that couldn't wait. Not after a lifetime of wondering. Not when his *father* stood before him.

'That day. The day you … the one that you spoke of. I've been told things about it, heard stories, remember small fragments. There was a great black hole above the city, like the sky itself had been torn wide open. Nobody knows what it was, they only know of the destruction that followed …' Joss choked on the thought.

His father regarded him solemnly. 'It was a terrible and traumatic thing. You may not want to hear –'

'No. I *need* to know,' Joss told him. 'What happened?'

His father seemed to sag. 'Chaos.' He spoke the word as if it were a curse. 'Carnage. The end of everything I'd ever known and loved. And all on a day that had started bright and blue and clear. A day of celebration.'

'Celebration?'

'*Ramera*. The Remembrance. When all ships are called back to Daheed, when all its citizens gather for seven days of commemoration and celebration. A holy time.'

Joss's father – Father? Darra? Naveer? 'Naveer' felt the most comfortable to Joss – rested his weight against one of the nearby tables, as if needing the support. There was some small part of Joss that wanted to go to him, to offer him some kind of comfort or understanding. There was another part of him, no less small, that wanted to shake him to hurry up. Joss returned to pacing the library and, thankfully, Naveer returned to his tale.

'It was on the morning of the seventh day, the day of feasting, that the darkness descended. It all happened so quickly – a dream that sours into a nightmare between breaths. We were gathered by the Thousand Sacred Stairs when a shadow fell across all the island, so dark that at first I thought an unexpected storm had set in.

There was a sound of a thousand thunderbolts striking as one, shaking the earth and setting all the children to tears. All the children but you. You remained so calm, so brave, even as the great black tear that you spoke of ripped open the sky above us.

'And I'll tell you this now: I've been an ethereon all my adult life, and an islander from birth. I've studied all manner of supernatural phenomena and weathered all sorts of storms. But I've never seen anything the likes of what I witnessed that day. It was something altogether ... *different*. Like some force from a place beyond our understanding was trying to tear its way into our world. You may not have been scared by it, but I was terrified.

'Your mother's instinct was to flee for the harbour and escape on the small boat we kept moored there. But I wasn't ready to abandon Daheed. Not when the winds were pulling people up into the sky, into the black vortex. Not while I had an idea of how to save everyone. I told your mother to take you and get to the boat, that I would follow if I could, but to sail to safety if I delayed too long. She begged me to come with her, but I insisted that she take you and go. It was only then that you started to cry.

'I ran home to gather my instruments. If I could perform a warding spell for a ship, surely I could do the same for an island. I set about marking the streets with the required sigils, using paint in place of coal and chanting as I went. The wind was an invisible beast by this point, howling louder and louder as it grabbed everyone and everything it could. I forced it out of my mind, focused on the task at hand. And the spell: it took! A barrier of mystical energy rose up to shield the island from the vortex. The winds eased. I was allowed one all-too-fleeting moment of relief. And then the black vortex surged.

'I must have miscalculated. There was something wrong with my spell. It reacted unpredictably to the vortex's presence, drawing the black tear against itself. But it didn't end there. The two forces struggled against each other, my barrier pulling against the vortex, pulling it down, pulling it under … and pulling Daheed along with it. The vortex was below us now, the mystical barrier a dome above us.

'Waves crashed over the city skyline, held back by the dome that was forcing us under. I prayed that you and your mother had escaped before it was too late. Buildings crashed all around me. People died screaming. Neighbours. Cousins. Lifelong friends. They all perished as Daheed was sucked down into the water.'

Naveer fell silent while Joss watched from across the room, unsure if what he was hearing and what it led him to believe were the same thing. 'Does that mean …' Again he had to wrench the words loose, his heart a swollen lump. 'The Destruction. You caused it?'

The effort it had taken Joss to ask his question paled in comparison to what it now took for his father to look him in the eye. When he did, it was with such a sense of defeat and shame that it left Joss startled.

'Daheed was doomed, one way or the other,' he said, an edge of defiance flashing beneath whatever other feelings tortured him. 'I'd tried to save everyone and instead I'd only sealed our fate, staying the execution in favour of a watery dungeon. It was the last thought I had before a piece of debris struck me in the head, knocking me unconscious.

'When I came to, I searched for survivors. Only two people had lived through the city's sinking, but their injuries were fatal. So many had died. I spent what must have been weeks collecting the bodies and burning the remains. The fires blazed for twice that time, fuelled by fat and human flesh. The smell … *the smell* …'

A shiver so powerful ran through Joss's father that it found its way across the room to his son. Biting back the revulsion, Joss pushed for more answers. 'What about Ichor?' he asked, starting with the most immediate threat before them. 'When did he arrive?'

'Long enough after the city's sinking for me to have

grown so mad that at first I didn't know if he was just an illusion,' his father said, his words still soaked in sorrow. He glanced up long enough to register Joss's shocked expression. 'I'm sorry. It's a difficult truth, but true nevertheless. This place infects the mind. Poisons the soul. I was the lone inhabitant of a forsaken tomb, and I would be lying if I said it didn't affect me. I became so lost that I considered ending it all – and most likely would have, if not for Ichor's arrival. Though it was never his intention, his appearance here gave me purpose.'

'What do you mean?' Joss asked.

Naveer stood, regaining his rigid posture. 'Let me show you,' he said, walking to the one doorway that had been left unbarred. He disappeared into the shadows gathered there, leading the way down a flight of stairs lit with lamps that had been nailed to the walls and hung from the bannisters. The lamps grew increasingly sparse the further down they climbed, reminding Joss of the black cavern where he and the others had left Salt and the Mighty Bhashvirak. Would the two of them still be there when the time came to escape?

'I know you must have many more questions yet,' Naveer said, his voice bouncing around the walls despite how softly he spoke. 'And I can answer them all in time. But I was hoping that you might consider … well …'

'You have questions of your own,' Joss said, and Naveer slowed down. Nodded. Joss stopped five steps behind him. 'Go on.'

Naveer picked up his pace again, his feet scuffing the steps, but he didn't speak.

Joss could still scarcely believe that the man before him was real, that he was flesh and blood and bone and not some figment of his overstressed mind. But then, could Joss have ever imagined the fate that had befallen Daheed? Or the tragic role that his own father played in its demise?

'How did you come to be here?' Naveer finally asked. 'This is the last place in the world I would ever expect to see you.'

'It wasn't the easiest journey. Or the most direct one,' Joss said, and went on to explain all the events that had led him there. He spoke of the attack on Crescent Cove, the abduction of Edgar, the voyage with Qorza, the path through the Northern Tundra, the guidance of Salt, and the taking of his Bladebound Brethren.

'Your Bladebound brethren?' Naveer said, seizing on Joss's turn of phrase. 'I took your form of dress to be of Thunder Realm, but not that you were actually training to be a paladero. Is that really so?'

'Would it be a problem if it was?' asked Joss as they came to the end of the stairwell and stepped down into an empty antechamber with an iron vault set into its opposite wall.

'No, I just never … it wouldn't have been what I imagined for you, is all. It's a world away from here. And a very different path.'

'But that's not want you want to ask me about. Not really. Is it?' Joss said.

Naveer flinched and faced the vault as he asked his question. 'Your mother. She …' He wavered, unable to continue.

'She – didn't make it,' Joss said. 'She saved my life. Even though it cost her own.'

The revelation sent a tremor through Naveer's body. But again he asserted control over himself, straightened his back, thrust out his chin. 'She would have it no other way,' he said, then added, 'Here. Follow me.'

He marched with renewed strength across the antechamber to the vault's iron door. The lock thumped and grumbled as he unbolted it, then pulled the hefty metal door open. Joss approached with trepidation. What was in there? What he saw was the least likely thing of all.

Rows upon rows of shelves had been filled with small clay pots. As bulbous as overripe fruit, they stretched on further than the eye could see, as dense as an orchard and just as deep.

'What is all this?' asked Joss, peering into the room but stopping short of actually entering it. Naveer drew close beside him to regard his handiwork.

'My plan. Nearly a thousand pots of liquid fire, all filled by hand, ready to rip this island apart and send it tumbling into the abyss. And Ichor will never see it coming.'

Joss saw the wild look in Naveer's eye, heard the cold fury that frosted his words. It was enough to make even a half-starved tyrannosaur take pause. 'You want to destroy Daheed? After all you went through trying to save it?' he asked.

'If I couldn't rescue it, then the least I can do is put it out of its misery,' said Naveer. 'This was a beautiful place once. A place of learning. A cradle of civilisation. We filled the seas with vessels as swift as the creatures that inspired their designs. Taught the world to master the tides. Traded our way into our enemies' good graces. We raised families, honoured our forebears, sang ancestral songs, told tales of times past, and feasted through every season.

'There was a special magic that came with pulling into dock at twilight, just after the sun had set but while its afterglow still lingered. The water and the sky would be the same shade of indigo, a liquid mirror streaked with golden lamplight. Sailing home on nights like that felt like gliding into the crystal canals of Paradise itself. It was for all this and more that we were known across the seas as the Gleaming Isle.

'Better it be remembered that way, don't you think? Rather than this ruin, to be used as a sacrificial altar for whatever abhorrent blood magic that Ichor and his stone-faced accomplice hope to unleash? I've heard them call this their city of night neverending. I would bring it a fiery dawn.'

Naveer's gaze was a lighthouse beam, pinning Joss in place and burning away the shadows of doubt in his mind, his residual shock and dismay.

'We would need to get the hostages to safety,' Joss told him firmly. 'All of them.'

'And we will. After all, what better distraction is there than setting a torch to all your enemy's plans? The chaos will provide the opportunity to liberate everyone before Daheed is granted its final rest.' Naveer took hold of one of the clay pots and brandished it with purpose.

Joss looked down the rows of shelves. He closed his eyes, pictured Daheed the way that Naveer had described it, the way he faintly remembered it. This was the place he'd been dreaming of all his life, the place to which he thought he could never return. A place that had died along ago.

Joss opened his eyes. 'Where do we start?'

CHAPTER TWENTY-SIX

A STARTLING REVELATION

'WE'LL need to set the pots at these locations,' Naveer said. He crouched and drew a map of Ichor's camp in the dust on the floor, marking an X for every target. 'If I'm correct, the chain of explosions will have multiple effects. First and foremost, they'll provide the distraction we need to break out the prisoners. Secondly, they'll safeguard our escape. But, most importantly, the force should be enough to destroy the sigils I marked out on the day when the vortex first appeared. With that done, the barrier will fall. And the island along with it.'

'Won't we drown if we do that?' Joss asked.

Naveer shook his head. 'The barrier should recede slowly enough for us to retreat to the cavern where the pyrates' submersibles are docked.'

'You know about the harbour?' Joss noted with surprise.

'Of course.'

'And you never tried to steal a vessel and escape?'

'They always kept too close a watch. It's only recently that their security has grown so lax. But if we're to have any chance now, we'll have to make sure we get to the cavern first and secure it before Ichor and his men can.'

Joss thought of Salt waiting down there, spear at the ready. 'That shouldn't be a problem,' he said.

'Good,' Naveer replied, dusting off his hands. 'I have a lot of work ahead of me if I'm to get everything done before any more hostages are threatened.'

'I can help,' Joss offered, noticing how much closer he'd drifted towards Naveer as they crouched together beside the map.

'Priming the pots is delicate and dangerous work. I wouldn't risk you being injured. Better that you go back up to the main chamber and rest. You'll need it.'

'But –'

'Please, Josiah,' Naveer said. 'Trust me.'

Joss chewed his bottom lip, flicked his thumb with his forefinger, shifted the balance of his weight to his other leg.

'It's Joss. Everyone calls me Joss. Well, most everyone.'

Naveer seemed to turn the word around in his head, examining it with care. 'Joss,' he said quietly, his eyes flickering like twin flames. Joss watched them closely as he pushed again at the edges of his memory.

'There are things I remember and things I don't,' he ventured. 'I remember what must have been our house, with the fig tree in the front courtyard …'

'And a bright yellow door, with wind chimes by the window,' Naveer added softly.

'That's right!' Joss said with perhaps too much excitement. Hunching back on his heels, he continued: 'I remember sailing on what must have been your boat. I remember coming here to wait for my mother to finish her work and take me home. I remember her smile. I remember her last words. But of all the things I remember, I don't … I can't –'

'Yes?'

'I can't remember what I used to call you,' he said. 'Was it "Father"? Or "Darra"? Or –'

'Actually,' Naveer said. 'It was "Paap".'

'Paap?'

'You were young.' A soft smile warmed Naveer's face. 'Though you'd be most welcome to call me that again. If you like.'

'It would feel strange to call you that now,' Joss admitted.

Naveer's smile flickered with pain. 'We can start with "Naveer" if that's your preference,' his father said. 'And then work it out from there.'

Joss nodded. 'All right,' he said.

Naveer's smile recovered its strength, though it was different from before. He rose to his feet and Joss joined him.

'I have to admit, this isn't how I imagined our reunion,' his father said. 'On the rare occasions that I would allow myself to imagine it, I pictured you as you were. Small and bright, full of wonder. I even dared to picture your mother returned along with you, *my Isra*, and that together we would be a family again. As if nothing had ever happened. The more time passed, the more foolish that felt, and it was too painful to keep hoping. Being trapped here has eroded much of me – many of the softer parts. Perhaps, when we're free of this place, we can find a way towards that happy reunion, even if it looks a little different than I thought it might.'

'I'd like that,' Joss said, before they lapsed into a moment of strained tension. Should they hug, perhaps? *It doesn't feel right yet*, Joss thought. And he didn't want to force it.

'I'm going upstairs,' he said. 'Let me know if you need any help.'

'Of course,' Naveer said, and again there was a moment of tense indecision as neither of them reached out for the other, broken only by Joss leaving for the stairs.

As he climbed his way back up, he thought about all that Naveer had told him. While he had never considered it possible, he too had imagined what a reunion with his parents might be like. But this experience hadn't matched those dreams in the slightest. Even with the tenderness that Naveer had ended up showing, there was something in his manner that set Joss on edge.

Perhaps it was the rigid formality with which he held himself. Maybe it was the touch of madness that bubbled to the surface when he spoke of his plans for Ichor and his devotees. Or perhaps it was just that Joss was inherently suspicious of them finding each other again, in this darkest moment, when Joss so sorely needed an ally. What were the chances of such a thing? How could his fortune be so favourable, even with what Qorza had said about fate?

He took a moment as he returned to the chamber to regard its emptiness. The cobwebs he'd noticed earlier heaved in the air like lungs suffering from a chest infection. Theirs was the only movement in the room, which looked untouched by any living soul, and yet Naveer said that he'd been hiding out here for years. Curious.

Joss scanned the room, hand pressed firm against the wisp mark that had been nagging him ever since his arrival in Daheed. He took note again of the curving shelves, the piles of texts, the barricaded exits. But then, concealed among the stacks, he saw a door set discreetly into the wall by his right. A trace of green light was escaping from around its edges. Joss took a quick look back down the stairwell. He could hear a distant scraping and the occasional grunt, which he took to be Naveer hard at work readying the explosive pots.

Satisfied that he could go ahead without interruption, Joss quickly crossed to the door. Its hinges squealed as he pushed it open, a cloud of dust pouring from its frame. A hallway awaited him on the other side, dark but for a few orbs strung from the walls to guide the way down its length. He took one step inside. And then another. No alarms sounded, nothing gave away his presence. He continued, passing the first of many doors that ran along the hallway. He tested its handle, found it locked, moved on to try the next.

Every door he came to was the same, handles rattling in his grip but refusing to turn. He was questioning the point of all this effort, when he came to the second-last door in the hall and saw a brass key sticking from the lock. To his astonishment, the handle turned without resistance and he stepped into the room.

Though dark, he could see it was a sizeable study with bookshelves lining the walls and an oak desk at the opposite end. Unlike the rest of the library, the texts here had remained in place thanks to the glass doors that fronted the inbuilt shelves, which had somehow remained intact. Joss recognised the Kahnrani script that decorated many of the book covers, though he couldn't read it. That wasn't a problem for the books that had been written in the Sleeping King's tongue, with titles like *Scrolls of the Ancients* and *Deciphering the Unknown*.

As Joss looked about the room he wondered why it hadn't been sealed off too. What was he missing? It looked like a typical office belonging to any academic or senior librarian, though even dustier than the main room had been. A simple illuminator was perched on the edge of the desk, the kind of device that couldn't be used for anything but playing back recorded images. Picking up the bronze ball, Joss pinched a nodule on its side and a rainbow of imagery burst from the device's crystal projector. The first thing he saw was a baby, its skin the same shade of brown as his own, its smiling face bright and bubbly.

That's me! Joss realised, staring with wide-eyed amazement. And this must have been his mother's office. The image then cycled over to one of his parents, which he recognised as being from their wedding day.

It was the same moment that Qorza had shown him on her Scryer, with Naveer and Isra exchanging matching marital necklaces. Only now did it occur to him that he hadn't seen Naveer wearing his, though perhaps he kept it hidden beneath his tunic. Or perhaps it carried too many painful memories.

The image cycled again, back to the recording of Joss as a giggling baby. He watched it over, bemused to see himself so happy and carefree. When it cycled back to the footage of his parents' wedding, he turned to investigate the rest of the desk, though he hesitated in disturbing any of the things on it. The way all the papers were laid out made it look as if his mother had just stepped away from her work for a moment. The idea came with an awful pang, like an instrument hitting the wrong note. Squeezing his eyes shut, Joss gave himself a moment to recover, then began sifting through the paperwork.

Renewal notices. Event invitations. Official memoranda. The documents heaped upon his mother's desk were both fascinating and banal, showing a life rich with duty. From the amount of correspondence and the respectful tone in which it was written, she looked to have been highly esteemed in her field. It gave Joss a bittersweet sense of pride, as well as a burning curiosity to know more.

Beside the paperwork, he found two books. The first wasn't written in the King's tongue, or in Kahnrani, or any other dialect that Joss recognised. The script was a rough assemblage of blocks and dots, an early and forgotten language that would have surely been known to only a handful. The other was a journal, its every page filled with notes written in the most elegant and flowing hand.

Joss touched the journal lightly. He turned its pages with reverence. He marvelled at the idea of it having once belonged to his mother, that it was where she worked through her ideas and research. And then, settling in as if to study a sacred text, he began to read.

But there was nothing of personal significance to be found. No diary entries about her family, or her life on the island. Only the translations of old scrolls and obscure poets. Interesting though it may have been, it wasn't what Joss had been hoping for. He was considering closing the book again when he came to the final set of pages, which had been titled *The Rakashi Revelations*.

On the left was what must have been the original text – the Revelations themselves – written in the same indecipherable block-and-dot script as the book left open beside the journal. On the right were what appeared to be the same passages but now translated into the royal language. His curiosity piqued, Joss started to read.

'From beyond silver seas, from out of blue skies, from the ruins of a lost life,' the text began, 'there will come a galamor.'

The passage broke off as several suggestions to the meaning of *galamor* were scrawled in the surrounding margins: 'saviour', 'protector', 'hero'. Each suggestion was coupled with a question mark, indicating just how uncertain the possibilities were.

'With right hand marked by fate, and carrying a vaartan rhazh –' Joss paused again to read the suggestions for what *vaartan* might mean. 'Victor'. 'Conqueror'. 'Champion'. And then, his hand now slightly trembling, Joss read all the words that *rhazh* could be.

'Weapon', the list began. 'Sword', it continued. 'Blade', it finished.

Joss's hand hovered over the final word before skimming back to *vaartan*, then bounced between the two before he came to the only conclusion that he could.

Carrying a Champion's Blade!

His mind was spinning, his interest now honed to a razor-tipped point. He read what remained of his mother's translations.

'Only the galamor *will stand when all else fall, and rise when all else kneel. Only the* galamor *can bring light to the oncoming darkness, and draw hope from a dying dream. Only the* galamor, *and the* galamor *alone.*'

Joss flicked over the page, found the next blank, flicked back again. He read the entire passage over and over, trying to piece together some kind of coherent picture. A saviour from across the seas prophesied to stand against some dark threat, armed with a Champion's Blade, right hand 'marked by fate'. Joss looked at his own right hand, palm scarred from his binding ceremony. Did all of this mean what he imagined it might? Or was it mere coincidence? And who or what was this Rakashi, and how much stock should be put in its vague prophecies?

Deciding that Naveer might be able to shed some light on the matter, Joss picked up the journal to take it back down to the storeroom with him. As he passed behind the desk, however, the tip of his boot caught on something on the floor.

Crashing painfully onto the polished stone, he landed on the bundle of rags and crinkled leather that had tripped him. Or at least that was what he assumed it to be. Eyes focusing in the dark, Joss saw what had been hidden away in here the entire time.

He must have screamed. And it must have been loud. He could still hear his voice echoing out into the main chamber as he scrambled back against the wall as fast as he could, horror spreading through him. Within moments, he heard footsteps running towards him.

'Josiah!' Naveer called out. 'Josiah, are you all right?'

Vaulting to his feet, Joss grabbed his mother's journal, stuffed it into his jacket, then drew the Champion's Blade from its scabbard and angled it at the door. He squeezed the sword handle tight with one shaking hand and held his grip steady with the other. When the door flew open, he readied himself for the struggle to come. He would not go without a fight.

'Joss, what's wrong? It sounded as if –' Naveer panted, gazing around the room at what could have caused such distress. His eyes flicked to the Champion's Blade. 'Is that aurum?'

'*Who are you?*' Joss demanded.

The man with his father's face looked at him in utter confusion. 'I'm Naveer Sarif. I'm your father,' he said as if the answer should be obvious.

'Then who in the unholy pits is this?!' Joss said, pointing at the ragged pile hidden behind his mother's desk. Naveer peered at it, and when he did his face fell in what looked to be shock.

Propped against the wall, a corpse had been left to atrophy. Though the hues of its garments had faded, they could still be discerned. Bright sky blue. Deep ocean green. Threads of sunrise red. And if that weren't enough, the thunderbolt necklace that dangled across its chest made it all too clear who this was, or once had been, even with its features withered to little more than a skull.

'I – I don't understand …' Naveer stuttered, feigning surprise so deftly that Joss wondered for a split second whether or not it was genuine.

'Then allow me to explain,' Joss said. Adjusting his grip on the Champion's Blade, he forced any trace of doubt from his mind. The monster standing before him didn't deserve the benefit of it. 'This is Naveer Sarif. *This* is my father.'

He pointed the tip of his sword at the impostor's heart.

'So what does that make you?'

—

CHAPTER TWENTY-SEVEN

A PALE AND TWISTED THING

'ADMIRAL Ichor has need of the prisoners,' said the pyrate with the mechanoid eye as he approached the cells with a regiment of armed muscle in tow.

The guard with the blade for a leg looked lazily up from his stool. 'You'll have to be more specific. We got a lot of prisoners here.'

'Don't try my patience, Gnash,' the pyrate sighed as his glowing eye whirled in its socket. 'You know who I mean.'

'Ain't trying nothing, Gnarl,' the guard spat back. 'Just doing my job as it's meant to be done.'

The mechanoid eye jerked to a stop, its pupil contracting to a fiery little point. 'I require the two intruders. If you would be so kind.'

Grinning, the guard called Gnash pulled himself up from his seat. 'Was that so hard?' he asked, and unclipped the keychain from his belt. 'No doubt it would bring a tear to our old man's eye to see his two boys getting along so well, Sleeping King keep him.'

Gnarl's piercing red pupil grew even more pointed in its gaze. 'You speak sacrilege in the house of our dark lord. And on the eve of his arrival.'

'Don't go getting preachy on me, brother,' Gnash said. 'It was only a turn of phrase.'

'See that it's so,' Gnarl told him. 'Now – the prisoners, if you wouldn't mind.'

Watching the altercation from the back of the cage, Drake and Hero found the crowd of hostages that surrounded them melting away. The armed guards moved quickly to take their place, swords drawn to keep the inmates at bay. Not that anybody attempted to resist them. They all knew better than that.

'On your feet,' Gnarl said.

With no other choice, Drake and Hero picked themselves up. But they weren't alone.

'I'm coming with them,' Edgar said, pushing forward to stand at their side. Gnarl's mechanoid eye homed in on the boy as if to study some strange new species of suicidal sea creature.

'And why would I allow that?' he asked.

Drake leant in, took Edgar by the elbow, told him firmly, 'Don't.'

'Because I'm their steward,' Edgar said, shaking Drake off.

Gnarl and his brother swapped incredulous glances. The blade-legged Gnash shrugged. 'Take him then, if he's so eager to meet his maker.'

As the prentices were led away, Lilia found the opening she needed to whisper to them. 'Remember, all they need is an excuse. These are cruel and violent men.'

'I can be pretty violent myself at times,' said Hero, glaring at her captors.

'Quiet!' Gnash ordered, slamming the cage shut again once the three prentices had been removed. As they were marched across the plaza, they passed the masses of pyrates huddled before the swirling vortex, still chanting. They were lined up along the staircase that descended into the abyss, with the masked Thrall again leading the congregation from the bottom step.

'It worries me what that stone-faced freak is doing here,' Hero murmured to Drake.

'Me too,' he whispered in reply. 'But I think we have more immediate concerns.'

Neither of them noticed the way Thrall stared at them as they passed, his followers growing more feverish in their recitations, the vortex swirling hungrily at his feet.

Naveer looked at Joss in astonishment, mouth agape and raised hands trembling. No, not Naveer. The *impostor*. Joss had to remind himself every other second not to think of this man by that name. This was his punishment for daring to trust.

'That – that can't be …' the impostor was stuttering, acting as if he hadn't known about the body that he'd stashed away to be forgotten. The whole act would have been very convincing if it wasn't so infuriating.

'But it *is*,' Joss told him, weapon glinting.

'Joss, please. I mean you no harm, I swear!'

'Then why pretend to be my father? Why play out this sick little game?' he said, and when the man who wore his father's face didn't respond, Joss demanded, 'Answer me!'

'I'm not pretending!'

'What other explanation is there?'

'I – don't know. I'm as baffled as you are.'

'Baffled? Baffled is not the word I would choose. Shocked. Deceived. Betrayed. Any of those would do. Feel free to choose your favourite.'

'Please, son, you have to believe me,' Naveer said, reaching out for Joss.

'Stay back!' Joss ordered as he pulled away, his wrist

brushing Naveer's hand. The protective charms fixed to Qorza's bracelet made contact with Naveer's skin, and the effect was as sudden as a lightning strike. Naveer howled as all his flesh quivered to reveal his true face: a pale and twisted thing with pointed black teeth and burning eyes.

Hissing, the impostor tried again to grab Joss.

'Don't touch me! *Monster!*' Joss screamed, the wisp mark burning into his chest. Spinning around, he shoved the creature back into the bookshelves. The glass shattered around him and heavy tomes fell like hailstones as Joss brandished his sword, taking one step back, then another.

He kept a wary eye on the creature with every move, waiting for it to lash out at him. It never did. It just gaped at Joss, skulking helplessly in the corner, its features shifting back into those of his father's face. Joss stepped into the hall. Slammed the door shut. The creature made no sound as Joss locked the door and removed the key, pressing his forehead to the hard wood.

'I was a fool to trust you,' he whispered, as much to himself as to the creature. He screwed his eyes shut to keep any tears from escaping, waiting until he was sure he had control of himself again. Still no sound of struggle came from within the study. So, Champion's Blade in hand, Joss ventured out into the main chamber.

It was just as empty as it had been before. No other monsters were waiting for him, or any of Ichor's men. But if all this had been some sort of elaborate trap, he wasn't going to wait around to find out. Sheathing his sword, he made for the rope hanging in the centre of the room. With great effort he climbed it, his hands and arms burning hotter than they had on the way down, and then clambered through the broken skylight and out onto the domed roof.

Joss stopped just long enough to check that he wasn't charging into an ambush. When he was more or less certain, he started the arduous path down the chalky surface of the dome, making his descent in a curving pattern and using the grip of his boots to control his sliding. One wrong move, he knew, and the ground would all too quickly fly up to greet him with its cold, hard surface. Eventually he made it to the library's rooftop, and from there he began scaling down the scaffolding and stacks of crates that the impostor had led him up.

His mind was like a broken kaleidoscope with its mess of fragmented thoughts. How had the creature known so much about their lives? Was it true, what he'd said about the fall of Daheed? Probably it had all been a lie, a way of confusing and manipulating him, as well as tarnishing his father's memory. But to what end he couldn't possibly imagine. A direct attack from a known enemy would have been far preferable to this cold-blooded deception.

Coming to the edge of the final landing, Joss leapt to the ground below. His feet hit the oyster-shell paving and his boots slid beneath him. He twisted to keep his skull from cracking on the gutter, dusted off his hands and knees, and pulled himself up to his full height.

And then he ran.

He didn't know where he was going, he didn't have any plan for what he would do to save his friends, to escape the city, to return to sanity. He just ran. And he kept running, through the endless night that engulfed the Gleaming Isle, into the unknown.

CHAPTER TWENTY-EIGHT

—

A FRIENDLY CONVERSATION

RAKE, Hero and Edgar were led into a darkened dockside tenement with brickwork that was as pockmarked as a plague victim, guards flanking them at every turn.

'Reminds me of where my father works,' Drake said, before being jabbed into silence by the butt of a spear.

'Talk again and we'll cut out that curly tongue of yours!' Gnarl warned him, the glow of his eye painting his face red. The prentices remained silent as they were led through the building's entrance hall and up a flight of stairs to the top floor. The expansive room would have once enjoyed sweeping views of the harbour and the ocean beyond it. Now its smashed windows looked out at the cage full of prisoners, and its rotten floorboards creaked underfoot with every step.

'Ah! There you all are.' A molasses-rich voice drifted from the dining table that had been positioned across the room, a mammoth-tusk candelabra serving as its centrepiece. The three prentices were pushed towards their places at the table, and as they rounded the candelabra, with its sputtering light, they got their first proper glimpse of their host.

Admiral Ichor sat with his back to the peeling plaster of the wall behind him, an oversized oyster in one hand and dagger in the other. He didn't need to look at what he was doing as he cracked the shell open with ease and plopped the oyster into his mouth, its juices spilling onto his beard. Instead, he kept his eyes on the three of them as they were each forced to stand beside a chair and wait.

'Please, have a seat. Rest your weary bones,' he said.

'I'd rather stand,' Hero replied, head held high. Drake and Edgar followed suit.

Admiral Ichor took his blade, wiped the salt water from its surface, then slammed the tip into the surface of the table. He stared at Hero with a cold fury as the handle of the knife trembled from the force of his strike. Each of the prentices looked at one another, then slowly and begrudgingly took a seat. Wrenching his knife from the tabletop, the admiral returned to shucking his oysters.

'Mmm! These would have to be the most succulent morsels I've ever tasted. So fat and creamy!' he said through a mouthful. 'I would offer you some but we're in short supply …' He chewed thoughtfully for a moment, cracked open another shell, scooped out the contents. 'Actually, that's a lie. I just don't feel like sharing with interloping scum who invade my city and spoil my plans. A fair sentiment, I'd say. Wouldn't you agree, Gnarl?'

'Yes, Admiral. More than fair.' Gnarl's pupil dilated with a motorised whir as he stood by his leader.

'We saw your masked crony outside. Too busy to join us?' asked Hero.

Admiral Ichor gazed at her curiously. 'Lord Thrall will be along shortly, if his duties permit. And when he arrives, I would refrain from calling him such things if I were you.' The admiral's lips twisted in a sinister grin, his teeth a busted mosaic of brown and grey. 'But we don't require his presence to enjoy a friendly conversation. I'd like to start with an apology for my earlier outburst. I was exasperated, rightly or wrongly, by your undoing of a lot of hard work, which I'm sure you can appreciate. And I'm just as sure that you would also like to apologise to me for the reckless disregard you showed in interrupting when you did.'

Admiral Ichor sat back in his chair and waited, while the prentices gaped at each other. Hero's astonishment quickly bubbled over into anger, though as she drew breath to spit what would certainly be an acidic reply she was stopped by a gentle touch on her hand from across the table.

'If it were any other ceremony we'd interrupted, Admiral, you would certainly have our apologies,' Drake said, his hand sliding from Hero's wrist to rest beside it. 'But you were murdering innocent people. We couldn't just sit back and watch.'

Admiral Ichor grinned. 'An idealist, I see,' he said, then pushed back his chair to circle the table, keys jangling against his hip, knife spinning around in his hand. 'Young, too. Which is good. Idealism is for the young. I remember I was much the same. All I ever dreamed of was a boat of my own, a crew to man it, and a wide blue ocean to sail. And for years I had everything I hoped for. But then the day came that I watched from the deck of my ship as the sky tore open above this very city and ripped all the life from it, like the flesh of an oyster sucked from its shell.

'For the first time I knew just how small I was. How truly insignificant. But more than that, I knew in one divine revelation of the greater force that existed out there, in the dark, beyond our dreams, preparing to subjugate and destroy all those who were foolish enough to try standing against it. So I gave up my name, gave

up my life, and I sought out this holy place – this land first graced by His Majesty, though his touch meant its doom – so that I might dedicate my life to something greater than my own wretched self. Something greater than us all …'

The keys fell silent as the admiral came to a stop behind Drake's chair, forcing Drake to crane his neck to see him. 'There are things I want to know. Things you're going to tell me. We'll start with how you found us here. You'll resist at first, I'm sure, but then you'll find I can be very persuasive. And once you've answered that question, you'll then tell me who your friend was who escaped us, and where we might find him.'

'You sound very confident about that,' Drake said, and Ichor laughed.

'If only because I've seen this little scenario play itself out, oh, *countless* times now. You're not the first band of malcontents I've had to parlay with and, until we've built our glorious new world, you won't be the last. So what do you say, my idealistic young friend? Want to start with telling me how you came to find us here?'

Again, Drake looked at Hero and Edgar. Then he turned back to address their host. 'I'm sorry, Admiral. You may have done this countless times before, as you say. But as you also pointed out, I'm young. And I'm only just getting started.'

The admiral laughed again, deeper and darker this time. 'I thought as much,' he said, and drew his knife up into the air to slam it back down into the table, straight through Drake's hand.

CHAPTER TWENTY-NINE

A GHOSTLY VISION

SWEAT ran down Joss's face, stinging his eyes. His breath was a tortured knot in his chest, worked tighter with every step he took on his aching feet. How long had he been running for? How far had he gone? It felt as if he'd doubled back on himself more than once. Thankfully the dome of the library was nowhere to be seen, giving him some cold comfort that he had at least put a degree of distance between himself and that wretched place.

He thought again of the deception that he'd all too eagerly allowed himself to believe, and for the hundredth time he cursed himself for a fool. Yes, he'd been wary at the start. First of 'Darra' and then of 'Naveer'. Deep down, he had felt the whole situation was too good to be true.

But he'd ignored that doubt. And it had cost him dearly. His mind was poisoned by seeing the transformation of Naveer's face from fatherly concern to leering ghoul. It soured his stomach and made him want to cough up his heart.

Stopping for breath, he tried to shake away the fog of his thoughts. Where was he?

To his left there was what looked to have once been a schoolhouse, its clay bricks crumbling, its doors hanging from their hinges. Many of its windows had been smashed, knocked out like teeth in a brawl. But in the few untouched panes hung a collection of children's paintings. On curled parchment and in swirling water-colours, now faded, they depicted sailboats floating beneath smiling suns, pterosaurs with tundra-blue plumage scooping up fish by the beakful, families gathered together beside palm trees, standing outside their island homes. Joss was struck by the same eerie sense of familiarity that he'd had when standing in the middle of the Imperial Library.

The yard that surrounded the schoolhouse was swamped with weeds. A playground could just be seen among the thistles and wild grass. The tilting sailboat, the whirling mermaid, the bouncing plesiosaur – they had all been choked to a standstill, paint flaking from their hides, eyes faded, spring-mounted joints rendered solid.

Turning to his right, Joss saw an olive tree at the corner of the street. It was little more than a withered husk now, its dead branches pointing down the adjoining avenue like a bony hand. Heeding its advice, Joss turned in that direction.

He walked down the new street with purpose, keeping a watchful gaze as he went. The feeling he'd had of walking through a dream was shifting now to something else. It wasn't a dream that he'd stumbled into. It was a memory. A memory of this very street, peopled with friendly faces, its sights and sounds filling his head in dazzling bursts.

There was the hut where a kindly old woman had lived, who used to give him candied figs as a treat. What was she called? Bara Jin? Baba Jeer? The name played at the edges of his mind like someone plucking at a tapestry's loose thread. That sensation only grew stronger as he passed the next house, which had belonged to a large family.

Grandparents, great-grandparents, nearly a dozen kids and their ever-harried parents had all lived under its roof, but they had all seemed contented despite the bedlam. He remembered the games of Capture the Kronosaur and Starfish or Swordfish he had played with the kids on lazy afternoons, pushing past sunset and the increasingly irate calls to dinner.

He remembered one boy in particular, his best friend in the world, and the day they declared themselves sworn brothers by sharing so many goblets of salt water that they were retching the rest of the night away. The memory brought a faint smile to Joss's face, even as the boy's name eluded him. Though it was only a small smile, a fragile smile, it was hard won. And it was just as easily lost as he came to the next house on the street.

It was the yellow door that he saw first. While the courtyard had grown as untamed as the school's playground, the paint on the door was unscathed. It was as bright and glossy as he remembered, even though it had been left hanging open. Uneven brickwork led out from the front step, winding through the dry grass up to the gate where Joss stood, his hand resting hesitantly on the latch. With much uncertainty, he pulled open the iron gate and stepped onto the overgrown path.

As he came to the front door, he was surprised to see the fig tree that he'd reminisced about with Naveer's impostor. Again he wondered how the creature could have known so many details about their lives. But despite how much that troubled him, he nevertheless marvelled at the small miracle of the tree and the fruit that it somehow still bore.

Reaching for one of the ripened bulbs, his arm brushed an overhanging branch. Wind chimes clinked musically above him. The sound was enough to send him tumbling back into memory, but rather than losing himself all over again he forged ahead into the hallway, pocketing the fig as he went.

Centipedes and silverfish scattered at his approach, with even the boldest insects shying away as he removed Qorza's Scryer from his pocket. The receiver signal was a flat line but that wouldn't affect the illuminator function. Triggering it, Joss cast some light in the darkness. He could almost hear his younger self giggling as the projection of his naming day shimmered before him while he explored the cottage. Outside, the wind chimes continued to ring and tinkle, scoring his journey as he went from the hallway into the parlour.

As it had been in his mother's study, it looked as if someone had only just stepped out of the room and was expected back at any moment. Firewood was still stacked beside the small hearth. A quilted blanket had been left strewn across the upholstered settee, its squares depicting clear skies, full fishing nets and endless oceans. Dark brown leviathan oil still filled each of the lamps that were in every corner and on every tabletop, waiting to shed light on the pages of all the books that had been piled up around the room. Joss was about to stop and scan some of the titles when the Scryer cycled over again.

'Ancestors save me ...' he said without thinking, staring up at the recording of his parents' wedding day as it was cast against the whitewashed ceiling, the timber beams bifurcating both his mother and his father. He watched as they again looped their matching necklaces over each other's heads, and squeezed the Scryer so hard that the casing threatened to crack, cutting off the illumigram and plunging the entire room into darkness.

The sounds around him grew louder. First the Scryer's little whirring motor, then the chittering of the insects, and then the beating of his own heart, which resonated in his ears like the footsteps of a thunder lizard. Only when his heartbeat had slowed did he open his hand again, letting the light out. The image of himself as a baby had returned, and it was with that joyful face floating before him that he continued exploring.

He passed the washroom, with its dusty copper tub and mould-spotted washbasin, and came to a room that was fairly humming with significance. His childhood bedroom. A short iron-frame bed, with a pterosaur mobile hanging above it, a matching chair and table, a toy box, and a soft cotton rug on the timber floor. Unsteady on his feet, Joss lurched into the room and sat down on the feather-stuffed mattress.

The Scryer was still buzzing in his hand. Holding out his palm, he watched the illumigrams dance around him as if he were stargazing, while with his other hand he plucked the fig from his pocket and pressed it between his lips. The taste was so bitter he wanted to spit it out, but he forced himself to swallow.

On the wall opposite him, his parents smiled and laughed, while somewhere out there in the unnatural night his friends were in a cage. And all he could do was sit here, on the edge of his childhood bed, and grieve for everything that he'd lost, and everything he was yet to lose.

CHAPTER THIRTY

An Executioner
Dressed for Duty

DRAKE screamed and thrashed, but the knife in his hand held him fast. Admiral Ichor stood unmoved by the cries of pain, while Gnarl grinned with wicked delight.

'Come now, boy. Surely you've experienced worse in your life,' the admiral said. 'I didn't so much as graze a bone! I'm more precise than an ethereon with my instruments.'

'Let him go!' Hero demanded, jumping up from the table.

'Nobody said you could move,' Ichor replied, while Gnarl gestured for the guards to hold her back with their swords and spears.

'*Let! Him! Go!*' she said again as she lurched against the blades that barred her way.

Admiral Ichor looked blankly at her as he leant across the table, took a jug of seashine, and ripped the cork out with his teeth. Spitting the cork onto the floor, he took a swig before speaking. 'Well ... the last thing I would ever want to be is a bad host. If you wish this delicate butterfly unpinned so badly, young lady – so be it!'

Grabbing the handle of the dagger, Admiral Ichor yanked it loose. Drake tumbled back in his chair, gripping his hand as tenderly as he could while trying to stem the bleeding. Hero again surged against the guards keeping her in place. A single gesture from Ichor was enough to have them stand down, and she was immediately at Drake's side to help him with his injury.

'Let this be a warning. Start answering questions or start counting your scars.' The admiral turned to Edgar. 'What about you, boy? Anything to say that might prick up my ears?'

Edgar looked at Ichor, looked at Drake and his bloody hand. 'His name is Josiah!' the young prentice blurted.

'Josiah?' Admiral Ichor said. He looked taken aback, and shared a curious look with his man Gnarl, though he was soon chomping on another toothy grin. 'Well, I'll be a sonovasiren! How do you like that? I'm not the only Josiah sailing the Silver Seas, as it transpires. Whaddya say, Gnarl?'

'My interest is mightily piqued, Admiral.'

Ichor chortled, before turning his attention back to Edgar. 'Go on, lad. Tell me more.'

Drake and Hero were staring at Edgar in shock, both of them taken aback by his readiness to talk. Ignoring their silent admonishments not to say anything else, Edgar continued: 'Well, he may go by Josiah … but he's better known as "the Rex".'

'*The Rex?*' Ichor said, lifting a shaggy eyebrow, while Drake and Hero's expressions shifted to confusion.

'That's right,' Edgar replied. He looked at the admiral with defiance as he explained. 'They call him that because he's the King of Thunder Realm. He took down a tyrannosaur single-handedly with no weapon but a single bola and his wits. I saw him do it with my own eyes, tracking the beast through a rocky maze so that he could corner it and overpower it. He's the greatest hunter that Thunder Realm has ever seen, and if he's here it's because he tracked you down and is now just biding his time until the exact right moment to strike. If I were you, Admiral, I wouldn't bother trying to find him. I would take my men and I'd run as far from here as I could get. And don't say I didn't warn you.'

Ichor stared at the pale young prentice. He stared at Gnarl. The slightest hint of doubt clouded his face. And then he unhinged his jaw to expel the most raucous laugh that any of the prentices had ever heard.

'The Rex! Oh, you almost had me there!' The admiral sighed when he'd regained himself, wiping tears from the deep wrinkles around his eyes.

'Laugh all you like. We'll see how funny you find it when the Rex has you cornered and at his mercy,' Edgar told him.

All the colour drained from the admiral's face. 'Now don't test me, son. You may have tickled me with that fanciful little story of yours, but I find threats a lot less amusing. Unless I'm the one making them, of course. Then they're the damned height of entertainment. Speaking of which ...' Admiral Ichor fixed his gaze on Hero. 'What about you, lass? Got anything to say about this "Josiah", or "Rex", or whatever fool name you call him? Or need I make a threat, and then make good on it soon after?'

'Tend to his wound first,' Hero insisted, holding Drake's hand between hers.

Ichor only rumbled with impatience. 'Very well. We'll start with sterilising it, shall we?' he said, taking the jug of seashine and pouring it over Drake's hand. The clear liquid practically hissed as it hit his flesh, making him cry out in pain all over again. 'There. Sterilised. Now, let's discuss the whereabouts of Josiah the Rex, shall we? Or maybe I'll just let my knife slip again.'

'Why trouble yourself, Admiral? Surely it's obvious

that they'll resist you to the last,' a voice echoed from the corner of the room, where a dark figure now floated from the shadows. He regarded them from behind his stone mask, his black feather cloak shivering as if alive.

'Lord Thrall,' Admiral Ichor said, and bowed his head in respect. 'I was merely questioning the prisoners so that we might better locate the fugitive.'

'You were making sport of it, Ichor. You know as well as I that we have far more effective means of hunting down the intruder, as well as more pressing matters to address. The preliminary rituals are almost done. The time of sacrifice grows near.'

'Apologies, my lord,' the admiral said, bowing low.

But Thrall's attention was quickly stolen by the scoffing noise that came from Hero. 'Just our luck to run into you again,' she sneered at him. 'It might have been impressive that you'd found someone to order around if he wasn't such scum-sucking guttertrash.'

The masked man regarded her coldly, with a gathering tension in his fists. She glowered in response, staring him down.

'Enough of this foolish nonsense,' Thrall snapped, turning away from her. 'If this Josiah is too cowardly to return for his allies, then we'll just take matters into our own hands. Ichor? Release the beasts. They'll find our quarry for us.'

A small cough came from the corner of the room as Gnarl cleared his throat. 'Lord Thrall, if I may …' His mechanoid eye glowed bright as it widened as far as it could. 'Do we really need to concern ourselves with this boy? Surely it would be best to focus our efforts on the ceremony.'

Thrall turned his predatory gaze on him. 'You're questioning my orders,' he said as he crossed the room, his robes cutting the air like a razor.

'Orders, my lord?' Gnarl replied, eye twitching. 'It was my understanding that we all kneel as one before the majesty of the Shadow God.'

Thrall loomed before the trembling pyrate, an executioner dressed for duty. Drake, Hero and Edgar looked at each other uncertainly. Even Ichor appeared tense, as concerned by what was about to happen as his captives were.

But then Thrall softened. 'You're right, of course,' he said, his benevolent tone allowing Gnarl a moment of respite.

Just one small moment.

'But some of us kneel lower than others.'

Thrall clamped his fist around Gnarl's face. The pyrate screamed, but the sound was muffled by the taloned glove pressed against his mouth. His flesh reddened, his screams growing more pained and panicked as the glove erupted with arcane energy. It steamed and spat and sputtered, frying Gnarl to a blackened crisp.

Edgar shrank from the gruesome sight as Drake and Hero watched on, transfixed. By the time Thrall was done, there was nothing left of Gnarl but his mechanoid eye, rendered blind atop a pile of ashes.

Clenching his fist and cracking his knuckles, Thrall didn't even turn as he addressed the admiral. 'Ichor?'

The pyrate leader, his gaze fixed on the ashes, struggled to find his voice. Luckily for him, it didn't take too long. 'Yes, my lord?'

'I trust there's no need to repeat myself.'

'No, my lord,' the admiral replied, shaking off his daze. 'We'll release the beasts immediately. The boy will be in our custody even sooner than that.'

'See that it's so, Admiral,' Thrall said, walking from the room. 'Or it will be your ashes I'm dusting from my hands next.'

—

CHAPTER THIRTY-ONE

A Thunderbolt Out of a Clear Blue Sky

A GREAT black wave rose into the sky, hiding the sun. Joss stared up at it, his feet sliding uneasily on the gilded roof of the Tower Memoria, his grip on the peak slipping. He could see faces in the water, all sharp teeth and dark intentions. He felt the first wet drops fall on his head. And then he woke up.

He was lying in his childhood bed, soaked in sweat, the pterosaur mobile hanging motionless above him and the purple rays of Naveer's protective dome streaming in through the window like moonlight. His mother's journal was propped on his chest, still open on the so-called *Rakashi Revelations*. The warnings and predictions they made whirled about inside his head.

Perhaps if Naveer had been who he'd said he was, Joss could have asked him about his mother's work, could have gained some insight into these seemingly ancient prophecies and their connection to the modern world. But with 'Naveer' revealed as an impostor, it was as if Joss had lost his parents all over again. The thought struck him with the force of a cannonball, knocking the breath from his lungs as the wisp scar flared again. It burned his skin beneath the pages of his mother's book, and though he rubbed at it to alleviate the discomfort, it continued to ache.

A noise sounded in the distance. Still kneading his chest, Joss dismissed it at first as being the wind – until the stationary wooden pterosaurs overhead reminded him that there was no wind down here at the bottom of the ocean. He climbed off the bed and unsheathed the Champion's Blade. If Naveer's monstrous double was looking to cause more strife, Joss would be all too happy to accommodate it.

In the hallway he heard the same noise again, clearer this time. It sounded like it was coming from outside, possibly down the street. He walked out into the courtyard to listen. Again the noise sounded, and to Joss's ears it was disturbingly familiar. If he were to guess at it, he would have said it was the snarling and sniping of a raptor on the hunt. But surely that wasn't possible here, so far from Thunder Realm – was it?

Despite how foolish he felt in doing it, he sheathed

the Champion's Blade and drew his humming knife. The knife felt minuscule by comparison, but he knew it would offer him more protection if the alarm he was feeling turned out to be warranted.

Then, from the darkness of the street, there emerged the largest and wildest raptor that Joss had ever seen, with scarlet feathers that flickered like flames. It had probing little eyes that were alight with an uncanny intellect, its nostrils flaring as it searched out its prey. And it wasn't alone. Two more creatures of almost equal size followed it.

Though they were predatory animals by nature, these three looked to have had those instincts honed by a master's hand. There would be no escape once they'd found their victim. Not when they were so close. Joss gripped his humming knife tight and readied himself for what was to come.

As one they saw him. The alpha's lip curled, baring a mouthful of thorny fangs as it snarled at him. Joss had grown so used to raptors that it surprised him how frightening they could sound. But they weren't the only ones who could make an intimidating noise. Shifting his feet into position, he assumed the first stance of a pacifying song, and began.

The humming knife carved the air around him as he flowed from one position to the next, the small spriggan runes on its blade twinkling like stars at twilight. The metal quivered in his grip, scattering vibrations up his forearm, while a melancholy tune resonated throughout the empty street. The raptors' heads bobbed and swayed in time with the music, though it wasn't enough to keep them still. While they hadn't attacked him, they were still drawing closer, one purposeful step at a time. He ignored the chuffing noises they made, the rattle of their tongues against their teeth, and focused solely on the song his knife was singing.

Still the raptors advanced, slow but steady, and their movement was enough to splinter his concentration. Sur Verity wouldn't struggle like this, Joss knew. She would have these lizards completely under her spell and running in formation by now, each of them eager to do her bidding.

The alpha was so close to Joss that he could feel its moist breath on his skin. It looked as if it was struggling against an invisible chain, desperate to get at Joss, to tear his flesh apart and lap up all the mess left behind. The only thing keeping it from tackling him to the ground and ripping open his throat was the song Joss was singing with his humming knife, though how long that would last for he couldn't say. Already his muscles were growing weary, the repetitive act of slashing the air with his blade exhausting him. He wondered if he could keep the song going as he backed away. How far would the raptors follow him, struggling against the tune that was meant to lull them into submission? Could he outrun them? Trap them? His mind searched desperately for a solution.

It came up empty.

Then, like a thunderbolt out of a clear blue sky, an arrow zipped past Joss's shoulder to strike the alpha raptor in the neck. The beast let out a shriek that was cut short as it tumbled to the ground. The other two raptors looked around in confusion, unsure of what exactly had happened to their leader, before both were similarly felled. With all three thunder lizards subdued, Joss drew his song to an end.

'Quite the performance,' a familiar and unwelcome voice said, and Joss turned to see Naveer standing behind him with his crossbow resting on his shoulder. 'I'm impressed.'

'I'm not,' Joss replied, drawing the Champion's Blade so that he stood with dual weapons in hand. The impostor blinked in surprise but said nothing. 'You didn't have to kill them. But then what should I expect of such a cold-blooded monster?'

'The arrows are tipped with a natural sedative. They'll be sore and groggy when they awaken but they'll wake all the same.' The impostor dropped the crossbow so that the stirrup was resting on the ground beside his boot. 'Joss, please. Let me explain.'

'No! You don't get to call me that. Do you understand? You're not my father. You're just a changeling!'

The impostor's face fell, and Joss knew he was right.

'I worked it out, didn't I? That's what you are. A changeling!' The snippets of information that Qorza had shared. The skiff at Crescent Cove, sent out as burning tribute to the wraiths and to the spirits and to the changelings that *steal the faces of our fellow men*. It all added up to one inarguable truth, and he was repulsed at the notion. 'A mindless creature that drains mortal emotions like a leech sucks blood. What could I possibly have to say to a leech? What could ever justify the way you deceived me?'

Though the face that stared back at him was only an imitation of his father's, it was a perfect one. Not just in its likeness but also in its profound sorrow. The anguish the changeling showed was enough to make Joss doubt for a moment, to be sorry for saying what he had, but he had no time to think this through.

A shout rang out. 'Halt! The both of you!'

Joss and the changeling looked over to the corner of the street. Two pyrates were stalking towards them, weapons drawn and ready, their faces shadowed with ill intent.

—

CHAPTER THIRTY-TWO

A DISTANT SHORE OF A PROMISED LAND

'NO need for hostility, gentlemen. We'll come quietly,' the changeling said, dropping his crossbow and raising his hands behind his head as the pyrates advanced on them. Joss could only gape at the ready act of submission, betraying the creature for what he truly was. Whatever flicker of compassion Joss may have been feeling for him was swiftly and thoroughly snuffed.

'What'd you do to my poor beasties? Eh?' one of the pyrates demanded. He was wearing steel arm bracers and a leather chestplate, the claw marks that scarred his face revealing him as the raptors' trainer.

'Everyone's showing so much concern for such cold-blooded creatures,' the changeling said with a bittersweet smile as he looked at Joss. 'I hope I can expect the same consideration.'

'You'll be lucky not to find your teeth busted at the heel of my boot, friend,' said the second pyrate. 'Now get on your knees. The both of ya.'

'One slight problem with that, I'm afraid.'

'Oh? And what problem might that be?' the scarred pyrate asked. The two of them were now closer than the raptors had been, their stink so potent it wafted around them like a cloud.

'Well ... *nothing*, to be perfectly honest,' said the changeling, his frank reply making both the pyrates pause. 'I was just stalling until you were near enough for me to do *this*.'

Whipping his hands out from behind his head, the changeling hurled a pair of throwing knives hidden within each of his sleeves. Both blades hit the pyrates in the throat, dropping them beside their stricken animals. Joss, staggered by the speed with which everything had just happened, felt his legs shake beneath him. The changeling showed no such uncertainty as he treaded over the fallen pyrates to stare at the little yellow-doored cottage.

'I haven't been back here in years,' he said so quietly that Joss strained to hear him.

'You ... you remember this place?' asked Joss, still unsure of the limits of the creature's understanding.

The changeling pointed past the gate, past the fig tree. 'I remember painting that front door. Your mother was busy gardening, planting the tree that our neighbour, Baba Yin, had given her as a birthday gift. I remember coffee brewing and fish stew cooking on the stovetop, listening to the rain pelt against the warped glass of the kitchen window. I remember telling you your nightly bedtime story, and how you'd always find some way of introducing a tyrannosaur into the plot.

'I remember back to a day long before that, when you were born in the parlour, your little face red and squalling as you emerged into the world. We cleaned you up and wrapped you in a blanket, and when I held you in my arms you looked up at me with such questing curiosity. I remember how you took my finger in your whole hand, smaller than a ripening fig, and you squeezed it like you never wanted to let go.' The changeling stopped, his voice cracking with sorrow, and drew a ragged breath.

'But I remember more than that,' he went on when he'd finally regained himself. 'I remember the day I lost everything, and every torturous day that followed. I remember being wounded in a skirmish with Ichor's men and retreating to the library, to your mother's study, where I thought I remembered lying low to recuperate. And then the next thing I remember is seeing you in danger and knowing that I had to help you. And the reason for that is simple. The reason my memory goes black is that it was in the library that Naveer Sarif died.'

Joss flinched despite himself. The changeling noticed.

'Whatever I may be, I had no hand in that. I promise you,' he said, holding a clenched fist against his heart. 'Just as you can't remember the day you were born, I promise you that I can't remember claiming his identity. Until that moment in your mother's study just now, I had no more clue of my true nature than you did.'

'But how is that possible?' Joss asked, his earlier certainty fading. 'How can you remember so much, and feel so deeply?'

'I was –' The changeling stopped. Reconsidered. '*Your father* was an ethereon. And given the circumstances I don't think it's arrogant to say that he was a gifted one ...'

'So he summoned you?' Joss guessed. 'So that he could live on somehow?'

The changeling shook his head. 'Not at all. He wasn't the kind of man who would try to cheat death like that, with some black magic trick. But he did know things, such as all the beasts and bogies that could threaten a ship and its crew, including the creatures that nest in places of death and despair, waiting for unsuspecting mortals so that they may take the form of a departed loved one.'

Joss thought again of Vaal, the Ghost City, and of the spectres he'd encountered there. As much as the experience had haunted him before, it took on a whole new meaning now.

The changeling continued: 'If your father were here, he could quote you whole chapters of the books he'd read on the subject. He could tell you all the names by which they're known throughout the world, such as in Mraba, where they're known as shadowkin, or how the Norvish of old named them doppelgangers.

'We simply call them changelings, and we know them as deceitful creatures that feed on the psychic energy of mortals. They use arcane abilities to draw on spiritual echoes of the dead and to invade the minds of the living, presenting themselves in a form that's familiar to their prey. They plunder memories, torment souls, feast on the turmoil. And when they're done, they move on to their next victim. Their next meal.'

The changeling fell silent, still looking at the cottage.

'I may not be your real father, Joss. I may not even be a man,' he said. 'But I am no monster. I did not search you out or prey upon you. Whatever I was before you set foot in this city, I have no sense of that now. And while I can't promise you much, I can at least swear to that.'

As he looked away from the cottage, Joss almost gasped at the expression the changeling wore. He'd only ever seen it before in flashes stolen from a mirror, in unguarded and unobserved moments. He knew that pain. He'd carried it with him all his life.

'My friends are in danger,' Joss said hesitantly, as the maroon eyes before him glistened. 'I could use some help in saving them.'

———

Edgar was the first to be flung back into the cage with the other hostages, then Hero after him. Drake was the last, his injured hand crudely bandaged with rags already soaked through with blood. He landed with a painful crash into the bucket that had been left in the corner, its contents slopping over the rim.

Gnash, the blade-legged guard, sniggered at his misfortune.

'Let me help you up,' Edgar said, slipping beneath Drake's arm to take his weight. Hero was quickly beside them, ducking under the other arm to help Edgar pull Drake up onto his feet.

'Don't be fretting over him too much now,' Gnash chided them as he slammed the cage shut. 'Admiral's fixing to feed him to the void first, from what I hear.'

'Then I'll have lived longer than your brother, at least,' Drake shot back through clenched teeth.

Gnash stared through the bars, his gusto gone. 'Something happened to Gnarl?' he asked.

'Thrall killed him,' Hero said, refusing to mince her words. 'Just so you know the breed of monster you serve.'

Gnash's head dropped as he considered the news. 'My brother – dead?' he said, before raising his face again in a wide, toothless grin. 'Bless the Shadow God and all his hallowed court! I never could stand that smug, insufferable prig!'

The pyrate laughed heartily to himself as he bolted the cell shut and hobbled away, leaving the prentices to struggle in what little light filtered through the bars. The other hostages cleared a path, allowing Lilia to push forward and inspect Drake's hand as Hero and Edgar gently deposited him on a pile of rags in the corner of the cage.

'Such barbarism,' the physician sadly noted as she examined Drake's injury. 'Though thankfully a clean wound.'

'Thank you,' Drake said to her as she went about patching him up, while Hero ran a gentle hand over his cheek, her concern radiating through her dark goggles.

'We need to get out of here,' she announced, looking at Edgar. 'Now.'

'If you have a plan, I have more ears than a herd of blind mammoths.'

Hero arched an eyebrow at his choice of words, the quickly shrugged them off. 'Simple,' she said. 'We steal a set of keys and bust out when the guards aren't looking.'

'I see one small problem with that idea,' Edgar replied, though whatever he was about to say next was quickly cut short as Hero reached into her sleeve and produced the keys that had adorned Admiral Ichor's belt.

'Really? Because I don't.'

—

A SNOWFLAKE FALLING INTO A FIRE PIT

J OSS and the changeling swept silently through the
streets of Daheed, moving with speed. While the
changeling ran ahead with crossbow loaded, Joss had
sheathed both his weapons, though he kept a wary hand
on the hilt of his humming knife – partly due to the
chance of encountering more raptors, partly because of
the crossbow.

Earlier, when he had traversed these streets on his
own, they were a confounding maze in which he'd lost
countless hours. But with the changeling's guidance they
unfurled before him like a scroll with a broken seal. He
could already see the library dome, which sat off to the
east, while they continued on towards the south.

'Don't we need to stop at the library first and collect

all the liquid fire pots?' Joss asked, keeping his voice low as he drew closer to the changeling.

'I took the initiative before coming to find you, and transported everything we would need to Ichor's campsite,' replied the creature. 'I had a lot to contemplate after you left. It was good to keep busy.'

'You carried all one thousand pots by yourself?'

'Hardly,' the changeling said. 'I worked out I only needed to plant a dozen or so in key areas. The spreading fire should set off the rest of the stockpile, with hopefully enough time for everyone to get to the submersibles.'

Joss noticed that the changeling avoided saying anything about 'us' or 'we', but decided not to question it.

'I've been meaning to mention,' the changeling went on. 'What you did back there was very impressive. With the knife and the raptors. I'd heard tell of paladero ways and of course seen illumigram recordings, but it's quite a different thing in person. Who taught you how to do all that?'

'Sur Verity Wolfsbane of Round Shield Ranch, the paladero to whom I'm prenticed,' Joss answered, keeping his answer as formal as he could. Though he wouldn't be impolite for as long as they were allied, that didn't mean he had to be warm and friendly.

'I'd always – your father, I mean – he'd always hoped you might some day show interest in spellcraft. That you might learn to be an ethereon yourself. In seeing you weave that magic on those raptors, it feels you weren't too far off.'

'I hardly wove any magic. They still kept coming for me. I may have only had a humming knife instead of a proper song sword, but Sur Verity could have used a twig and still brought them under her control.'

'You're young,' the changeling said, with a return of that same knowing smile. 'You'll learn.'

Joss could feel his face betraying him, a similar smile tugging at his lips. He frowned it away, along with the peculiar sense of pride that came with the changeling's comment. They continued on, the library receding into the distance, while the hot bonfire glow that emanated from the Thousand Sacred Stairs grew brighter.

'We're getting close,' the changeling said, even more hushed than before. 'We should approach from the rooftops. That way we'll have a better vantage point and less chance of being spotted.'

The changeling led the way again, up the side of a ramshackle hut and, from there, upward again to the city's skyline. Hopping from one roof to another, they quickly came upon the encampment. It looked just as crowded as before, though now all the pyrates were lined up to chant and sway in unison, their dark hymns gaining strength and resonance.

'We need to plan our move,' the changeling said, handing Joss a brass cylinder with a red orb embedded in its barrel.

'What's this?' he asked.

'A shadowscope. Normally a useful etherical tool for spotting spirits on the high seas at night. Now even more useful for spotting Ichor's cronies. Look and see.'

Joss turned the device over, extended it to its full length and pressed it to his eye. The camp was lit up before him in bright red tones, allowing him to see everyone up close, in perfect detail, despite the gloom.

The majority of the camp was on its knees, bowing as low as possible while reciting the same guttural, indecipherable words that Joss remembered the Stitched Witch using as part of her attempted blood ritual. He shuddered at the memory, as well as at the thought of what a whole legion of dark disciples could accomplish if left unchecked. He then caught sight of Thrall, who had once again assumed the stage on the First Step to deliver the same sermon he'd been giving back when Joss and the others had first arrived.

'I've already deposited six explosives on the outer edges of the camp,' the changeling explained, pulling out a sack of carefully wrapped balls of cloth. 'But that won't be enough. I'll need to infiltrate the camp and hide more of these pots around the Thousand Sacred Stairs to create a wall of fire between Ichor's men and the hostages in the cage. If we can trap the pyrates behind the fire lines then we stand a chance of getting everyone to the submersibles before the flames spread too far and set off the cache back at the library. I'll need you up here keeping a watch over everything and covering me with the crossbow. When I'm done, we can ignite the pots using the incendiary arrowheads I brought. Can you handle that?'

Joss lowered the shadowscope and looked at the changeling. 'No,' he said.

The creature wearing his father's face blinked. 'Well, it's quite simple,' the changeling replied, pointing at the bow. 'You load the bolts here, using the stirrup for leverage –'

'No. I'll do it. I'll go down and plant the explosives.'

'Joss, I don't think that's wise. There's a whole army of ruthless cutthroats down there, not one of whom would hesitate in running through his own father.'

Joss furrowed his brow and the changeling winced.

'Poor choice of words,' he said. 'But the fact remains that if you're caught down there you'll be lucky if you're killed on the spot. If you're unlucky, they'll make you suffer first. There's no way I'm letting you take that chance.'

'I'm not going to sit up here out of harm's way while my friends wait in a cage to be executed,' Joss replied.

'Joss, please try to understand –'

'No, *you* understand. You're not my father. There's no way you'll *let* me take that chance? There's no way I'm trusting you not to throw that chance away!'

Again, the changeling's face was bruised with a look of deep hurt. Joss refused to let it rattle him. Not when Edgar's, Drake's and Hero's lives were hanging in the balance. Of course, the changeling wasn't willing to concede the fight just yet. He was still holding the bag of explosives with a firm grip. They stood staring at each other, a tense standoff only interrupted by a scream of fury that rang out from the campsite below.

'What was that?' the changeling exclaimed while Joss spun around to use the shadowscope again.

It was Ichor, his face a mottled shade of red as he charged from one of the derelict buildings across the plaza towards the cage. He was accompanied by a pair of guards who ran ahead of him to clear a path. Joss watched, his blood running cold, as the guards threw open the cage door and Ichor marched straight in to confront his Bladebound brethren.

———

'Who did it?' Ichor demanded, grabbing Edgar by the scruff of the neck and yanking him to his feet. 'Was it you, boy? Was it you who stole from me?'

'What – what do you mean?' Edgar gasped in pain.

'My keys!' the admiral said. The words slipped from between his ruined teeth like a snake through a hole in a fence. 'Were you the nimble-fingered muckrunner who made off with my keys? This whole island is my prison, you artless little beggar! You can no sooner escape here than you can grow gills and swim to Mraba! But then who am I to deny the existence of miracles? Mayhap we should load you onto a submersible and kick you out the hatch, see how fast you can swim. What do ye say, boy? Feeling fishy?'

Edgar grunted, unable to speak as his face burned red and spittle flecked his chin.

'Leave him alone!' Hero shouted, and Ichor looked at her with the same wildness as a thunder lizard readying to charge. Reaching behind her back, she produced the keychain, the keys ringing in her grasp. Drake sagged at the defeat, while Edgar watched in horror. Neither of the guards needed any order to step forward. One of them struck Hero in the gut with a cudgel, doubling her over in pain, while the other snatched the keys from her.

'I should have known it'd be you, y'mouthy trollop,' Ichor said, his leather glove creaking as he squeezed Edgar's neck even tighter. 'I think a lesson is in order.'

'You can't! They're only children!' Lilia pushed forward,

her protests quickly silenced by another swift strike from Ichor's guards.

'I can and will. Starting with this little runt,' the admiral said, jerking his arm so that Edgar twisted painfully in his clutches. 'But don't worry, son. Your friends can come along too. Take them.'

The guards grabbed Drake and Hero, while the admiral kept firm hold of Edgar. Together they dragged the prentices down along the Thousand Sacred Stairs and through the chanting crowd, towards Thrall, who was coming to the grand finale of his sermon.

'We give this sacrifice willingly, that we might please our master and hasten his arrival into this world!' the masked man cried out, his voice resounding across the masses gathered before him. 'Darkness take us!'

'*Darkness take us all!*' the crowd responded, with many of them breaking out into cheers as they spotted the three young faces being pulled towards the vortex. Ichor went first, hauling Edgar behind him like a panicked hatchling trying to avoid the branding iron.

'No, please! Stop!' Edgar kicked and thrashed, but there was no escaping Ichor's iron grip.

'Calm yourself, boy. It will all be over soon. And then you'll be one with the darkness.' The admiral grabbed Edgar by the throat and pushed him out onto the very edge of the step. The tip of Edgar's boot scraped a pebble, which was sent bouncing over into the swirling vortex below. It disintegrated like a snowflake falling into a fire pit, leaving no trace of having ever existed.

Ichor offered one last toothy grin. 'As you go, so goes the world.'

And then he let go.

—

CHAPTER THIRTY-FOUR

A Slight Change of Plan

JOSS could only watch in horror as Ichor herded his brethren from their cage and down towards the First Step.

'He's going to throw them all into the vortex!' Joss gasped and looked up at the changeling, whose face was creased in what looked to be resignation. 'We have to help them!'

'There's no time, Joss. We're too far away,' the changeling said.

'I'll show you too far away,' Joss said. Grabbing the crossbow from the changeling's hands, he immediately set to loading one of the incendiary bolts. He had only just pulled the string taut when he heard a shriek from below.

'*No!*' He spun around to see Edgar being thrown from the step.

'Darkness take us!' Ichor roared in triumph.

Like good little minions, the crowd all shouted in turn. '*Darkness take us all!*'

But all Joss could hear was a high-pitched screech in his head. Edgar was gone. And if he didn't act quickly then Drake and Hero would soon share his fate. He marched to the edge of the rooftop.

'Joss, don't –' the changeling said, but Joss shrugged him off. Standing with one foot on the parapet he raised the crossbow, drew in a lungful of air, and bellowed as loud as he could.

'*Josiah Eichmore!*'

The entire camp looked up. The pyrates, the hostages, the admiral, Thrall. Drake and Hero both stared at him in shock, though the guards that flanked them on either side kept them held firmly in place.

'*If the darkness won't take you, maybe this will!*' Joss shouted, and sent the crossbow bolt flying. It shot across the plaza with astounding speed, the pointed head bursting into flame only moments before impact. It struck Ichor in the shoulder, throwing him back as it set his coat ablaze. The pyrates gasped. The admiral screamed. Guards rushed to his side, tearing the coat from Ichor's back to stamp out the flames. By the time they'd wrested the burning clothes off him and pulled the bloodied bolt from his flesh, he was staring up at Joss with wild-eyed fury.

'*Kill him!*' he screamed, his words almost unintelligible. 'Kill him *now!*'

The pyrates all pulled out their weapons as they charged for the building on which Joss and the changeling were standing. With their rusty green armour and grotesque helmets, they looked like a rampaging horde of monsters from the deep.

'So. A slight alteration in the plan then,' noted the changeling.

'Only slight,' Joss replied, tossing him the crossbow. 'I'll go for the hostages. You clear me a path.'

'And how do you suggest I do that?' the changeling asked. Already the pyrates were clamouring at the base of the building, the first wave of attackers using the handholds of the rough brickwork to scale their way upward.

'You set up those explosives, didn't you?' Joss said as he inspected an old copper line that ran up from the street, the kind that delivered illumigram signals before receiver dishes had replaced them. He tested its strength and found that it held just as firm under his weight as the guy-wire had back in Crescent Cove.

'True,' the changeling replied, and quickly loaded

another bolt into the crossbow. He paused, staring in disbelief as Joss stepped up onto the ledge of the building. 'What are you doing?'

Unbuckling his sword-belt, Joss threw it over the copper line and gripped it on either side.

'Something stupid,' he said, and launched himself off the building, just as the changeling let loose his arrow. The bolt struck a stack of barrels on the edge of the encampment and exploded, casting fireballs into the crowd. Joss zipped through the flames, hair lashing his face, the street rushing beneath his feet, the pyrate horde preparing its attack.

———

Chaos whirled around Drake and Hero like a tempest. Ichor had been dragged to shelter by his guards and was now shrieking from beneath a tarpaulin as his personal physician tended to his wounds. While the rest of the admiral's regiment had rushed off to either join the fray or to put out fires, Thrall had simply vanished. That left a lone pyrate to watch over Hero and Drake, his seashell chain mail hanging from his scrawny frame like a sheet on a clothesline. It clinked every time he jumped at an explosion.

Drawing close to Hero, Drake whispered in her ear: 'Follow my lead.'

'What are you –' she began, stopping short as Drake fell to the ground with a cry of anguish, clutching his hand.

Startled, the pyrate guard took a tentative step forward. 'What's happening?' he asked.

'His wound – it must be infected!' Hero said as she rushed to Drake's side. 'Quick, help me get him to the physician's tent.'

'I don't think –' the pyrate replied uncertainly.

'He'll die if you don't help me right now! You want to explain that to your admiral?'

Looking all around for help and seeing that none was coming, the pyrate lurched forward. He knelt down beside Drake and was just about to inspect the wound when the two prentices jumped up to overpower him. Spinning his helmet around to obscure his vision, Hero pinned his arms to his sides while Drake wrestled the cudgel from the pyrate's grip. Three quick smacks and the scrawny pyrate slumped unconscious with a groan.

'Good job,' Hero said, untangling herself and straightening her jacket. Looking up, she caught sight of a stack of supplies that had been left piled up along the First Step. 'My bandolier!'

She wasted no time in retrieving her property, leaving Drake to stare distantly at the black vortex.

'Poor Edgar,' he muttered.

'Poor Edgar is right. And we'll be next if we don't hurry up and get out of here,' Hero replied, tossing Drake his sword-belt with the humming knife strapped to it, then looping her bandolier around her chest.

'How can you be so brusque?' He shot her a rueful glance. 'Don't you care about anyone other than your damned self?'

'Of course I care!' she snapped. Drake took a half-step backward, while Hero ran a hand over her face. 'But standing here crying about it now does us no good. First, we escape. We go help Joss. Then we mourn. It's the only way to –' Hero stopped. 'Do you hear that?'

'Hear what?' Drake strained to listen.

'*Help!*' someone was faintly crying.

'Hear *that!*' Hero said as she rushed to peer over the edge, then burst out in a grin. 'It's Edgar!' she shouted.

Drake hastened to her side to see the young prentice clamped to the rough underside of the step, just a few scant feet from the vortex below.

'Thank the liege!' Drake sighed. 'Edgar! Are you all right?'

'Not really,' the boy replied in a small, wavering voice.

'Can you climb up?'

'Not really ...' he said again.

'Can you take my hand?' Hero asked, lying on her stomach to reach out to him. Edgar grimaced as he hunkered against the rocky surface.

'I know I'm repeating myself, ma'am, but –'

'Not really,' Drake concluded.

Hero caught his gaze. 'We need a rope,' she said, already searching for whatever she could find that might help.

'Aye, you could use a length of rope, all right. And a yardarm from which to hang!' a voice boomed behind them. Spinning around, Drake saw how quickly Ichor's physician had performed his work. His patient was standing bare-chested before them, a bandage wrapped tightly around his shoulder, cracked teeth bared in an animalistic snarl. Though his guards had gone to join the mob charging on Joss, he was no less dangerous for the lack of reinforcements. Not with the familiar-looking weapon he was wielding.

'That's my family's spear,' Drake said, cold as a tundra wind. 'It belongs to me.'

'Oh?' Ichor replied. He hefted the Icefire spear with such ease it could have been a shaft of light rendered solid, the tip aimed at Drake's heart. 'I'd be happy to return it, lad. Just say where.'

Drake drew his humming knife. The admiral merely laughed.

'Lord Thrall was right. I've been aching for sport down here. I thought before that you were only good for breaking. But I see now how much better suited you are for dying,' he said, spinning the spear around in his rough hands. 'Just don't do it too quickly now.'

'I don't intend to,' Drake replied, holding Ichor's gaze as Hero slipped a zamaraq from her bandolier.

The admiral laughed again, quieter this time, and with far more menace. 'They never do.'

CHAPTER THIRTY-FIVE

―

AN UNCAGED MONSTER

JOSS hit the ground running. And ducking. And rolling. The pyrates were converging on him with such speed and strength that he already knew he'd made a grave mistake. It was foolish to try taking them head on, just as the changeling had said. There were simply too many of them. His only tactic was to sprint as fast as he could, to hit and run and keep running.

Joss could still hear Edgar's terrified, heartbreaking scream as he'd been thrown over the side. It was enough to keep him moving forward through the fear and panic that buzzed in his head like a wounded tiger wasp. That buzz became a full-throated roar as a wave of pyrates surged towards him.

'*Take the devil's eyes!*' howled a hook-handed brute at the front of the pack. Joss was now surrounded, the pyrates' numbers too great to overcome. He could already feel the cold shadow of death settling over him, and shivered at its touch.

But the changeling proved as true in his aim as he was in his word. With a sputtering hiss, a crossbow bolt shot past Joss's head to strike another concealed pot.

'Black and bloody depths!' the same brute cursed in the single moment of silence that followed, before the whole camp erupted and everyone was thrown off their feet.

Joss was caught up in the force of the explosion, flung far across the stairs to land painfully on his back, the breath knocked from him. He had no time to recover. Off-balance and gasping for air, he pulled himself up onto his feet.

'Over here!' he heard someone shouting through the ringing in his ears. He approached the nearby cage to find the hostages crowded against the bars, with one silver-haired woman gesturing emphatically at him.

'How many fingers am I holding up?' she asked him, hand raised before her.

'Lilia, there's no time for that now!' said the man beside her. 'We need him to break us out of here, not pass a physical examination!'

'Great chance he'll have of helping us if he's suffering from a brain haemorrhage,' the woman, Lilia, shot back.

'Three. You're holding up three fingers,' Joss answered in the hope of ending the argument. Lilia smiled, satisfied.

'Can you get us out of here?' her companion asked.

Joss wished it was as easy to answer that question as Lilia's had been. Maybe if he'd brought one of the exploding pots with him he could have blown open the bars. Hero might have had some luck in picking the lock, but there was no way of reaching her with all the pyrates that divided them. If he was going to do something, he had to do it now. Searching desperately for an idea, his mind landed at the *Rakashi Revelations* and the promises they'd made about a *vaartan rhazh*.

'Stand back,' he said, raising the Champion's Blade high. Gripping it as tightly as he could, he brought the sword smashing down on the lock.

———

Ichor moved like an uncaged monster. His every swipe and slash was delivered with lethal intensity, keeping Drake constantly on the defensive. It didn't help that their weapons were so mismatched, with the Icefire spear easily outclassing Drake's humming knife. The few strikes that Drake managed to parry almost broke his arm from the force alone, and the idea of getting close enough to the admiral to land a blow himself was laughable. Ichor's constant chuckling, broken only by the occasional grunt, was testament enough to that.

'Face it, boy. You have no chance of victory. Best surrender now and I promise a quick and honourable death.'

'I don't give up so easily,' Drake huffed.

'Then you'll die screaming,' Ichor replied with a grim smile. 'How splendid.'

The admiral paused, cracked his neck and backbone, before he launched at Drake with renewed strength. He rained down blow after blow, strike after strike. Drake moved as fast as he could to deflect and dodge. But he wasn't fast enough. The tip of the Icefire spear slashed him across the hand, sending his knife hurtling.

'*Ah!*' he cried out in pain, clutching his hand to his chest. Ichor grinned triumphantly as he swaggered forward, pressing the spear against the flesh of Drake's throat.

'Any last words?' the admiral asked.

'Just a question,' Drake said, eyes flicking around Ichor. 'What's that behind you?'

Ichor sniggered. 'That's weak bait. But I'll bite. What exactly is behind me?'

Drake didn't answer. But Hero did.

'Me,' she said, and the admiral spun around just in

time to take a zamaraq to the face, the bladed weapon burying itself in his cheek. Roaring in anguish, he let go of the Icefire spear. It clattered to the ground beside Drake, who quickly scooped it back up.

'*You cowards! You malformed mongrels!*' Ichor screamed as he rolled on the ground, hands wrapped tightly around his face and the weapon sticking from it. 'I'll have your flesh for my overcoat! You hear me? I'll see you both flayed alive for this!'

Hero flicked open a second zamaraq, the blade ringing between her fingers. 'No doubt you could use the surplus skin after having your own so thoroughly punctured.'

'Ignore him, we need to help Edgar,' Drake said, gently placing his bandaged hand on hers. 'Have you found any rope?'

'No. But I've worked out the next best thing.'

Collapsing the zamaraq and tucking it into the hem of her pants, Hero unbuckled her bandolier. The leather strap uncoiled from her chest, the end of it dragging across the ground as she returned to the island's edge.

'Edgar!' she called out to the boy, whose grip looked to be weakening by the second. 'Catch!'

She tossed one end of the bandolier to him while holding on to the other. Though the length was just a few inches too short to reach him comfortably, it was still within grabbing distance. But Edgar wouldn't budge.

'I can't.'

'You *will*,' Hero told him.

Hesitantly, he grasped for the strap.

The rasp of a blade being drawn from its scabbard was followed quickly by a furious howl. It was Admiral Ichor, sword in hand and charging, ready to hack them all to pieces.

'*DIE!*' he screamed as he ran for them, the word a drawn-out battle cry.

'Not today!' Drake told him. 'Not by your hand!'

Dropping onto his back, he kicked up at the admiral's gut at the same time that he slammed the grip of the Icefire spear against Ichor's chest.

'No!' the old pyrate gasped as Drake rolled him up and over. With one quick motion, the admiral was sent sailing right over the edge of the step.

'*Darkness take m—*' was all he could scream before he was swallowed by the vortex, all his flesh and bone disintegrating at once. And then, as if the vortex disagreed with what it had just ingested, the island rumbled violently.

Hero looked around in alarm. 'Was that an earthquake?'

'Either way we need to get out of here,' Drake said, sliding the Icefire spear into the sling on his back as he joined Hero to reach over the side. 'Edgar! Come on! It's now or never.'

Edgar nodded. 'Yes, sir,' he said, taking one last deep breath before coiling against the rock face, then springing upward. Hand outstretched, he grabbed for the leather strap, just as the entire island began to roar.

—

CHAPTER THIRTY-SIX

A PURE JOY

JOSS had only struck the lock twice and already it was showing signs of buckling. One more blow and the cage was sure to open. He was just about to take that final swing when the ground started to lurch and heave beneath him. There was a sound of bones splintering as fissures ruptured open across the plaza, tearing apart the brickwork and sending hordes of pyrates scattering.

'What in the –' Joss was interrupted by a cry from within the cage.

'*Look out!*' Lilia shouted.

Acting on instinct, Joss ducked. Sparks rained down on his head as a twisted red blade struck the bars of the cage. Without even looking, he knew exactly who was behind him.

'I don't know what you're doing here,' Joss said, turning to face his attacker. 'But whatever your plan is, it ends now.'

Thrall stared at Joss through that infernal stone mask of his, as enigmatic as ever. Again he swung his blade, and again Joss scrambled to escape its touch.

'You are a small and lowly thing to aspire to be of any significance to my master or me, even with all the damage you've wrought today. Damage that you'll pay for, I hope you know.' His voice sounded different from the first time Joss had heard it. Darker. More powerful.

'That mangy ginger pyrate is your master now?' Joss asked, keeping his eyes locked on Thrall as he circled away from the cage. 'You're moving down in the world.'

Thrall laughed. Or made a shrill, hacking noise. It was hard to distinguish. 'That sewer-mouthed reprobate is no master of mine. He is merely a means to an end. I serve a greater power,' he said, slicing the air in front of Joss's face. 'As will all the kingdom soon enough. Not that you'll live to see that day.'

'That day being when raptors fly and the moon dances with the earth below.'

'Make jokes,' Thrall said, taking another swipe at Joss, forcing him backward. 'And we'll see who's laughing in the end.'

The ground shook again, far more intensely. A nearby

stone tower creaked, tilted, then all at once collapsed on the pyrates gathered at its feet. Joss was blinded as a rolling cloud of dust engulfed the campsite. Thrall, however, was unaffected by the debris, taking advantage of the distraction to slash at Joss with his blade.

Joss raised the Champion's Blade just in time to avoid having his head severed, though the strength of the blow still sent him reeling. Squinting through the grit in his eyes and panicked, he wondered how he could fend off this obviously superior swordsman, even as Thrall stalked forward to renew his attack.

'I can already feel a chuckle coming on,' the masked man said, failing to see the small clay pot sailing through the air above him. Joss watched the pot trail a stream of dust as it curved high over the campsite, before a sputtering crossbow bolt pierced it.

WHOOM!

The explosion hit with the intensity of an earthquake. It ripped open the tattered lock on the cage, blew in the bars, rained fire on yet another wave of pyrates and sent them screaming from the plaza. Joss, already unbalanced from Thrall's attack, found himself lying on his back and wondering how he got there. Head swimming and vision blurred, he looked up to see a shadowy form hovering before him.

It was Thrall, pierced through with a chunk of

splintered wood, his torso covered in a thick, dark substance that seemed like it should be blood, but wasn't. His head was rolling around on his shoulders as if it were about to drop off and, as he stood weak and unsteady before Joss, he uttered only one word.

'*Mesmerising …*'

'What did you say?' Joss asked through the ringing in his ears, just as another explosion sounded nearby. When he turned back to Thrall the masked man was gone, as if he'd only ever been a trick of the mind. In his place, a second figure came running through the haze, clothed in Daheedi colours. By the time Joss had found his feet again, the changeling was by his side with crossbow in hand.

'Are you injured?' he asked.

'Where's Thrall?' said Joss, searching around the immediate area and finding it empty.

'The man in the cloak? I lost sight of him through the explosion. He must have fled, though his wounds would keep him from getting far.'

'I wouldn't be so sure of that,' Joss said, as a cry for help came from the cage, reminding him of the more immediate matter at hand. The hostages were trying to wrestle open the twisted metalwork of the barred door, which was hanging from its hinges but still blocking any escape.

'It's too heavy!' Lilia exclaimed as Joss approached.

'We may have more luck together,' the changeling suggested, surprising Joss again with his eagerness to help. He watched, stunned, as the creature with his father's face rushed forward to lend a hand, before snapping out of his stupefied state to do the same. They had moved the door less than an inch before he heard yet another familiar voice calling out.

'Wait for us!'

He had never been so relieved to see the faces of his fellow prentices as when they came running across the wreckage of the plaza. But as happy as he was to see Drake and Hero, it was with pure elation that he spotted Edgar following two steps behind them.

'What? How? *Edgar!* You're alive!' Joss grabbed the boy for a rough hug which was heartily returned.

'Thanks to sir and ma'am here,' Edgar said, beaming. 'You should have seen it! They saved me from the vortex and threw Ichor into it like they were making a trade with the Sleeping King himself.'

'You really need to stop calling me ma'am,' Hero said.

Drake nudged her with his elbow and offered her a sly grin. 'Would you prefer he call you "the Rex"?'

'The Rex?' asked Joss, and Drake nodded at Edgar. The boy was turning the brightest shade of red that Joss had ever seen.

'Your young friend here has a very high opinion of you. Which shouldn't be too surprising, given that this whole rescue effort was your idea.'

'Is that true?' Edgar asked, and before Joss could respond the boy's arms were clamped around him. The most he could utter was a breathless squeak, followed by a deep inhalation as Edgar finally let him go again.

'Don't get too excited,' he said, reaching into his coat pocket. 'I knew you'd be wanting your glove back, is all.'

He handed the mud-stained, green leather glove back to his friend, and as big as Edgar's eyes had been before they were even wider now.

The changeling that wore his father's face shuffled into view, and Joss watched as Drake and Hero took stock of him.

'You said Ichor was thrown into the vortex?' he asked with concern.

Drake's expression shifted into one of defiance. 'It was him or us,' he said to the changeling, clearly wondering who he was and why he was expected to answer to him. 'And I can't bring myself to feel bad about it.'

'That's not what I'm saying,' the changeling replied. 'Ichor made himself one of the spellcasters responsible for the ritual's completion by playing such a prominent role. In being thrown in himself, the spell has now been disrupted. The vortex is becoming unstable and all the island with it. It won't be long before the entire city is destroyed – permanently this time!'

'Then we have to get these people out of here – now,' Joss said, addressing the silver-haired woman who'd called out to him. 'Are you ready?'

'We're not as strong as we could be, but we can do this,' she answered.

'I know you can, Lilia,' Drake told her, his words giving her cause to smile, as everyone trapped in the cage gathered again around the door. Joss and the others did the same on their end, each of them grabbing the frame with both hands.

'All together now!' the changeling called out, and as one they hauled the door from the cage. It shrieked as it scraped against the bars, proving as heavy as a giant's hammer, but then finally it gave. With a satisfying *clang*, it dropped to the shell-paved street. The hostages wasted no time in pushing their way out, looking to Joss and the others for guidance, all of them talking in a rush as they asked what to do, where to go, how to get out.

'Everyone, *listen!*' Joss called out over the noise. 'We don't have much time!' As quickly as he could, he described the subterranean harbour and the path to find it, as well as the man who would be waiting there for them.

'His name is Salt and he can guide you onto the

submersibles that we'll use to escape – if the pyrates haven't already made off with them. We may encounter some resistance on the way, but we can fend off any attacks if we band together. Understood? Then let's go.'

As if they were back in Thunder Realm mustering livestock, the prentices herded the hostages from the plaza. Keeping their weapons drawn, they marched together in a line, making sure that the weaker members of the group who stumbled among the debris weren't lost along the way. Drake kept the tip of the Icefire spear held low as he approached Joss.

'It occurs to me,' he said. 'In all the commotion, I didn't get your friend's name.'

Joss looked over at the man by his side, who looked back at him uncertainly.

'He's not a friend,' Joss said.

Drake's confusion only doubled as the stranger, crestfallen, slowed his pace. Joss lent him a comforting hand, bringing him back in step.

'He's Naveer Sarif … My father. Or "paap", as I used to call him.'

Naveer blinked. Slowly, a look came over his face that Joss had only briefly glimpsed before. It started in his eyes, which widened and sparkled as they drank in the light, before it travelled down his face like honey pouring from a hive, turning his reserved smile into a radiant grin. It was the purest expression of joy that Joss had ever seen.

For his part, Drake looked utterly baffled. But he proved as courteous and tactful as ever, offering his hand to Naveer in a hearty shake.

'An honour to meet you, sir. Especially given the circumstances.'

'It's always a pleasure meeting one of Joss's friends,' Naveer replied. 'And it's reassuring to know that he's surrounded by such stalwart companions.'

Drake lowered his head bashfully. 'I don't know about "stalwart". But I do know that someone of Joss's character demands a certain standard in the company he keeps.'

Now it was Joss's turn for modesty, though he couldn't resist adding a little bite to it. 'That's either one of the nicest things anyone's ever said about me, or one of the worst.'

Drake, Joss and his father shared a laugh, the moment feeling so real that Joss had trouble reminding himself of the situation they faced. They could have just as easily been gathered around a campfire or at a kitchen table. It was as if the quiet family life for which he'd always envied others was now within his reach.

It gave him much to consider as they marched on through the fiery night, weapons at the ready, vigilant for whatever lurking threats the shadows may yet unleash.

—

CHAPTER THIRTY-SEVEN

A FINAL MEMORY

EXPLOSIONS sounded in the distance, triggered by
the flames that were tearing through the city. But
for all that mayhem, the road to the underground
harbour was relatively quiet. Only a few scattered
bands of pyrates offered any resistance, with the ragtag
battalion that Joss and his brethren had made of the
escaped hostages quick to fend off their attacks. They
used pitchforks and pickaxes for weapons, upgrading
their armoury with every victory. Joss couldn't believe
their luck. At this rate, they'd be loading into the
submersibles and sailing to freedom within moments.

Or they would have been, if not for the Tower
Memoria.

A massive band of pyrates had fortified the site, firing
at anyone who stepped out from behind the cover of the

surrounding buildings. The first sign of trouble came when one of the hostages charged ahead, only to take an arrow to the knee. Under a hail of crossbow bolts, they dragged the fallen man back behind the corner of a crumbled building, where Lilia set to treating him.

'*Muck!*' Joss cursed, stealing a glance at the tower from behind the cover of a stone wall. Even from this distance the pyrates could be heard hurling threats, insults and slurs. 'We're never going to make it to the harbour if we can't find a way to get past those pyrates or flush them out of there.'

'Impossible,' Hero said as she surveyed the tower through her binoculars. 'They have too strong a position. And they're fanatical enough to hold it right to the end.'

'Is there another path we can take?' Edgar asked, and everyone looked to Naveer.

He shook his head. 'This is the only way.'

Another earthquake ripped through the island, fracturing the ground. Everyone leapt out of the way as a fissure split open beneath their feet and the brimstone stench of sulphuric steam spewed into the air.

Joss slumped against the stone wall. They had come so far, prevailed against overwhelming odds, and now here they were at the end of the road. Trapped. He tried to think of a solution, some kind of strategy, but his mind was a blank, save for the sense that someone was watching him. He looked over to see Naveer staring at him with deep concern.

'I can keep them distracted while you continue on,' he said, stepping forward. 'Then I can double back towards the centre of the city and make sure the last of the protective sigils are destroyed. It's the only way of ensuring that the vortex will close once the island has been consumed.'

Joss frowned, hoping that he was misunderstanding the plan in some way. 'But ... that means you'll be taken with it.'

Naveer said nothing, his look of concern shifting into something else. Perhaps sensing the conversation that was to come, Drake turned to the others. 'Let's give them a moment ...' he said, ushering everyone over to where Lilia had finished treating her patient's wound and was now wrapping it in fabric that she'd ripped from her own tunic. Edgar offered Joss a look of commiseration before going to join them.

'Joss, I –' Naveer began, but Joss didn't want platitudes. He wanted answers.

'You're going to sacrifice yourself?' he asked, relieved that everyone was out of earshot so that they couldn't hear his voice cracking.

'It's the only chance you'll have to escape,' Naveer said, adding uncertainly, 'You didn't think I'd be able to return to the surface, did you? I imagined that would be the last thing you'd want.'

'Yes. No. I don't know. I'm not sure what I thought ...'

Naveer fixed Joss with a resolved gaze. 'Joss – I'm not mortal. There's no way of knowing just how long I can retain this form and the memories that come with it. Changelings aren't known for their sentiment. As much as it pains me to admit it ... you were right to be wary of me.'

'But you saved my life! You know things that it should be impossible for you to know ...' replied Joss, trying somehow to bargain his way out of the problem, even as he knew it was hopeless. 'Maybe the hold that this spell has on you is permanent. Maybe if you came back with me, you could –'

But Naveer wouldn't budge. 'It's not the spell that's proven so strong, Joss. It's simpler than that.' The changeling reached out, held his son's face one last time. 'It's a parent's love.'

Tears were running down Joss's cheeks, pooling at Naveer's fingers. Retreating from his grief, he took hold of the brass cylinder that he'd stuffed into his belt earlier. 'I still have your shadowscope,' he said, shaking as he offered it to his father.

'You should keep it. You'll get far more use out of it than I would. Speaking of which –' Naveer slipped a hand into the satchel at his side. 'I took this before I left the library. I wanted to give it to you when the time was right. And if that's not now, I don't know when it ever will be.'

He pulled loose a familiar necklace, the silver thunderbolt catching the light. Joss stared at it in awe.

'That's not –'

'It is. And you know I speak the truth when I say that he'd have wanted nothing more than for you to have it.'

Naveer handed Joss the necklace. The pendant was heavy. Solid.

'Your mother and your father will always be with you. You'll keep them alive in your heart,' Naveer said. 'But you shouldn't let them rule it. Let the past be past. Live for today. Look to tomorrow. And remember: you can take hope from tragedy –'

'And build something new from the old,' said Joss, finishing the words that had comforted him through his darkest days.

Naveer looked at him with wonder. 'You remember that?'

'Of course I do.' The tears were a flood now. Joss used his sleeve to wipe them away. Then, acting on impulse, he threw his arms around Naveer, hugging him tightly, only to be hugged back just as fiercely.

Then Naveer turned back to Drake and the others.

Lilia had helped the wounded man to his feet, and he was now being guarded by a pair of armed companions.

'Ready?' Naveer called out.

'When you are,' Drake replied as the ragtag battalion prepared to charge.

Naveer hefted his crossbow, the incendiary bolts loaded and the string drawn tight. He looked again at Joss. 'Remember what I said.'

Joss wanted to say so many things in return. He wanted to tell him that he was sorry for his cruelty. He wanted to say how much Naveer's sacrifice meant. But the words wouldn't come. All he could do was nod. Satisfied with that, Naveer returned the gesture, then walked the length of the wall to stop at its edge. Father and son shared one last look and then Naveer prepared to move.

'Wait!' Joss called out to him, and Naveer stopped. He cocked his head, curious, expectant. 'Whatever you were,' Joss said. 'Whatever else you may have been – you're my father. And I'll never forget that.'

The joy that had lit up Naveer's face earlier flared again, tempered this time by the surrounding darkness. Joss could feel his Bladebound brethren at his side, but he kept his gaze fixed on Naveer, who offered one last bow of the head, then jumped out from behind cover and ran.

The pyrates were on him in an instant, loosing

arrows and firing off their flamecannons. Naveer fired back, his crossbow bolts piercing the darkness of the Tower Memoria. Screams and shouts of panic rang out as flames erupted within the building. He kept running, heading in the opposite direction of the harbour.

With the pyrates amply distracted, the prentices and the escaped hostages made their move. Joss led the way quickly, following the path that Naveer had avoided, but once they were out of the worst danger, he gestured the others on and drew to a stop. He could still see Naveer in the distance, shooting fiery crossbow bolts as he ran on towards the flames that were engulfing the city. He was shouting at his attackers, doing everything he could to keep them focused on him.

'*You cravenly sons of demons! You fathers of dust and ashes! Come out here and face me, if you have the mettle!*'

A crash came from within the tower, as if barricades were being ripped away and thrown to the floor, then the pyrate with the bladed leg burst outside, a pack of cutthroats following close behind him.

'*Come on, lads!*' he shouted, taking off after Naveer. 'Let's gut this cocky loudmouth and feed him his own entrails!'

Naveer drew the pyrates away, leading them into the furthest reaches of the island. It was this image that Joss chose as his final memory of his father.

He watched him for as long as he could, watched until the man whose face so closely resembled his own had slipped away into the shadows, and then he followed the others, past the ruins of his childhood, knowing that he would never be the same again.

CHAPTER THIRTY-EIGHT

A RISING SHADOW

THE tunnel to the harbour was just as slick and suffocating as Joss remembered. It forced everyone into single file as they marched down into the abyss, with each shadow hiding – in Joss's mind – a feathery black cloak, a pair of empty eyes, a stone mask that betrayed no emotion.

But Thrall was nowhere to be seen. Perhaps Naveer had been right. Perhaps Thrall's wounds had proven too severe to overcome. Or perhaps he'd already made his escape, having fled a city that was growing more unstable by the moment. The tremors were sending rocks tumbling loose, the smaller ones bouncing away harmlessly, the larger ones hitting with deadly force.

Already one hostage had been struck senseless, and was being carried with Edgar's help. Hero was at the end of the line, guarding the rear, zamaraq in one hand and humming knife in the other. That left Drake and Joss leading the march, constantly looking ahead for any sign of trouble. All that Joss found in this weak light, however, were the many puddles that had been spattered on the chiselled stone steps and across the rough, craggy walls.

'See this?' Drake quietly asked, tapping at one of the puddles with the toe of his boot.

'Smelt it more like,' Joss replied, his nose wrinkling at the coppery stink of blood. Maybe Thrall hadn't been so quick to escape after all.

'We need to be cautious,' said Drake. 'There's no telling what could have caused it.'

Joss responded only with a troubled nod, wary that he already knew what awaited them. But still they trudged downward, the earth folding in over their heads even as it continued to tremble.

When they finally emerged into the cavernous harbour it was to the sight of bodies strewn across the ground like discarded ragdolls. Weapons at the ready, Joss signalled for the others to remain where they were while he and Drake scouted ahead. They had taken only a few short steps before Joss was met with a blade to the throat. Keeping as still as possible, he stole what might be his only glance at his assailant.

'Salt!' he exclaimed with relief, and the spearhead at his jugular was lowered.

'Ganymede! Josiah!' Salt said. His face and hands were covered in fine cuts, but otherwise he looked unharmed. 'I had all but given up hope of seeing you again.'

'And we didn't know if you'd still be here,' replied Drake.

'That I am.' Salt gestured to the fallen pyrates. 'Though not without some effort.'

'What about Bhashvirak?' Joss asked, while Drake returned to the stairs to let everyone know it was safe to proceed.

'Gone. Took off the moment the island began to shake.' Salt peered over Joss's shoulder. 'I see you've brought company.'

The hostages were pouring out of the passageway behind them and gawking at the bodies, as well as at the armed and unkempt man responsible for all the bloodshed.

'It's all right. He's with us,' Hero assured them, though everyone maintained their distance, standing with their backs against the rocky cavern walls.

'Salt, are all the submersibles still here?' asked Joss. Naveer would surely have eluded his pursuers by now, which meant he'd be doubling back to the city to destroy the protective sigils. Time was running out.

'All but one. A pair of marauders was able to pass me as I was busy dealing with their comrades. They had a pack of raptors with them.'

'Does that leave us with enough to get everyone to safety?'

Salt scanned the vessels moored along the harbour, his expression uncertain as he then counted the people lined up against the wall. 'We'll know soon enough,' he said.

Wishing he had more assurance than that, Joss addressed the hostages. 'Is anyone here capable of driving one of these things?'

A few doubtful hands were raised, while a couple of others were coaxed into doing the same by the people who knew them.

'But I'm just a navigator on a fishing trawler! I'd never even set foot on a submersible before being abducted on one,' a bearded young man objected after a friend had volunteered him.

'We don't have a lot of other options,' Joss said, 'Captain.'

The young man seemed stricken to have such a title imposed on him, but he consented to it all the same. Soon everyone was gathered into small groups and began boarding the submersibles.

'Salt is going to lead us all out of here,' Joss called to those aboard their vessels, his voice bouncing around the cave while he stood on the dock. 'We'll have to navigate single file through the tunnel. Once we've cleared that we'll head for the surface, where we can regroup and then sail for shore.'

'Be safe, everyone!' added Edgar, while Hero gave the final command.

'Lock your hatches and power your engines. We're shipping out!'

Doors slammed shut and were fastened tight. The cavern grew smoggy as each of the submersibles rumbled into operation. Standing at the edge of the dock, Salt gave a small salute to the prentices, who had not yet boarded a vessel, before shifting into his animal form and diving into the water. The first of the submersibles soon followed, with each of them trailing in turn.

'I'm going to need help with getting these two on board,' Lilia said, gesturing to the injured hostages and the last submersible. Joss, Hero, Drake and Edgar were quick to help her carry them down the dock. They were almost to their craft when another quake ripped through the island, knocking them off balance and unleashing a rain of spear-shaped stalactites.

'We need to get out of here. *Now.* We don't have much time left.' Joss helped Lilia back onto her feet, only to be struck dumb by a dark and haunting voice from the water, the wisp scar blazing against his flesh.

'You're more right than you know, boy.'

A shadow rose from the bow of the submersible. It was intangible at first, a black shape without form or face. But then it began to solidify, feathered cloak twitching into existence, curved sword swishing the air.

Thrall stared down at the ragged band of survivors before him.

And then he attacked.

CHAPTER THIRTY-NINE

A BLACK VORTEX

L IKE a pterosaur after its prey, Thrall dived upon the prentices. Drake only just raised his spear in time to keep his face from being split in half, and then he was driven backward by a relentless barrage of blows.

'Leave Mister Drake alone!' Edgar shouted as he rushed forward to help, and was quickly rewarded with a sharp kick to the gut that sent him flying. Hero had to sidestep the airborne steward and raise her zamaraq in the same motion, then cursed as Thrall flung Drake straight at her, knocking them both senseless as they slammed into the rocky cavern wall. That left only Joss.

'How are you still standing?' he said, searching Thrall for any sign of injury. All that remained of his wounds were the rips in his vestments, and the dark stains that coloured them. 'I saw you impaled right in front of me!'

'It would take more than that to fell a servant as faithful as I,' Thrall said as he smoothed out his feathered cloak. 'You, though? You I imagine to be a far more fragile thing. Easily crippled with just a snap of the neck. And when that's done, I'll drag you and your *brethren* here back to the city, where you'll be surrendered to the darkness as tribute to His Majesty.'

'Tribute to His Majesty?' Joss said, thinking back on what had happened to the other people who'd served in Thrall's ritual. It hadn't looked like a peaceful death, but it had been a quick one. Certainly more merciful than what his parents and all the people of Daheed had suffered.

'It would be quite the honour, boy. Believe me. So put away that gaudy little sword of yours and save us any further trouble.'

The masked man's words came with flashes of memory: Joss's first encounter with Thrall all the way back in Tower Town, and the glowing orb the strange man had held that offered visions of glory; the sight of Thrall conducting his sermon upon the First Step of Daheed, his devout followers gathered at his feet.

Thrall's stony gaze was fixed rigidly on Joss, his empty eyes as black as a shark's. Feeling a tug inside his soul, Joss sheathed the Champion's Blade.

Thrall nodded with approval. 'Smart lad,' he said,

moving forward. 'Perhaps I underestimated you. Perhaps someone of your talents is in want of a master. I watched you through the ruins of this dead city while I gave myself time to heal. I saw how you dealt with Ichor's men. Very impressive for someone so young.'

'It was?' Joss asked, against the unnatural whispers in his brain. He shook his head, dispelling them for a moment, while Thrall continued to advance on him. The whispers crept back in, growing louder.

'The truth is, I've long found this pyrate scum to be ill-suited for His Majesty's service,' the masked man said, blade flashing beside him. 'All this sacrifice, all this death. It hasn't been in vain. It's all been towards a greater good. And I could use someone as able as you at my side, ensuring that all this effort is not wasted.'

Joss frowned through his confusion and the whispering in his head. He could feel a bead of sweat trickling down his temple, though he knew he couldn't risk wiping it away. One false move and Thrall would end him. 'You made an offer like this before, back at Tower Town,' Joss said, the glowing orb and its glorious visions flashing again in his memory. 'You told me that chances were like lives. We don't get more than one. Don't you remember?'

Thrall lost a step as the earth rumbled all around them, but recovered quickly. 'And yet here I am, offering you a whole new lease on life. What say you, boy?

Are you prepared for more power than you could have ever possibly hoped for?'

Joss turned his gaze over to where his Bladebound brethren were only just starting to stir. 'What about my friends?' he asked.

Thrall waved away Joss's concern. 'A necessary sacrifice for a greater cause. Though the hostages may have escaped, a price must still be paid. But why should that worry you? You'll find soon enough that with great power comes little need for friendship. Only obedience.'

Joss stepped back, the whispers in his head growing silent. Thrall followed, and Joss retreated. Thrall moved again, and again Joss stepped away. Slowly, one move at a time, Joss backed his way along the wharf, his eyes fixed on Thrall as the masked man followed him.

'I see I rushed too soon to praise you,' Thrall said, his voice taut as he maintained a moderate distance from his quarry. 'If you're so determined to die alongside your collaborators, then so be it. This little game of yours only delays the inevitable.'

Planks creaked under Joss's feet as he edged down the pier that ran out into the centre of the lake. He circled both hands around the grip of his humming knife. With great concentration, he whipped the blade through the air. It flowed from one position to the next, the runes glowing in his face, and a lilting tune floated into the air.

'What is that?' asked Thrall, stepping onto the pier to continue his unhurried pursuit. Joss didn't answer, concentrating instead on his form, his fluidity. Even the smallest mistake would be enough to silence the song, and he couldn't allow that. Not now. Not with so much hanging in the balance.

'Is that …' Thrall hesitated, searching the air for answers. The tune grew louder. He continued towards Joss, boots thumping the boards.

The humming knife was shining so bright now that it was blinding Joss. He kept going. With every backward step he swiped his blade, swung it, twirled and slashed it. He could hear the water churning beneath him, waves lapping at its pillars, bubbles popping in time to the song his knife was singing.

'Is that a summoning song?' asked Thrall in disbelief from halfway down the pier, laughing in his choked, raspy manner. 'You truly are desperate, boy. What could you possibly hope to summon down here?'

Joss made no reply, he just kept carving his spell into the air. Thrall laughed again, heartier this time. Joss's brow twinged as he wondered what was so amusing, only to realise as his heel searched for firm ground and found nothing. He was at the end of the pier with his back to the great beyond and nowhere else to go. Worse, his faltering step made him lose his place in the song, his humming knife falling instantly silent. He realised now that despite all that Thrall had offered him, the masked man had only been playing with him, biding his time until Joss was at his most vulnerable.

'It would seem your impromptu performance is at an end,' Thrall said, sword hovering at his side. The bent red metal resembled a tongue, its tip glinting thirstily. 'Perhaps you'll allow me to perform the encore.'

The water was swirling now. Joss dropped to his knees and held the pier.

'Sorry,' he said. 'Show's over.'

Thrall drew breath to reply. It would be his last.

'MIGHTY BHASHVIRAK IS ARRIVED!'

The great shark rose up like a tidal wave, white and grey and sleek and deadly. It opened its mouth, as black a vortex as any that Thrall had worshipped.

And with one cataclysmic bite it swallowed the man in the stone mask whole.

CHAPTER FORTY

AN END TO THE DREAM OF DAHEED

THE pier shattered as Bhashvirak snapped it in half and slammed back into the water, his fin slicing through what little remained. Joss was left clinging to the one wooden pillar, struggling to stay afloat as Bhashvirak dived back beneath the surface. But he couldn't help grinning triumphantly.

He'd done it! With only a humming knife and an ounce of hope, Joss had slipped free of whatever spell Thrall had cast and somehow managed to summon the King of the Seas. He wondered what Sur Verity would think if she were here. More to the point, what Naveer might say if he'd seen what his son had done.

But Naveer wasn't here. And he never would be again. Joss's triumph evaporated as another earthquake ripped through the island.

'Joss! Are you hurt?' Drake called from the shore while gingerly rubbing the back of his head.

'I'm all right!' He looked at the wrecked pier, at his lone pillar. 'Stranded. But all right.'

'You're not the only one,' Hero replied as she joined Drake. 'The submersible's damaged!'

'What?!' Joss whipped around to see the craft bobbing in Bhashvirak's wake, its tailfin and propeller both so bent that it would be impossible to steer. The great shark must have damaged it in his attack. How were they going to escape now?

Joss considered their options, few as they were. Closing his eyes, he quietened his mind and called out. 'Mighty Bhashvirak, are you still there?'

'*MIGHTY BHASHVIRAK REMAINS!*' the shark answered, his fin rising from the depths to slice the water surrounding Joss. '*AND HIS HUNGER IS SATED. FOR NOW.*'

'That's a relief,' Joss muttered to himself before addressing the great beast. 'Thank you for all your help –'

'*MIGHTY BHASHVIRAK DOES NOT "HELP". MIGHTY BHASHVIRAK DOES AS MIGHTY BHASHVIRAK WILLS!*'

The fin, large as a catamaran's sail, cut past Joss's pillar. Joss shifted his weight, repositioned his hands.

'In that case ... would Mighty Bhashvirak be willing to perform one last act?'

Joss explained his plan, first to the megalodon and then to everyone on shore. His voice was hoarse from shouting and his arms were growing weary from holding on, so he was grateful at how quickly Drake, Hero and Edgar snapped into action.

First they retrieved a mooring rope from the wharf, tying one end around the submersible's cabin. The other end was then given to Lilia, whose agility took Joss by surprise as she hopped onto Bhashvirak's back and quickly secured her end of the rope to the great shark's lifechamber, linking it with the submersible.

'Ready!' she called, dodging around falling rocks as she tugged on the rope to make sure it held. With Joss's guidance, Bhashvirak circled back around to the wharf, where the other prentices lent a hand to load Lilia's patients onto the giant shark.

'Careful ...' Joss muttered to himself, watching the infirm hostages struggle into place. When they had finally made it across, Lilia then helped them into the lifechamber, which she sealed shut behind them.

That left Drake, Hero and Edgar to clamber into the inoperative submersible, with Joss still clinging to the pillar in the middle of the harbour, the water so cold it felt as if it was biting him through his boots. The waves only grew larger as Bhashvirak swam past, spraying Joss with speckled foam. He stole one last glimpse of Lilia and the others sprawled inside the glass lifechamber before the great shark dived beneath the dark marbled surface of the water.

The rope that Bhashvirak was trailing behind him pulled tight, dragging the submersible from its dock. The rudderless craft whished past, and with the last of his strength Joss sprang from the pier just as the cavern rumbled and sent the largest salvo of rocks yet crashing down.

'*Gah!*' he grunted as he landed clumsily on the slippery metal, a small but sharp rock hitting him on the back of his knee. The rest of the rocks pinged off the submersible's riveted surface, while Joss grabbed one of the protruding steel rungs to pull himself up and into the hatch, which he quickly slammed shut behind him.

Inside, he sealed the door tight before dropping down into the main cabin. Drake, Hero and Edgar were waiting there for him, cheering as he emerged beside them.

'Welcome aboard!' Drake said, clapping him on the arm.

'I can't believe we made it!' Edgar grinned.

'We're not in the clear just yet,' said Hero, and pointed out the porthole. The shower of rocks was becoming a

hailstorm, with loud bangs and thumps echoing off the cabin. One large boulder rolled down the cavern wall, bounced into the air, then smashed into the window, spraying a web of cracks across its surface.

'*Merciful liege!*' Edgar yelped, his eyes bulging.

Squeezing past him, Drake gently ran his fingertips along the glass to inspect the damage. 'It hasn't penetrated the whole way through.'

'Will it hold under the pressure?' Joss asked. The cabin was already suffocating enough. The last thing they needed was gallons of water rushing in to drown them all.

'Can't say,' replied Drake, drawing back his hand.

'Then I guess we'll find out,' Joss said.

He and the others watched as the rope drew them ceaselessly towards the mouth of the cave, paused, then dragged them under. The glass held. Still, nobody took their eyes from it as Bhashvirak towed them through the underwater cavern, the submersible banging against the rocks with alarming regularity. With nothing left to do but wait and pray, Joss settled back into one of the padded seats. Though he stared at the porthole window the entire time, he couldn't help but think of Thrall.

Now that the terror was at an end, it didn't seem real. And yet there was no denying it. He'd seen the man consumed with his own eyes. But it was another man who loomed larger in Joss's mind and, as the submersible bounced its way through the tunnel, he found himself wondering where that man was right now …

———

His breath ragged and his hand clutched tightly to his side, Naveer limped into the city square. Blood was oozing from the wound the remaining pyrates had bestowed upon him before he'd managed to escape. He could hear them now, somewhere off in the distance, shouting for his head even as the earth continued to rumble and fracture.

It wasn't just the island that was breaking apart. The energy dome that had long kept Daheed preserved was rapidly weakening. Torrents of black water were rushing in, drowning the ruins. Looking up, he saw a great shadowy figure gliding past the dome. It was dragging what looked to be the last of the submersibles, the rest of the fleet having already made its escape. Naveer sighed with relief. Josiah was safe. There was nothing left to do but destroy the last protective sigil and bring this madness to an end.

But first he raised his hand. Touched his cheek. His firm brown skin was gone. There remained only the ashen, waxy skin of his true form. His memory, however.

That remained. He looked down at the sigil beneath his feet. He could remember the day that he'd inscribed that mark, the chaos that demanded it. But the memory was evaporating, bit by bit, bubbling away like foam on a sandy shore. His wife's face. His son's birth. His every blessing, every brightest moment. They were disappearing into the ether. Soon all that would be left was a mindless husk. A memory of a memory, quickly forgotten.

He refused to let that happen.

'Let the past be past,' he murmured to himself as he hefted the last pot of liquid fire from his satchel. He squeezed it tight, imagining it to be a hand as small as a ripening fig, wrapped around his own.

And then he dropped it.

The clay pot burst like a falling beehive, unleashing a swarm of flames that set the sigil ablaze. Overhead, the dome quivered, then ruptured. The black water came tumbling down in vast curtains, drawing to an end the dream of Daheed, while the man who called himself Naveer Sarif closed his eyes and waited for the darkness to take him.

—

CHAPTER FORTY-ONE

AN OPEN GRAVE

JOSS watched from the submersible's window as the dome surrounding Daheed disintegrated, its purple lights flickering to nothing, leaving the city to be crushed under the surge of water. The vortex opened up like the mouth of a ravenous beast, swallowing whatever hadn't already been decimated by the deluge. Stone by stone the island was consumed. Every street, every home, every last pebble. All of it went tumbling into the void, where it was devoured.

Joss felt as if it was his own heart that was being eaten piece by piece. He imagined Naveer down there, lost in the wreckage of the city. The thought was so sharp and painful he pressed his hand to his chest. But still he stared, watching as his island home was taken from him for a second time, watching as the void claimed it for itself.

With every piece the vortex consumed it grew smaller, until all that remained was a rift the size of a small lifeboat. And then, when the last chunk of rock had been consumed, the rift began to eat itself. The shockwave it unleashed slammed into the submersible, tossing the prentices around like beans in a tin can.

'Hunting herbivores, that hurt!' Edgar muttered as he rolled over and rubbed his skull, while Drake and Hero both pulled themselves up beside him.

'Daheed …' Drake asked, rotating his shoulder. 'Is it –'

Joss peered again through the window. They were flying from the trench now, its maw wide open and empty, iridescent jellyfish lighting their way.

'Gone,' he said, finding the answer hard to believe. 'The city, the island. Even the vortex. All of it. Gone.'

It was true. As if nothing had ever even been there. As if it had all been some grand illusion, some dream now faded. The City of Night Neverending. The Gleaming Isle. *Home.* It was a place that had been called many things, and had meant even more, but all of that was past now. Joss sank to the cabin's floor, his strength spent. He was alone again. The last survivor of Daheed, same as it ever was. The idea made him want to weep.

'We've got trouble,' Hero said, leaning past him to take her own look out the porthole. She pointed to the towrope that linked them with Bhashvirak, and the halfway spot where it was fraying apart.

'*Muck!*' Edgar gasped. 'It's going to snap any second!'

'Joss, can you talk to Bhashvirak?' asked Drake. 'Maybe he can swing around and snag us.'

Joss cleared his mind to focus on Drake's question. 'I don't know.' He tried reaching out to the great shark. 'Mighty Bhashvirak – can you hear me? Mighty Bhashvirak, this is Joss – this is the mortal boy. The rope is breaking! We need you to –'

The cabin shuddered, then jerked as the towrope snapped apart, whipping up a trail of bubbles. It coiled in the water before them, then sank. And Bhashvirak didn't notice at all. He just kept swimming, his tail beating against the tides as he gradually disappeared into the distance.

'Bhashvirak! This is the mortal boy. Bhashvirak! Can you hear me?' Joss tried and tried again, but there was no response. The great shark could barely be seen now through the dark water. Its fin was little more than a fleck of grey on a black canvas. It flashed one last time through the gloom and then was gone, leaving the submersible to fall towards the open grave of Daheed.

'Ganymede, quickly! Can you get this bucket running?' Joss leant over the navigator's chair to jab blindly at the control panel. The craft was picking up speed, sinking into the trench with the velocity of an anchor thrown overboard.

'I tinker with machines, I don't pilot them,' Drake replied as he sat down to run his eyes over the wide array of instruments.

'Will we be able to catch up with the others?' Edgar asked as he and Hero crammed in alongside them.

'The rudders were damaged, remember? We won't be able to steer it anywhere,' Drake said, still studying the controls.

'We don't need to steer,' Joss told him. 'We just need not to sink.'

Tentatively, Drake began to poke at buttons, tap gauges, switch levers, but nothing happened. Not until he balled up his fist and punched the console. Then the whole thing sprang to life, its readouts lighting up, the engines humming into operation. Even the external headlights switched on, lighting the water and revealing the drifting algae and all the little microbes that rushed past as they continued to fall.

Joss, Hero and Edgar all looked at Drake, each of them astounded.

'We were overdue for a little luck,' he said, reaching for what looked to be the accelerator. 'Let's hope it holds.'

The cabin screeched with effort while the motor grumbled, sputtered, farted a cloud of bubbles.

A chopping sound emanated from outside as the rotor blades kicked into gear, keeping the vessel from falling any further. The submersible bobbed in place for a moment before, miraculously, it began to ascend. The prentices let out a whoop of victory, each of them rushing in to give Drake a congratulatory hug.

'That's one problem solved,' he said, his grin fading. 'Then there's the issue of being stuck out in the middle of the ocean with nobody to rescue us.'

The cabin fell silent again.

'Maybe –' Edgar ventured, thought better of it, and shut his mouth.

Joss watched him for a moment, then reached into his pocket to pull out the necklace that Naveer had given him. His father would have known what to do. Between his years of sailing and his natural resourcefulness, he would no doubt have had some kind of plan, some failsafe strategy. Joss turned the thunderbolt pendant around in his hands, considered its radiance, felt dull by comparison, then reached up to place the necklace back in his pocket. And as he did, his fingers brushed against another recent keepsake.

'I've got it!' he said, jumping up from his seat. Everyone looked at him with puzzlement, Drake most especially as Joss said, 'If you can get us to the surface, I can get us home.'

'How?' Edgar asked.

'With this.' Joss smiled, producing the Scryer that Qorza had given him.

Drake's face lit up, elated and relieved. 'Then let's get out of here, shall we?' he said, and turned back to the controls to begin their ascent, carefully controlling their speed to avoid decompression sickness. Nobody spoke. They barely even breathed. They simply watched as the water outside brightened one excruciating shade at a time, while the receiver signal on the Scryer gradually ticked upward. When it finally beeped in his palm, Joss fired it up and activated the emergency beacon, just as the submersible breached the surface.

The vessel bounced around on the waves like a cork in a wine barrel. Edgar moved quickly to unlock the top hatch and fling it open, letting in a gust of fresh air. Everyone sighed with relief, the sound of circling gulls as musical to the ears as chamber hymns. Then, crowded together, they poked their heads up through the open hatch to stare at the twin shades of perfect blue that were the sea and the sky.

Joss closed his eyes. Leant his head back. Felt the kiss of the sun on his skin, the wind's caress. Daheed was gone. So was his family. But he was alive. And he would never forget.

'What do we do now?' asked Edgar, his joy at seeing

the bright blue world above dimming at the prospect of being left marooned at sea.

'We wait,' Joss said.

After all, there was nothing else to do but hope they wouldn't be waiting long. That hope diminished as the first hour passed, shrank even more as the second hour drew to a close, and all but disappeared as the third hour wore on past the point of counting. Until Joss spotted a hulking black mass on the horizon.

'*There!*' he shouted, pointing it out. The others clambered up to see.

It was the *Behemoth*, its sails full, its smokestacks pumping, its prow relentlessly cresting the waves. Within moments it was upon the submersible, circling the crippled vessel in a wide loop.

'Ahoy there!' Captain Gyver called out as she waved from the railing, with Qorza smiling beside her. 'Need a lift?'

—

CHAPTER FORTY-TWO

A Good Man, Through and Through

JOSS sat on the bow of the *Behemoth,* looking out at the horizon with his father's shadowscope in his pocket and his thunderbolt pendant in hand. His legs were dangling between the rails, his knees knocking against the beams, his heels brushing the monstrous figurehead. Qorza was doing the same, shivering through her fur-lined coat now that they'd passed beyond the Veil of Frost. They had been sitting together for an hour as Joss told her everything that had happened, from their arrival in Snowbridge to their swift exodus from the drowning ruins of Daheed.

Though he had ended up explaining Naveer's true nature to his brethren as they'd waited for rescue, he knew it was only Qorza who could offer him any true insight on the matter. Though for all her knowledge, she looked just as stunned as the others had been.

'The changeling sacrificed itself to save you?' she remarked with surprise.

'That's not something they might normally do?' asked Joss, fairly certain he already knew the answer.

'Not at all,' Qorza said. 'It'd be like having a tyrannosaur as a loyal mount. It's just not in their nature. They feed and they move on. That's all.'

'He said –' Joss hesitated. 'He said it was a parent's love. That it proved stronger than any other instinct.'

Qorza smiled with appreciation. 'What a lovely notion,' she said. 'But that was your father. A good man, through and through. Clearly that rubbed off on the creature. Though I doubt it would have if not for you.'

'Me?'

'The ties that bind us reach both ways. Your memories were strong, Joss. Buried, hard to retrieve, but strong nevertheless. You may not have had your family for very long. It may have hurt to have been without them all this time. But there's a joy at the centre of all that – a pure and particular love – that ensures you're never lost in the world. The pain of your past may initially have drawn the changeling to you, coupled as it was with the beacon of the wisp's mark. But it was the light you carry inside that truly transformed the creature. Love conquers all, in the end.'

Joss's nose wrinkled of its own accord; he was unaccustomed to hearing such open sentimentality. Folk in Thunder Realm seldom if ever spoke in such a way. But that didn't mean it wasn't pleasant to the ear.

'When we first met, you said our running into each other had something to do with fate,' he said, thinking now of another matter that had been weighing on his mind. 'Do you believe that?'

'I'm an ethereon, Joss. It's my job to believe.'

'What about prophecy, then? Can it be trusted?'

'It depends.' Qorza shrugged. 'Who's making the prophecy, for starters.'

Joss explained the discovery of his mother's journal, and her notes regarding the *Rakashi Revelations*. Qorza listened with rapt attention, her interest only intensifying when he showed her the book itself. 'Fascinating,' she said, examining each page in detail. When she was done she handed the journal back to Joss, and he tucked it away again. 'Clearly I have some research to do.'

'Whatever you can find out, I'd appreciate it. Especially if you can work out the translation of those words.' Joss had known that if anyone would be interested in his mother's research, it would be Qorza. He could only hope that she'd be able to shed some light on the mystery.

'Of course. But for now I must get on with my duties,' she said, pulling herself up. 'I'm glad, though. That you got a chance to meet your father. However unusual the circumstances may have been.'

Joss pondered what she'd said, then looked up at her with a soft smile. 'Me too.'

Returning the smile, Qorza crossed over to the stairs that led down onto the main deck, passing Drake as she left.

Drake came to a stop beside Joss, sharing the view with him for a moment before he spoke. 'We received a message from Stormport. Salt arrived with all the submersibles in tow. Everyone's safe. Even Bhashvirak showed up – I can only imagine the reaction. We'll be there soon enough, but in the meantime they're serving supper down on the main deck if you're hungry.'

'I'll be along in a moment,' Joss said.

'Something on your mind?' asked Drake.

Joss kept his eyes on the horizon as he thought through his reply. 'It feels silly now, but when we were back in Snowbridge with your family ...' Joss risked glancing at Drake before quickly looking away again. 'I envied you. Even with everything you'd been through – the heartache, the anger, all those lost years – I was still jealous that you'd had any of it in the first place. Does that make sense?'

'I … think so,' Drake said as he knelt down, sliding into the spot that Qorza had vacated. 'You wanted a family so much it didn't matter if it wasn't a perfect one.'

Joss nodded. 'And when your father gave you his spear … all I could think was how much I wanted something like that. Some inherited memento, some token of a family legacy. And now I'm here, with this.' He held up the thunderbolt pendant. 'And all I can think is that I'd trade it in an instant if it meant he was here instead.'

Drake sat absorbing what Joss had said. 'Family,' he said at last. 'It defines you in so many ways, doesn't it? Both good and bad. I thought for the longest time that I was the opposite of everything my family wanted me to be. Turns out it was more complicated than that. I don't know if I'll ever have a perfect relationship with them. In fact, I doubt that's even possible. But that doesn't mean it won't be a relationship worth having. And even if it's difficult at times, even if we fight or fall out, that doesn't mean I won't still have family. Because whatever we may lack in the home we were born into, whatever we may have lost along the way, there's one simple thing to remember – family is whatever you want it to be.'

Drake touched Joss's shoulder. 'You may not have your parents with you, Joss. That pendant may not be able to bring your father back. But you have us.'

Joss didn't know what to say. Though from Drake's warm expression, it seemed that he didn't have to say anything at all.

'*Land ahoy!*' The call came with a ringing bell from the crow's nest, and they looked again at the horizon to see Stormport ahead of them. It was little more than a distant constellation, its buildings twinkling silver, its wooden docks a ruddy brown in among the glacial blue of the landscape. Squinting, Joss could just make out the fleet of submersibles docked in the bay, their copper hulls gleaming in the light of the setting sun.

'Strange to think that we'll be in the Northern Tundra soon, back at the beginning.'

'And with all our training still ahead of us,' Drake said. 'Ready for it?'

'More than ever,' Joss said. 'You?'

Drake grinned. 'Just try and stop me.'

'Ganymede?' Hero called up from the bottom of the stairs. 'Edgar's onto his fourth helping of stew with no sign of slowing down. If you or Joss want any chance of eating anything, I'd come quickly.'

'On our way!' Drake replied, then turned back to Joss. 'Come on. There's still some time before we reach shore. We'll have some food and play some castes. You may even win a round this time.' His grin reflected Joss's own.

'You go ahead. I'll just be a minute.'

Drake nodded before taking his leave. Only when he was sure that he was alone, Joss again removed his mother's journal from his inside coat pocket. He was still amazed that he'd somehow managed to keep it safe through everything. Flipping it open, he re-read the *Rakashi Revelations* as written out in his mother's hand.

'*From beyond silver seas, from out of blue skies, from the ruins of a lost life, there will come a* galamor, *with right hand marked by fate and carrying a* vaartan rhazh. *Only the* galamor *will stand when all else fall, and rise when all else kneel. Only the* galamor *can bring light to the oncoming darkness, and draw hope from a dying dream. Only the* galamor, *and the* galamor *alone.*'

Joss closed the book, its words echoing in his head as he stared again at Stormport, where the next step of his journey awaited him. If what the revelations said were true, did that make him the *galamor*? And, if so, could the destruction of Daheed have fulfilled the prophecy? After all, he'd carried a *vaartan rhazh* – the Champion's Blade – while opposing a cult dedicated to an oncoming darkness. If that didn't fit with the prophecy, what else could?

Thrall had talked of a master, a greater power to whom all his sacrifices had been made. But Thrall was gone. Surely whatever looming threat he'd spoken of had perished with him. After all, the dead rarely finished what the living had started.

Joss tucked the book back away before slipping the thunderbolt necklace over his head and under his tunic. It rested cool against his chest, soothing the dull heat of the faded wisp scar.

And so, with the inheritance he'd received from his mother and his father sitting beside his heart, he pulled himself up from the edge of the ship and went to join his brethren. Whatever lay ahead, he couldn't hope to predict. But he knew one thing, at least.

He wouldn't be doing it alone.

EPILOGUE

TOGETHER the cloaked figures swept into the circular chamber, moving in perfect unity. Iron braziers ignited at their presence, spitting crimson flames, while the flickering candles on the overhanging chandeliers wept black wax. Stone markers were arranged in a circle at the centre of the room, each marker inscribed with its own unique rune. The cloaked figures formed a ring as they all took their positions atop their own individual markers, with the largest of them stepping up onto the rocky slab at the head of the chamber.

The marker beside his remained empty, the only untended place in the ring.

'One of our number has fallen,' he said, his feather cloak bristling as he addressed his fellows. 'May the darkness take him!'

'*May the darkness take us all,*' intoned the gathering.

'We commemorate his passing with the drawing of fresh blood ...'

'May it be so,' the others replied, and again in unison they drew their swords. The red of their crooked blades looked unremarkable in the crimson firelight, even as they crossed the steel along their gloved hands. Blood ran as black as the candles above, dripping into the channels that had been carved in the granite floor. It flowed like a river down into the drain set beneath the feet of the largest figure, who spoke up again to address the gathering.

'Though we now number fewer than we did before, we are not weaker for it. Every day His Majesty grows stronger, his time grows closer.' The figure drew back his hood, revealing his stone mask and the harsh runes that covered it, mirroring the characters carved into the circling markers. 'And we loyal servants of the Court of Thralls will have his eternal favour.'

'May the darkness take us!' the many Thralls said as they raised their hands, their wounds already healed. The largest Thrall stared at them, his grim satisfaction apparent even through his mask.

'May the darkness take us all.'

ACKNOWLEDGEMENTS

THIS book owes a great debt to a whole range of people. I'd like to start by thanking the Hardie Grant Egmont team for all their hard work. Special thanks must go to my publisher Marisa Pintado, editors Penelope White and Alison Arnold, and to Sarah Magee, Haylee Collins, Kristy Lund-White, Mandy Wildsmith and all the sales force. Many thanks also to my agent Clare Forster and her colleagues at Curtis Brown Australia for their guidance as well as to Hayley Crandell for her help and enthusiasm.

Despite a demanding work schedule, Jeremy Love returned to provide another beautiful piece of cover artwork with Milenko Tunjic joining the team to provide internal illustrations. Big thanks to both.

Similarly generous with her time was Tina Healy of Gender Diversity Australia (aka GenDA), who went above and beyond in reviewing the manuscript and offering her invaluable insights. I'm in awe of Tina's courageousness, which partly inspired the creation of Ganymede Drake. My immense gratitude to her.

As always, my family has been a great source of support. Thank you to Mum, Dad & Suze, both Nans, Judy & Carl and Nicole & George.

This is a book about fathers and sons. During the course of its writing, our son Max was born. And what a dramatic entrance he made. I'd like to thank all the staff at the Northern Hospital, Mercy Hospital and the Royal Children's Hospital PIPER team for their compassion, dedication and diligence.

To Max; I'm already so proud of you. There's a vast horizon out there waiting for you, and it will be my greatest privilege to help guide you towards it.

Finally, I'd like to express all my love and gratitude to Max's mother – my wife, Simone. This book is all the better for her influence. As is my life. And I can't thank her enough for it.

ABOUT THE AUTHOR

Steven Lochran spent his childhood writing stories and now he does it for a living. He graduated from Queensland University of Technology with a Bachelor's degree in Creative Writing, and has worked as a film critic, projectionist and DJ. He's spent the last decade in the publishing industry, during which time he's written the *Paladero* and *Vanguard Prime* series of books. He lives in Melbourne with his wife and son, as well as two spoilt cats, but you can find him at www.stevenlochran.com